Praise for *The Weirdness*

"Wonderfully weird and entertaining."   —*Esquire*

"An utterly charming, silly, and heartily entertaining coming-of-age story about a man-boy who learns to believe in himself by reckoning with evil . . . a welcome antidote to heavy-handed millennial fiction. Instead of trying to find profundity in party conversation or making his readers shudder in melancholy recognition of their thwarted lives, *The Weirdness* finds virtue in absurdity. Thank goodness—or darkness—for that."   —*The Boston Globe*

"Arriving as a practitioner of such supernatural humor, loaded with brio, wit, and sophisticated jollity, like the literary godchild of Max Barry, Christopher Moore, and Will Self, comes Jeremy Bushnell . . . An engaging reading experience."
                    —Paul Di Filippo, *Barnes & Noble Review*

"In many ways, this is an illuminating parable for these times . . . you'll just wish you had more of this delightful novel still left to read."
                    —*San Francisco Bay Guardian*

"A whimsical approach . . . an aspiring author in New York who wakes one day to find that Satan has just brewed him a cup of fair-trade coffee—and has a little deal to discuss."   —*Tampa Bay Times*

"[*The Weirdness*] is immensely entertaining, and more than being merely diverting, is truly funny."   —*Harvard Crimson*

"The novel is truly a 'weird' read, though unforgettable . . . An open-minded, modern reader will fully appreciate this bizarre and unusual work of fiction, the author's first novel."   —*Fairfield Mirror*

"Absolutely, positively one of the most original takes on the nearing middle age, suffering male writer bit . . . Bushnell manages to turn this story on its head in what should be the most ridiculous novel you've ever read."
—*The Picky Girl*

"A comedic literary thriller situated between the world of Harry Potter and the Brooklyn of Jonathan Ames, Bushnell's debut effectively mines well-trodden terrain to unearth some dark gems."
—*Publishers Weekly*

"*The Weirdness* manages to soar beyond the potentially familiar tropes of urban fantasy with a strong sense of style and character . . . Bushnell's debut novel is a clever, darkly satiric tale of the devil, literary Brooklyn and the human penchant for underachievement."
—*Shelf Awareness*

"This book is wild. And smart. And hilarious. And weird . . . in all kinds of good ways. Prepare to be weirded out. And to enjoy it."
—Charles Yu, author of
How to Live Safely in a Science Fictional Universe

"Jeremy Bushnell has written an irreverent, chaotic, comically inventive novel that makes New York City look like the insane asylum some suspect it is. It steadfastly refuses to bore you, and by the end has something important to say about the way we dream."
—William Giraldi, author of *Busy Monsters*

THE
INSIDES

ALSO BY JEREMY P. BUSHNELL

The Weirdness

THE
INSIDES

A NOVEL

JEREMY P. BUSHNELL

 MELVILLE HOUSE
BROOKLYN · LONDON

THE INSIDES

Copyright © 2016 by Jeremy P. Bushnell

First Melville House Printing: June 2016

Melville House Publishing
46 John Street
Brooklyn, NY 11201

and

8 Blackstock Mews
Islington
London N4 2BT

mhpbooks.com   facebook.com/mhpbooks   @melvillehouse

Library of Congress Cataloging-in-Publication Data

Names: Bushnell, Jeremy P., author.

Title: The insides : a novel / Jeremy P. Bushnell.

Description: Brooklyn, NY : Melville House, [2016]

Identifiers: LCCN 2015050058 (print) | LCCN 2016008295 (ebook) | ISBN 9781612195469 (paperback) | ISBN 9781612195476 (ebook)

Subjects: | BISAC: FICTION / Action & Adventure. | FICTION / Fantasy / Contemporary. | GSAFD: Fantasy fiction.

Classification: LCC PS3602.U8435 I57 2016 (print) | LCC PS3602.U8435 (ebook) | DDC 813/.6—dc23

LC record available at http://lccn.loc.gov/2015050058

Design by Marina Drukman

Printed in the United States of America

1   3   5   7   9   10   8   6   4   2

TO MY FAMILIES

There is a time in life when you expect the world to be always full of new things. And then comes a day when you realize that is not how it will be at all. You see that life will become a thing made of holes.

—HELEN MACDONALD, *H Is for Hawk*

You want to know what it's like in there? The fact is, you spend all those years trying to make something of it. Then guess what, it starts making something of you.

—M. JOHN HARRISON, *Nova Swing*

THE
INSIDES

PROLOGUE

When Ollie was eighteen she was given a decision to make. And she never would have made the decision to follow the warlock if it hadn't been for his dog, which was about the friendliest-looking dog she'd ever seen. She'd been sitting on the wide concrete rim of a fountain in Tompkins Square Park and the mutt came trotting up to her, his enormous brown ears alert. He put his massive paws up onto her knees, locked eyes with her, and plopped his muzzle into her waiting hand.

"Oh, hello," she said. She turned the dog's head this way and that, admiring the messy mix of gold and brown and cream in his face. He had a red bandanna tied around his neck, so she guessed he had an owner nearby. She looked up, in search of the owner, and then she found him. The warlock.

She never would have made the decision to follow him if he hadn't been young, like her. He might have been a little older: she guessed nineteen. When you're an eighteen-year-old girl spending most of your days wandering around the city, you come across a fair number of people, mostly men, who try to get you to follow them somewhere. Lots of them are older, sometimes way older, and Ollie had learned that the guys who are older almost always meant bad news in one way or another. Not that younger guys were ever totally safe: they weren't; she'd learned that, too. And so Ollie gave this guy the quick assessing look that by this point in her life she'd pretty much mastered. In quick succession she noted his grubby black T-shirt, his gray utility pants, his tattooed hands, his scruffy beard, his unkempt hair. None of it gave Ollie much confidence that he might be trustworthy, that he might be anything other than a threat in a city full of them (except maybe his hair, which mirrored her own in its kinky wildness). But having the friendliest dog ever half up in her lap had lowered her defenses just enough for her to give the warlock a second look, and this time she looked at his eyes, at his lips, and she noticed an openness there, a kindness. It's not that he wasn't looking at her with attention, with interest—he was—but he was also looking at her without cruelty. With intention, yes, but without calculation. She wasn't used to experiencing one without the other. She almost didn't know what to do with that. It knocked something loose in her sense of what was possible, in a way that was, frankly, a little bit scary.

So she wouldn't have followed him if she hadn't also been with her friend, Victor, a queer Colombian kid she knew from the group home, her companion all through that summer. He wasn't her protector or anything—he was only about half her size, so she was pretty sure that in the event of a real throwdown she'd be the one protecting him—but that wasn't the point. The point was that there was safety in numbers, always, that people were way less likely to fuck with you when you were with somebody else, anybody else.

So when the warlock—his name, they'd later learn, was Gerry—asked them what they were up to, Ollie said, "Nothing" instead of "Leave us the fuck alone." And when the warlock asked them if they wanted to see something cool, Ollie said, "Sure."

And then the warlock took them to the second floor of an abandoned building and showed them something cool.

It was something like an altar, or a workbench, or a shrine. It was a long flat table surrounded by a collection of symbols graffitied onto the walls behind it and by a set of eclectic artifacts arranged on the floor. A bleached cow skull, a cracked Virgin Mary figurine, an outlet strip, a belt buckle with a picture of a sixteen-wheeler on it. The friendliest dog sniffed around, pushed a few items out of place with his nose; Gerry didn't seem to mind.

"What is all this?" Ollie asked.

"Magic," Gerry said.

Ollie and Victor didn't say anything. Ollie didn't know if she believed in magic or not but she knew that the room was very beautiful and that it held within it a kind of meaning that she didn't often get the chance to experience. She knew that she wanted to spend more time inside rooms like this, if she could.

"What would you say," Gerry said, "if I told you that, using nothing more than the items in this room, you could get anything you wanted?"

"I'd say you were a fucking liar," said Victor.

Gerry smiled. "Fair."

"You don't look like someone who has everything he wants," Victor said.

"Don't I?" Gerry asked. He was sitting on the floor, cross-legged, scratching his dog behind the ears. Victor didn't answer.

"Let me ask you," Gerry said, "just to think about this question. If you didn't think I was a fucking liar—if you really did think that, after a period of apprenticeship, you could get whatever you wanted—what would you want? Don't tell me the answer. But think about it."

Ollie didn't know whether Victor was thinking about the question, or what his answer might have been. But her own answer came to mind immediately. *A family*, she thought. *I would want to be in a family.*

"You come up with something?" Gerry said, after an interval of time had passed. Ollie nodded, just the tiniest nod. She looked over at Victor and saw him offering his own tiny nod as well.

"OK," said Gerry. "In a minute, I'm going to ask you to decide if you want to join us, to embark upon doing a kind of work with us. If you do the work, you'll get what you want. You don't have to. I'm not twisting your arm. You can just walk out of here and go back to whatever you were doing before I came along. That's totally OK. But before I ask you to make the decision, I need you to think about one other thing. I need you to think about the Possible Consequences."

He paused for import, which made Ollie want to roll

her eyes, but then the pause went on, and stopped seeming silly. She listened.

"It's really important that you think about those, pretty seriously, before we get started," Gerry said. "Because that's the thing about magic. At first it seems awesome to be able to get what you want all the time, but getting what you want always has consequences, and you'd better know what those are, because they're going to bite you square in the ass, every time. If that's going to make you reconsider wanting what you wanted in the first place, it's better to know before you get started bending the whole Goddamn universe this way and that."

Ollie thought about it. But she was only eighteen. She wasn't very good at thinking about the far-off consequences of things that probably wouldn't happen anyway. *I just want a family*, she thought. *What's the worst that could happen?*

Fifteen Years Later

1

CARNAGE

The meat begins to arrive. It arrives in refrigerator trucks stenciled with the silhouettes of majestic steer. It arrives in plain white delivery vans driven by mellow Iranians, quiet masters of exsanguination. It arrives in the trunk of Ulysses's Buick, which has been lined with rubber blankets and packed with ice. He digs out four heirloom chickens beheaded this morning, upstate, and hands them off to Ollie, same as he's done every Friday this summer. They will later be artfully turned into eight plates and served in the private dining room, at around a 200 percent markup over what Ulysses gets paid for them, which is already a sum that does not fail to impress Ollie anew every time she signs off on an invoice.

Her name is Olive Krueger; she goes by Ollie; her signature, made in haste, is an elongated, runny O.

Even though Ulysses's beard has gotten a little gray and wild, and even though his teeth are as crooked as they've ever been, he is still, Ollie thinks, one awfully handsome man. His short-sleeved work shirt, patterned in a pink strain of lumberjack plaid, is worn tight across his chest: the sight invites her to remember what his body looks like, even though the memories are part of a thicket which is not without thorns. She turns away, hands the chickens off to Guychardson, her co-worker, a wiry Haitian with a rockabilly hairdo, who has emerged from the kitchen to help with the unloading. When she turns back, Ulysses catches her eye, gives her the look that asks if he's invited to stay for a minute. She gives him the look that says OK.

It's a qualified OK. Not: *OK, come on in, hang out as long as you want, like everything's normal, like we're back to fucking again*; more like *OK, you can stand with me, here in the loading zone, for exactly as long as it takes me to smoke one cigarette. Don't talk too much.*

And he doesn't. They don't have that much to say, these days. She doesn't want to talk about the past, and the future, in the absence of either of them making some major change, just looks the same as this. So all they're left with to remark upon is the present.

Ulysses leans on the railing, squints up at the segment of hazy sky visible between the buildings. "Supposed to be in the nineties again today," he says.

"Fucking August," Ollie says.

She looks over her shoulder: Guychardson's still inside. She takes Ulysses's collar in her fist. Because they're unobserved, she feels at liberty to pull him away from the railing, pull him in close, kiss him ferociously on the mouth.

This is a thing she does with him only sometimes, often enough to be familiar but not so often that either of them can allow it to settle into an expectation.

She uses her tongue. He tastes like violet: it's that gum he's always liked. She probably tastes like a Marlboro Red. She never really enjoyed this style of vigorous kissing but she knows that Ulysses likes it, and she likes thinking that giving him a taste of her will give him something to remember as he heads back upstate. She likes thinking about him wanting her from 150 miles away. She might not even want him any more, but she still wants him wanting her. She's not entirely sure what that means but she doesn't feel like figuring it out right now, not at this point in her life.

And then she feels eyes on her. She breaks the kiss, looks over to see a Greek guy wearing a nylon Red Bull jacket coming up the stairs at the end of the loading dock. Greek dude is scowling, which makes her vigilance kick on: thanks to her fucked-up youth she still can't see someone scowling at her without trying to reason out exactly why, trying to figure out what exactly is coming at her. She suspects that what's coming at her, in this instance, is some racial shit, especially if he thinks she's a white woman, which he almost certainly does. White guys, like Greek dude here, don't always like it when they see white women making out with black guys, like Ulysses here. So it could be that. Or it could just be his face's default demeanor. She repeats a thing that Donald used to tell her: not everybody is your enemy. You live in a city, he would say, sometimes people are grumpy for reasons that have nothing to do with you.

Regardless: this man's appearance means that more meat has arrived. She slaps Ulysses on the shoulders and grins at him by way of goodbye, and once he's strolled back

13

to his Buick she takes Greek guy's clipboard and signs for six skinned and hollowed goats. Guychardson returns, and the two of them load goats up on their backs and head into the kitchen, out of the heat of the day.

Part of their job is to make all this meat go somewhere. She passes the three walk-in refrigerators without a look; space is at a premium in there and the carcasses are too large to fit. The rule at Carnage is that nothing goes in the walk-ins until it's been sundered. So instead she loads the carcass into the dumbwaiter. Guychardson is right behind her: he loads his goat next to hers in the dumbwaiter's double-wide car, and punches the button that kicks on the motor. Ollie heads downstairs.

The building used to be part of the waterworks system, or something; Ollie's not up on her New York City infrastructure enough to be able to say for sure. All she knows is that the Carnage basement is a huge length of semicircular tunnel, lined in clammy antique tile. Once the tunnel went somewhere, she presumes, but now it terminates at both ends in crudely masoned brick walls. Beneath her feet, ovoid grates mark out eight-foot intervals on the floor; through them she can hear the distant sound of water, running through some vast dank sequence of caverns beneath Manhattan. Above her are the hooks.

The room—windowless, subterranean—stays cool all year, even now, in the long, sweltering stretches of summer. Part of the reason Jon and Angel even set up in this building in the first place, as the lore goes, was because they saw this room as a quick-and-dirty solution to the problem of where to put all the meat they were going to need in order to make this venture work. Install some hooks on a track in a vast cool space and you got a start.

She lifts the goat. She can do this a hundred times a day: she's six feet tall and has her father's Germanic-peasant arms. She also has her mother's welter of wild curls. In a perfect world these would be minor entries in a long list of gifts she'd received from her parents: in this world, though, they're the two best things she got.

She returns to the dumbwaiter, where there are two more goats for her. This repeats until all six goats are on hooks, and then she heads back upstairs to start working on the pigs.

Storing meat in a cool basement is strictly short-term. If it's down there for more than four hours it starts to attract raised eyebrows from the Department of Health and Mental Hygiene, and if you run a restaurant called Carnage which uses "meat reenvisioned" as its high concept, you'd better be reliably getting DHMH to give you sheets of paper with a giant letter *A* on them or you're pretty much fucked. So the next part of her job is to take whatever heap of meat is on hand and reduce it down to manageable pieces, ideally pieces that demonstrate some level of finesse, pieces the chefs won't bring back to you and wave in your face while calling you a talentless abortionist.

She fishes her battered, seven-year-old iPod out of her apron pocket and slams it into the SoundDock that she keeps on the highest shelf in the prep area (Guychardson, who's about five foot four, can't meddle with it up there unless he gets a stool). She punches play on the work playlist, which kicks off with Swans. "Raping a Slave." As the kitchen fills with thudding, dirgelike percussion, she pulls her knife kit out from under her station and approaches the prep table, where Guychardson has arranged four sides of pork.

Together, they butcher.

She saws her side into thirds, grunts as she works the saw through the aitchbone. Takes the middle section and separates it: chops, ribs. Saws the chops from the backbone, then switches from saw to trimmer as the music switches from no-wave pummel to annihilatory black metal shredding. This mix is eight hours of the kind of music that keeps you from thinking about yourself too hard, which is why she likes it. Guychardson whistles a jaunty melody over the top of it, possibly to annoy her; when she looks up he is pretending to play a set of ribs like a xylophone. He looks like something out of a macabre old-time cartoon. She smirks, in spite of herself, and goes back to finishing the chops; she slaps them down on a twelve-inch platter and racks it in the end-loading cart. She removes some belly fat and plops it into a steel bucket: Angel will turn it into something tasty later.

She gets the loin out and drops it on another platter, racks it, moves to working on separating the bacon from the ribs. She spares a glance at Guychardson's work at the other end of the prep table, notes that he's begun on the rear third of his side, cutting out the hams. That's her least favorite task to perform on any pig; it takes time, and breaks up the flow of the work. She envies Guychardson his pace. He's faster than she is. At that part anyway.

They only work together two days a week, Friday and Saturday, prepping for the really busy nights. The rest of the week Guychardson's at a Caribbean joint somewhere in

16

Brooklyn and Ollie's on her own here. But even though they spend only two days a week together, they've developed a rivalry. They race. They track who's ahead, who's made more animals disappear into the walk-in, who's produced more finished cuts. It's friendly, sort of. Or, more accurately, it has the surface appearance of being friendly. In reality there's an edge to it. Guychardson wins almost every night. She thinks he must be cheating.

The competition has left its mark on her. At the end of one shift last winter, she was going too fast, trying to catch up, and she took off the edge of her left pointer finger, leaving a quarter-inch sliver of flesh on the surface of the prep table. She clicked her tongue once against the roof of her mouth and closed her eyes, and when she felt the blood begin to well out she clenched her right hand around the wound as if she could unmake her mistake through the application of pressure alone. When the chefs figured out what happened they poured her three shots of whiskey and made her stick the finger into a chafing dish full of kosher salt. She remembers the scream she let out. She doesn't remember what happened to the tiny filet of finger-meat; it amuses her to think that it might have ended up accidentally swept into a sausage bucket and served to some unsuspecting customer.

Before that, about a year ago now, just after she'd first started working with Guychardson, she'd asked him how he was able to bone out the hams so effectively. He gave her a grin she immediately thought of as *shit-eating* and said, "I'm a man, baby." She has tried to make herself believe that he'd said *I'm the man*, but he hadn't: she knew it then and she knows it now.

17

I'm a man. His stupid answer comes to mind at least once each time they work together, percolating up unbidden through the layers of scorching drone that her SoundDock fills the kitchen with, through the work, which is supposed to ground her, keep her mind from wandering. And each time they work together—every Friday and Saturday—she reaffirms that his answer is bullshit. Being a man has nothing to do with it. He's tiny. She's bigger than he is, she's stronger than he is, and she's pretty sure there's no other kind of inherent male advantage that could be helping him in this particular arena. And frankly, his technique isn't any better than hers either, at least as far as she can tell.

She takes a quick glance across the table, watches him separate a tough joint. She narrows her eyes, inspecting him.

Maybe it's his knife. He uses this weird knife in his kit for almost every task. The weird thing about it is that it has no spine; both sides are sharpened to an edge, like a fucking dagger or something. It's got no bolster to speak of and the handle looks like he cut it out of a piece of oak with a saw; the whole thing looks like he might have made it in shop class when he was a kid. It makes no sense. She can't see how anyone could get good action off that thing. But it's clear that he cares for it. He doesn't leave it at his station at the end of the day; he takes it with him, in a special lacquered box that only holds the one knife. So maybe there's something about it.

Maybe his knife is magic.

She's spent a lot of her life around enough people who used magic to cheat the world. She's done it herself, though that was a long time ago, and she tries not to think about

18

it too much, these days. And on an average shift, she stays busy—so it's pretty easy to keep from thinking too much about anything.

They work. They wheel filled racks into the walk-in. They drop the hocks and hams and bacon into the big brining buckets. They replenish the prep table with more meat from the basement. Angel and Jon show up. Jon, a curly-haired pirate-looking Caucasian, sticks his head in for only a second, beams a smile at them, then heads back to the front kitchen, where he will spend an hour or so planning the day's specials out on a whiteboard. Angel, a slender guy, half Puerto Rican, half Cuban, sits in the rear kitchen with them for a couple of minutes, watching them appreciatively. Watching her. Even without turning away from the task in front of her, she can feel something in that look. An invitation. Hers to respond to or to ignore. This note in the look is something new. It started about a month ago, which, she notes, somewhat uneasily, lines up almost exactly with the date Angel's wife moved out.

Don't shit where you eat, she tells herself this afternoon, as she tells herself every afternoon, when she feels the invitation in Angel's look. But on some other level she already knows that it's going to happen, that she will accept the invitation eventually, whether she wants to or not. It's just a matter of time. But she makes herself not think of that. Instead, she imagines smoking a cigarette. She imagines it in great detail.

Ollie's playlist moves into its final songs, long pieces of Louisiana sludge rock. The basement is finally empty now, the walk-ins nearly full. She's lost the competition again. Neither she nor Guychardson remark upon it, but she knows that he's noticed, and she knows that he's noticed that she's noticed. A couple of the cooks and the lead servers have shown up, congregating around Jon's whiteboard. Laughter and easy talk. Somebody's turning leftover bison into the family meal.

And at the end of that final hour she jams her iPod back in her pocket and joins everybody in the main kitchen and listens to Jon and Angel talk the staff through the plan for the night. Half-listens, really: her work for the day, at this point, is done. Sometimes, if they're shorthanded, she'll work an additional shift, but they don't need her tonight, so she wolfs down an enormous bowl of shepherd's pie and cleans up her knife kit and dunks her apron in the laundry bin. She receives a few claps on the back from the friendlier cooks and heads out through the service entrance. She has the cigarette she fantasized about earlier, her second of the day. She's trying to quit. Guychardson follows her out, lacquered box under his arm, and with one wave back over his shoulder at her he disappears, into the waning light.

And then she stands there, alone, her hair and fingers stinking of iron and offal and brine and smoke, her head ringing with the memories of the roaring noise which soundtracked her day's work. Now, on the evening air, she hears the murmur of a line out front, just beginning to form. People have come to dine on the food that she's handled and prepped. There's satisfaction in hearing that murmur, satisfaction in being exhausted from long hours of labor. This is as happy, these days, as she ever gets.

• • •

She rides the 6 back to the Bronx, walks the quartermile from the station to her apartment. When she gets inside she flips on the light and finds a little tableau that Victor has laid out for her: a Glencairn whiskey glass, a spoon, an unopened bottle of single malt Scotch, and a note. TREAT FOR YOU IN THE REFRIGERATOR, says the note. PAIR W/ THE SCOTCH FOR BEST RESULTS. XOXO

Well, OK. She opens the fridge and finds a table-setting card marked with an O, propped against a coffee mug filled with chocolate mousse.

She sits down, fills the glass halfway with Scotch, and takes a bite of the mousse. Holds it in her mouth, disassembling it, the way she knows Victor would want her to do. She detects honey, vanilla, but also the faintest note of something dank, like a rotting leaf; echoed by the bogginess of the Scotch that she uses to swish it away. It is a wholly Victor concoction: delicious, but delicious in a way that has a little bit of difficulty in it, something the faintest bit unlikable for the mouth to puzzle over.

She texts him as she's mulling through the second mouthful. He'll be at work, but somehow he manages to always be checking his phone, even in the middle of churning out God only knows how many desserts for a Friday night rush.

TREAT DELICIOUS, she texts. WHAT'S IN IT?

By the time he texts her back she's forgone the spoon and has begun scraping out the recesses of the mug with her finger.

INFUSION OF CAVENDISH TOBACCO, reads his response. It is so characteristically Victor that she has to roll her eyes. It's a little gimmicky; it excites on a kind of shallow level, designed as much for its attention-getting qualities as for anything having to do with the way the end result will actually taste. It's something that Victor would describe as *sticky*, something likely to get passed around on the food Tumblrs or whatever other Internet things he keeps up with. It's the side of the industry that she hates—just do good work, she thinks, and you will never need to worry about all that shit—and his engagement with it would make her insane if he didn't have the talent to make things that actually tasted good in addition to being, whatever, clickable.

His obsession with attracting and retaining attention: she chalks it up to his one brush with celebrity some years back. He'd created a confection that ended up as the *now* dessert for a season: the Black Cupcake, made from squid ink and a near-perfect dark ganache. The thing landed him a gushing interview segment on the Food Network, made his career at the tender age of twenty-one. Everything he's done since then has seemed designed, at least in part, to try to reclaim some of that glory, working hard to dispel the notion that he's the one-hit wonder of the dessert world even though the only person in all of New York who holds that notion is probably himself.

Excellent work as always, she texts back, and she means it. She waits a minute to see if he'll say thanks or anything, but she doesn't really expect him to, and he doesn't. She pours herself another glass of Scotch and downs it a little too quickly, and then staggers into her bedroom without brushing her teeth and presses her face into the pillow.

At around three a.m. she's awoken by the sound of

fucking: Victor's brought some boy home, as he's known to do. She groans with irritation and slaps the wall blearily, once, twice, and then she spins back down into sleep, not quite waiting to register whether the noise has ceased.

She dreams. Faces rise in her mind: the faces of people she doesn't want to see, churned up by the fitfulness of her sleep. People from her life before. They float up like leaves, dislodged from somewhere down below. They break the surface of the calm black water and they turn there in a wide slow gyre, disturbing the stillness, all night long.

2

DEMONSTRATION

Logan International, Boston, Massachusetts. Maja gets off the airplane, submits her form and her passport for inspection, answers the familiar questions, and, everything in order, she is once again stamped into the United States of America. She checks her watch, which she set to local time during the night, when she was over the ocean, sleepless. Her appointment with the prospective client is in three hours. She is right on schedule. Jet-lagged, of course, but she's come to prefer doing these initial consults that way. Get off the plane, get to the client: that's been her rule in recent years. A flight leaves her higher functions blunted and her nerves raw: put another way, it leaves her sensitized, sensitized in the exact way that makes it easier for her to do the work that the clients will be expecting.

She drags her suitcase and garment bag into the airport bathroom, inspects her reflection in the mirror, checks her gums for bleeding. She runs a hand over her ruff of short black hair, aiming to give it some mussy volume, hoping to better show off the few thin lodes of gray. She's forty years old this year, but flight draws out her premature markers of age, sharpens the network of lines in her face, enhances the sense that she's lived a life spent focusing with powerful intention.

You look good, says the Archive.

Well, she thinks back, *we all end up with the features we deserve.*

You sure about that? asks the Archive.

This she ignores. She washes her hands for a long time in the steel sink, aware, as always, of the ways in which airports facilitate the passage of bacteria, but she doesn't splash any water on her face: she doesn't want to lose the dark circles under her eyes; she wants as little color as possible to return to her lips. Jet lag legitimately helps her work but it also enhances the theater of what she does, it also makes her look more dramatic, scores another point with the clients. Clients—the kind of clients who want what she has to offer, anyway—like to see her this way. A little ragged at the edges. A little haunted-looking. It makes her look exactly like the person they're hoping will come in through the door.

So cynical, says the Archive.

You were always supposed to be the cynical one, she replies.

That was a long time ago.

Mellowing out in your old age, are you then?

She rearranges the strap of her purse, grabs the handle of her suitcase, and heads briskly back out into the flow of people moving through the airport. She stands in a designated zone outside and catches a shuttle to a rental car place, negotiates the pickup of the compact car she's reserved for the day. She declines the GPS that the rental agent tries to upsell her on; she curtly waves off the cheaply printed regional map that he tears off for her from a pad of same. "I know the area," she says, in her accented English.

The car's been sitting in August light all morning, and as she opens the door she can feel heat push out in a wave. She lowers herself into the sun-baked driver's seat, closes the door behind her, and smiles, allowing herself to enjoy the sensation of sudden sweat prickling in her armpits, beneath her dark blazer and her linen dress shirt. Outside of saunas she's only experienced this kind of heat three or four times in her life, and all of them have been here, in America. It's good to be back.

Somebody died the last time we were in America, says the Archive. *Am I remembering that right?*

They both know the answer to that, so she doesn't reply. Instead she starts the car and turns the air conditioner on as high as it will go, lets the crisp cooling streams blast against the exposed bone of her sternum with the force of a massage. She's almost embarrassed by the luxuriousness of it. She makes a series of precise, incremental adjustments to the mirrors and then heads out onto the road.

She lied before. Back at the counter, when she said she knows the area. Not strictly true. She's been to the States several times before but not to this sector, not to New England. Nor has she studied the area closely on any map. She could not tell you the name or number of the highway that she pulls onto to head south. She only knows that south, along this road, is the way to the client. Once she's exchanged more than a few e-mails with someone, she knows the way.

Before long, she's outside the city limits. Here, both sides of the highway are lined with trees and occasional lakes. The sky is blue, dotted with thick storybook clouds and a single distant helicopter. Summertime. The nearest vehicle on the road is a Jeep, loaded up with mountain bikes and a kayak made from florescent plastic, like an enormous toy. The spare tire is hidden by a cover which bears the legend LIFE IS GOOD. Maja has to marvel at this touching declaration of optimism, so unlike anything she'd see in Norway.

She pulls up alongside the Jeep, spares a quick look at the driver and passenger. Tanned girls, with plastic sunglasses and matching blond ponytails. They appear to be singing along exuberantly with something on the radio. Maja gives her head an almost imperceptible shake, expressing some admixture of bafflement and appreciation. She doesn't think poorly of the girls, she just can't imagine being them. She wonders what kind of person she would have become if she'd grown up here. Would she have soaked up solar energy and synthesized it into a greater enthusiasm for life, into the surplus of *pep* so evident in these two beside her?

She knows one thing. She wouldn't do what she does. She wouldn't have the skill that she has. The whole reason she has it, the only reason she discovered and honed it, is because she grew up in Hammerfest, where she suffered through two months of darkness each winter. As a child, she never trusted that the sun would return. It would be gone for so long that she would begin to believe that it had been obliterated, snuffed out utterly by some cosmic malevolence. The thought would deliver her into terrors from which no assurance could release her; she would sit in her closet and shudder for hours. Eventually she learned that the fear could be dispelled if she could sense where the sun was, if she could locate it in space somewhere. It didn't matter whether it was a few degrees beneath the horizon or on the far side of the planet; as long as she knew where it was she would feel better, breathe easier. And so it was the first thing she taught herself to find.

She's nearing the exit. She glances at a sign on the side of the highway, an unnecessary reflex of confirmation. She takes in no data other than the icons of fast-food restaurants emblazoned there, which make her smile wryly again with appreciation for this strange country, which embeds fast food directly into their institutional signage, as though it's part of their infrastructure. She clicks the turn signal on, takes the exit, contemplates actually stopping for a burger. She usually doesn't eat meat, hasn't eaten it regularly since puberty: it's too easy for her to know where it's been, too easy for her to trace it back to a cut-and-kill floor in some industrial packing plant. To feel animal pain and human overwork in every bite. But she wonders whether she will ever actually understand this country without eating a Whopper or a Big Mac. She should try one of each, maybe. It would be unpleasant, she's certain—it would *hurt*—but as an experience it might serve as a rite of passage in some way, a bit like getting a tattoo. Another tattoo: she already has a pair, one thin black band around each bicep. She got the left one when her mother died and the right one when her father died. She didn't get one when her brother died: she remembers him in a different fashion.

She checks the clock. Time is beginning to get tight

and she wants, as always, to be punctual. She'll have to explore the full extent of the American Experience some other day. She accelerates out of the turnoff ramp and blasts past the restaurants and gas stations clustered there; she hangs a right, roars down a few miles of ragged road, lined on both sides with sunken bogs, undeveloped lots, roughly cleared areas, scrub, stumps, brush piles, an occasional bulldozer or loader standing idle. And then, she rounds a bend and comes upon her destination: an office park, an expanse of mirrored buildings and wide green lawns, rising incongruously from the mud and sand of the landscape. She pulls up the long wide driveway and enters the mazy roads of the park.

To the eye, the place seems quiet. There's not another human being to be seen. The only activity on the lawns is the movement of water flung by sprinkler systems. She can feel the presence of people, though, workers, behind the glass and steel; she can feel the accumulated mass of their unfolding activity. It hangs in the air like a sort of atmospheric heaviness, like a subsonic thrum.

The involuted roads in here don't follow an obvious logic but they pose no more problem for her than any other part of the trip so far. All she has to do is keep following the trail that leads her to the client; it might as well be a series of arrows painted on the surface of the road, pointing the way. She is led, in the end, to a long brick outbuilding, one of a series of similar buildings unglamorously filling in the back of the park. It houses six separate businesses behind identical generic facades facing a strip of parking spaces.

Ten minutes early, she notes with satisfaction as she

pulls the car into a space. She looks in the rearview mirror and musses her hair again.

From her suitcase in the passenger seat she retrieves a box of black nitrile gloves; she opens the box and dons a pair.

She emerges from the car, strides across a sweltering strip of asphalt, steps up onto the curb. The glass door behind which lies the prospective client is stenciled with the words THE RIGHTEOUS HAND FOUNDATION.

A bell jangles as she pushes into the tiny lobby. It's cool inside, but even despite that the space seems swampy, as though there's mildew beneath the cream wallpaper, as though the rust-colored carpet has spent time under stagnating floodwater. She can feel the client, just one room away now; she turns her head to face the door set in the far wall and closes her eyes for a brief moment, perceives him as a shape in the darkness, which is a thing she couldn't do when they were communicating transatlantically, via e-mail. It's not like she sees a glowing silhouette or anything. It's more like she sees a kind of floating Rorschach blob. Not his shape, but rather the shape his personality makes in the world.

She is unsurprised when she finds the flaw, the part of this shape that tastes to her mind the way rancid oil would taste on her tongue. It repulses her, somewhat, but it generates no alarm; there's no surprise in it. Years ago, when she first began finding for others, it would startle her to peer into a client and discover *damage* there: some wound that never healed correctly, some emotional apparatus that had grown wrong, curled inward, rankled, bloated. But before too long she realized that those people—damaged people—

31

were the kinds of people who needed her the most, and that she wouldn't get far if she turned and walked back out the door every time she caught wind of something foul. Thus, she learned that sometimes you have to know when to stop looking inside someone, you have to know when to get out of someone else's head and get back to your own. And that's what she does now.

She opens her eyes and rests them on the small, unattended reception desk, finds the least interesting thing available—a selection of highlighters fanning out of a plain white mug—and she waits.

After a minute, the office door opens and she gets her first actual look at the prospective client, Mr. Hogarth Unger. He's sixtyish, ruddy complexion, wearing an ill-fitting navy suit that looks about thirty-five years out of date. Big brass buttons.

"Maja Freinander?" Unger says, in a voice pitched loud, bordering on a shout. The accent catches her off guard for a second: it's European, French, where she was expecting coarse Boston honk. "Yes," Maja says, taking the time of one blink to recover. "Mr. Unger. Hello."

"Please come in," says Unger, gesturing into the office with a sweep of his arm.

He does not offer her his hand to shake, which she takes as a sign that he's remembered the instructions that she laid out in their preliminary exchanges. So she might not have needed the gloves after all. A good sign.

Together they step into the office, into a space barely wider than the desk that Unger settles behind. She takes a seat in the molded plastic chair available to her, looks quickly over the array of items on the desktop. A large beige computer monitor dating back to before the era of the flatscreen. A letter opener with a wrought handle, resting atop three file folders stuffed thick with documents—old documents, some of them rotting at their edges, as though they've been recently salvaged from the depths of a forgotten basement. A statue of a peregrine or some other bird of prey, the very tip of one outstretched wing missing, lost to fracture. Each item swirls with tempting histories, but there's no time to read them. She takes one final moment to coolly examine the banner hung on the wall behind Unger's head—emblazoned with what looks like an archaic French coat of arms, featuring a crown—and then she looks Unger in the face.

Actually, she decides, the accent suits him: he looks like he could have enjoyed a comfortable life in some lower rung of French provincial government. His hair falls into a sort of rough bowl cut that gives off the strong impression that he cuts it himself. He has the chunky, somewhat toadlike face of a minor councilman, a face built by heavy sauces. Bulbous nose like a root vegetable. And yet there's something troubled in the face as well, something that deforms the picture. The sockets of flesh around the eyes look clenched. There's an angry welt forming over his cheekbone, something that suggests interesting stresses, convolutions, pain.

We all end up with the features we deserve, she thinks again, although she knows that the Archive was right: it's not as simple as that. She's looked through enough history books, seen her share of Nazi soldiers looking into the camera, blithely pretty although God only knows what they'd done. She's worked for psychopaths who smiled at her with telegenic faces, smoothly untroubled. It's not what you've done that changes your face so much as how you feel about it, what you think about it. And when she looks at Unger, even willing herself not to look beneath the surface, she sees someone who has done bad things, but who has done them with some degree of discomfort, who has done them knowing that they were wrong, fully anticipating to be troubled by them but electing to do them anyway, in the name of some greater good. This, Maja knows, makes him more dangerous than the usual psychopath, not less. So she'll have to be cautious.

Unger's face breaks into a broad grin. "So how do we begin?" he says.

"I was under the impression that you wanted to use this meeting to address some final questions," Maja replies.

"A demonstration," Unger says. "I would like to ask you for a demonstration. If that is all right with you."

"Of course," Maja says. This is the part that she's used to. The clients always want a demonstration. "Do you have something in mind?"

"I do," Unger says. Of course he does. They always do. "Shall we begin?"

"Certainly."

"And it works like you said? I can ask you to look for something? Does it have to be something specific? Can I say *find something interesting in this room*?"

"Yes," Maja says.

"Then let's begin there."

"That's fine," Maja says. She closes her eyes, feels her way around the room. Picks over the desk, the statue, the file folders, the monitor. Of course, viewed a certain way, everything in the room is interesting. The folders are full of fat veins of information but she's guessing that he's not asking after anything intangible like that. She follows the cable from the monitor to a big CPU stashed on the floor, hidden from view by the desk. More intangible data there, finely ranked, but for now she skips over that as well, instead letting her perception flow to the back wall, where there is a heavy hard-walled suitcase; she guesses that her fee is inside and quick probing confirms it. Bundles of American currency. She probes a little deeper, checking for anything extra in the case, something tricky, a surprise. But she finds only the usual baseline that most people consider *nothing*: dust, bits of skin, microbes, rich histories of exchange.

Moving on, she finds a long crate, next to the suitcase. She looks inside, and an instant later her eyes snap open. "Guns," she says. "Two guns."

"What kind of guns?"

She needs to close her eyes and concentrate a moment for this, but it's easy enough: the guns appear to her wrapped in a radiant layer of information, spiky with facts, just waiting to be peeled. "One is a Beretta M9A1 9mm pistol," she says. "The other is an M4A1 carbine rifle."

"What else can you tell me about them?" Unger asks, quietly.

Cautiously, she closes her eyes again, looks back into the gun, follows the through-line of its travels. She gets glimpses and fragments of scenes. It is a bit like the process of remembering a dream in the morning, or pulling something up out of memory. Only not her memory: the memory of the thing itself.

"They were stolen," Maja says. "Stolen from a National Guard armory here in Massachusetts."

"Stolen by whom?" Unger says, leading her.

Maja frowns, goes deeper. "A man," she says. "A young man."

"Can you identify him?"

She tries extracting the history of the man from the weapon, but it's hard. Sometimes she can pull knowledge about a person she's never met or seen out of an object that that person has handled, but the traces tend to quickly get obscure, and so it is here. She gets a glimpse of a head, shaved, the shape of a skull. A tattoo. Some number, some heavy black bars. Not much more. She opens her eyes, flicks her attention away from the weapons, back to Unger. If he knows the man, the information's probably there, in his skull, just waiting to be read. She doesn't really want to go there, but for the sake of the demonstration she looks, and, sure enough, she finds a whole history there, years of it, piled up in heaps, strata.

"Your son," she says, intuiting this just from the volume of the material alone.

"Correct," Unger says, his face threatening to beam. "Martin."

"You've mentioned him before," Maja says. "You're sending him with me. He'll be serving as the agent of retrieval?"

"Yes, that's right," Unger says. He looks at his watch with a degree of evident irritation. "He was supposed to be meeting us here this morning; I expect that he'll be here soon."

"He's in the National Guard?" Maja asks. She's guessing now, rather than looking. She still wants to spend as little time in Unger's head as possible.

"No, no," Unger says. "He was in the Marines for a time, but that was, oh, ten years ago now. He retains some contacts from those days—including some helpful ones in the Guard. However, Martin has realized—wisely, I think—that his talents are best deployed, shall we say, more flexibly than is usually encouraged within a traditional military structure. It's outside of those structures that he can do actual good, that he can really do his utmost to address the concerns that face the civilized nations."

He pauses here, looks expectantly at her. Maja assumes that he's waiting for her to take the bait, to ask something like *And those concerns are?* Or maybe he wants her to fill in the blank, to meet him halfway. Maybe it's a kind of test. She's not very interested in being tested in that way, though, and so she waits, her face blank.

"I speak, of course, of degeneracy," Unger says, right as the pause begins to grow uncomfortable. He looks down at his folded hands with a tinge of remorse, as though to even utter the word is somewhat shameful. "The rise, globally, of degeneracy. A tide which it is in the interest of all civilized peoples to stem." He lifts his amphibian gaze to her face once again, and waits.

Maja nods, to show she's heard. She's heard these sorts of ideas before, of course: those old nationalist ideologies never quite died out entirely; you can't live in Europe without coming across them every now and then. You can't read the news without eventually seeing some hint of them smoldering at the periphery. Smoldering, and occasionally flaring up: she remembers Anders Behring Breivik, back at home, who first killed eight people with a bomb and then went on to shoot and kill sixty-nine more, mostly teens. Not that long ago. She remembers reading excerpts from his manifesto in the paper, remembers his remarks against Islam, against multicultural Europe. Repellent—but perhaps that's the test; perhaps Unger is waiting to see whether she'll balk, whether she'll show some sign of distaste that would give him reason to question her commitment to the job. But she can keep neutral when it's necessary. All she has to do is wait the moment out.

Sure enough, Unger eventually claps his hands together and says, "So! I am impressed by your demonstration. I suppose I would like you to offer me one final assurance that you can find the—how did you put it—the target item?"

"It will be complicated," Maja says.

"You said as much in our correspondence."

Maja continues as though he hasn't spoken: she wants to make sure she is perfectly clear. "You haven't handled the item," she says. "You don't have access to anyone who has handled the item. So it will take me some time to find it."

"I accept this," Unger says. "But you *can* find it."

"Yes," she says. "I've done the preliminary work. At this point I know something. An area. If I go to the area, I'll know more."

"And the area is—where, exactly?"

"For that answer, you pay me."

A thoughtful look clouds Unger's face, then passes. "I have a final stipulation," he says. "There are two parts to it. Either part may serve as something of a sticking point."

Maja leans forward incrementally, a little irritated. She doesn't appreciate surprises.

"As we've discussed," Unger says, "Martin will be traveling with you, serving as the agent of retrieval."

"As we've discussed," Maja says.

After a hesitation, Unger offers this: "People can find Martin—difficult to get along with."

Difficult how, Maja wonders, but she figures she'll be able to glean that information later. Everyone she works with is difficult in some way; it's in the nature of the job. And so she says the thing that she says when future difficulties begin to make themselves known, a prepared disclaimer: "If he makes it impossible for me to do my job, I take the first half of my fee and I walk away. You get nothing. No refund, no recourse, no second chances."

"I understand," Unger says. "Martin will not interfere with your work. I can make this clear to him. He *hears* when one tells him things, it's just—" He sighs. "Well, you know—*sons*."

Maja knows nothing at all about sons. She knows what it's like to have a difficult brother, but that information she opts not to volunteer. Instead, she waits until she's certain that no more is forthcoming. "And the second part?" she asks then.

"The second part," Unger says. He smacks his lips once, loudly. "He will be traveling with these guns."

She expected this. They didn't discuss weaponry in their correspondence but weaponry is almost always involved in any job she does. It does require her to embark upon a speech she's given before, a disclaimer. "I don't hurt people," she begins.

"I understand," Unger says.

"I don't hurt people," she repeats. "I just find things. You have to understand that or we call the whole thing off, right now."

"I understand," Unger says.

They hold one another's gaze for a moment, until she's certain he means what he's said.

"OK," she says.

"OK," Unger says, smiling as though taking pleasure in an unfamiliar idiom. "Then I suppose all that remains is the transactional portion of our conversation." He cranes about in his chair, hauls up the suitcase. Maja rises to take it from him.

She tightens her grip on the handle and feels the reassuring weight of the case. Even though it's only half of her total fee, the amount of cash here is considerable. It's enough for her to live on for a year: over a year, if she spends carefully. And she always spends carefully. She allows herself a moment to think of the time that this money buys her, just one moment to enjoy the sensation of her growing control over the future, the way money gives some structure to the imperceptible, the unknown, that which is always before her.

"Thank you," she says.

3

HEARTBREAKERS

When Ollie was twenty-three years old, she loved her life.

She was living then in the Hudson Valley, working on Donald's farm: long hours, every day, under the sun. It was difficult work, exhausting—hard on her joints, her wrists and her knees and her back—but she loved it.

She loved pulling carrots out of black soil.

She loved manning the table at the farmers' market on Sundays, passing food along to people who would just appreciate it, openly. People would just give her money and take the food she'd grown and they would smile happily at her in a way that was totally honest. Appreciation without guile; intention without calculation. It was her favorite way for people to look at her.

She loved the long August evenings. She loved sitting at the picnic table, eating fried potatoes, drinking vodka lemonade, watching Donald practice archery in the yard, holding her boy close in her lap.

She didn't love the mosquitoes, but she did love killing them, loved the little splotch of blood left behind on her arm after she'd smash them midfeed. Her blood. *Mine*, she would think.

She loved the sweat and the dirt and she loved falling into bed exhausted and entering a sleep so solid that no dream could get inside it.

Basically she loved the work. This was not a surprise: she'd always believed that work would be satisfying. For a long time she believed this on faith alone, a dumb faith that was nourished by just about exactly nothing in her childhood. Not watching her mom nod out on a bare mattress in a crumbling room in some squat. Not watching NYPD eviction task forces hit her dad in the lower abdomen with a plastic truncheon. Not being moved around from one Child Welfare Administration group home to another. Not, at age thirteen, fucking a grown-up who had nothing more to offer her than a way to get out of the rain.

But then she met the street magicians, the gutter witches and warlocks who found her in Tompkins Square Park, who invited her into their temporary encampments, erected in whatever empty lot or abandoned building they could find that week. In those spaces they would tend tiny shrines and salt-fires. These were the people who confirmed for her that work was worth doing.

Not *work* like *jobs*; they didn't do *jobs*. Of the dozen or so that she trained with, there were maybe like two who had ever held a job for longer than a week. Work, for them, was a thing that they called the Great Work, and they were dead serious about it. She could never get any two of them to agree on what the Great Work *was*, exactly, beyond that it involved *emancipation of the will*.

Magic, she remembers them saying, is about applying will. Basically using your will to bend the universe. They taught her how to try it, and she tried it, and for a while nothing happened, and she began to suspect that it was all a bunch of bullshit.

But then, at age nineteen, almost exactly one year into these studies, she met Donald, an NYU grad student who had started appearing and reappearing at the edge of their world, describing himself as a quote-unquote *participant observer*. He claimed to be writing something about the anthropology of transient punks.

She didn't realize that he was the thing she was asking for, not at first. The first detail she noticed about him was his soft little belly, which she wanted to pierce, as though she were a flint arrowhead. She'd spent all nineteen years of her life thus far developing contempt for soft people and their reek of easy living. And when she first met him, she thought his project was contemptible: the first time he explained it to her, he referred to the crusties as the *voluntary homeless* and she laughed in his face and walked off, wouldn't even look at him for the rest of the day. But he kept coming back. He kept coming back, kept observing, kept participating. He stayed through the summer and through the fall but it wasn't until winter that she really decided he was a serious person, because winter was when it got to be really tough to spend all day stamping around in the streets and the subway stations with no particular place to go. Nobody would do that voluntarily, she believed, unless they were a serious person, and this was how she came to believe that his project was, in its own way, a legitimate form of work, a legitimate expression of his will. This was how she came to respect him. And that was what made it OK to go home with him, when he invited her, to spend the night in his two-room apartment rather than in a homeless shelter or huddled over a steam vent.

He was willing to give her distance when she was sick of him, and that was what made it OK to talk to him when she wasn't. Importantly, he was the first person who she could talk to about family. About what it was like to have been taken away from her family at age nine. About missing her mom and dad even though they were drug abusers and fuckups and really did neglect her and really did leave her in harm's way. About wanting to have a family again one day, a real family. This was something she couldn't talk to the street magicians about, not really. If she would bring it up with them they would say *what do you need a family for, you've got us*. And there was some truth to that: they served as a family to her in many ways; they cared for her, they treated her with kindness—they *took responsibility for her*, which was more than she could say for her own parents, more than she could say for any of the foster placements that CWA arranged for her. Inherently she knew, though, that this was not enough, that a roaming band of like-minded souls is not a family. Any time she'd say this to the street magicians, though, they'd shout her down or laugh her off, which honestly she thought helped to prove her point as much as anything. But Donald listened, and he talked about his own family, about how money had fucked it up, about how he wanted to build something different for

44

his own kids, when the time came. And somewhere in those conversations she found herself thinking: *This. This is the guy.* She found herself with a goal toward which she could apply her will.

She hadn't really needed to use magic to make it happen, or not much, anyway. A couple of candles, a circle made from spices she'd pinched from a market, kid stuff, nothing advanced. She wasn't bending the universe so much as she was nudging it in the direction that it wanted to go anyway. They spent a year together, just the two of them, from one winter to the next, and during that year Donald's project stalled, which was maybe OK, because during that year they were busy drinking and talking and fucking and fighting. Growing comfortable together. And she was deciding that she wanted to have the boy.

The boy, she thinks at herself now, thirty-three years old, lying fetal in her bed in her muggy Bronx apartment, the stink of meat still all over her. She feels a bitter anger at herself for using those words, for reducing him to an abstraction. She demands that she think his name. She thinks his name: *Jesse*.

She demands that she look at the photos that she keeps in the cigar box, in the bedside table's lone drawer. She does not look at the photos.

The point is: another nudge and there he was, the boy—*Jesse*—just as she'd imagined him.

On Jesse's first birthday, around a cake—the first birthday of anyone's she'd ever celebrated with a cake—she had the idea that she wanted Donald to give up on the stalled dissertation, that she wanted the three of them to leave the city. On Jesse's first birthday she decided that she wanted to make a life on the tiny parcel of farmland that Donald's family owned but had practically forgotten about, that she wanted to take its attendant ring of deteriorating buildings and make them into her home, to take Donald and Jesse and make them into her family. For real for real for real. She wanted it, and she arranged it, and the universe provided, with infinite bounty. The universe provided her with carrots and picnic tables and goats and alpaca and pigs and the skills to slaughter. All hail. Twenty-three years old—just barely an adult—and her Great Work was complete. Twenty-three years old, and she was happy.

She was happy, so she quit using magic, and she concentrated instead on the farm, and raising Jesse, and loving Donald, and she told herself that she could be happy this way, doing this, for a long time. And she wasn't wrong.

But then at thirty she met Ulysses, who ran a homestead fifteen miles up the road.

Ulysses was smart; Ollie figured that out right away. He had gone to Harvard Business School, she learned, and upon graduation he very quickly began to amass a fortune doing day trading, and when this fortune reached a particular threshold he promptly left the Wall Street game and bought forty acres of Hudson Valley land. Eventually he would explain to Ollie that this had been the culmination of a long plan of his: his grandfather had owned a parcel of land, and the later loss of this land was understood, within the family, as being a consequence of racial injustice, and so the teenage Ulysses began reading up on Reconstruction history, and the long sad tale of black landownership in America. From this history he developed particular ideas about the relationship between property ownership and personhood; he developed a theory that black people should build up capital and then use this capital to purchase as much property they could, and that subsequently they should work this property fruitfully: that doing this, en masse, would be the thing that would move them along the path to being recognized, finally, as full citizens of what Ulysses called *this fucked-up racist country*.

It was exhilarating, frankly, for Ollie to hear someone talk like this. Her mother had been black, and for most of her youth and adolescence Ollie had been able to pass either as black or as white. She often presented, during those years, as ethnically ambiguous; but she'd also learned the ability to switch from one identity to the other when circumstances necessitated, when she could see some benefit to doing so. But by her eighth year on the farm, she'd stopped using that ability: she just presented as white all the time. Donald was white, and the college students who they'd hire to help out with the summer labor were usually white, and most of the people she talked to at the farmer's market were white, and her child looked white. Her skin was dark from long hours out in the sun but so was everyone else's, more or less, so no one seemed to notice: everyone treated her as white and after enough time she came to inhabit that identity reasonably comfortably. But the very first time she met Ulysses he looked at her with open recognition and she felt something inside that was unmistakably a note of doubt: doubt about whether she'd been right to let that aspect of her identity stay hidden for so long. It began to feel like a form of suppression. And after that, she started to meet with him more often, on some flimsy pretense or another, and Ulysses would start talking about black emancipation under neoliberalism, about learning the workings of capital as a way to master the tools of the white power structure, and she could feel these ideas touching something in her that nobody had ever touched before, and on top of being intellectually exhilarating she also had to admit that she found the entire thing to be impossibly, achingly hot.

It didn't hurt that Ulysses was just a beautiful man to begin with. He was smart, and he was beautiful. And although she loved Donald, and Donald was certainly smart, she had never really been attracted to him, not exactly, and she found herself believing that she deserved, maybe just once in her life, to fuck a man who she actually thought was beautiful. So she decided that it would be OK to give things just one more nudge. To cheat the world one more time. What she didn't think about, or what she chose to ignore, were the Possible Consequences.

She sits up in bed now, far away from Donald and the farm and their son, rubs her eyes. She opens the lone drawer in the bedside table.

Don't, she tells herself.

For God's sake, she retorts, against herself, *they're just photos. They can't hurt you.*

She pulls out the cigar box, opens it up. The photo on top is the most recent one she has. In it, Jesse is nine. He was a shaggy little metalhead at age nine, long greasy curly locks and a denim jacket with goat-head pentagram patches that she'd sewn on herself. *You're going to be a heartbreaker*, she used to mumble into his hair, not quite wanting him to hear.

She doesn't touch the photo, or look at any of the photos beneath this one. She knows the math: this picture of him is two fucking years old now. What he looks like, now, at age eleven, she can only guess. Donald's blocked her on Facebook and she hasn't been back to the farm. *I never want to see you again*, he'd screamed at her, the night she left. *Don't ever come back here*, he'd said. And she's consented to this: she hasn't been back to the farm in just over a year.

Unless you count the vision.

She's not sure she should count the vision. But she's not sure she shouldn't count the vision.

It happened last winter. It must have been a Monday or Tuesday because she had the night off. She was at a Goodwill in Harlem, checking out the scratch damage on a $7 coat, when, suddenly, a series of black pinpoints seemed to open up in the grain, as though the leather were spontaneously rotting in her hands. She had frowned, reinterpreted the spots not as holes but as tiny particles, specklets, attempted to brush them away. But they swarmed around her hand, tadpolelike, untouchable. It was then that she realized that they weren't a thing that was happening to the leather but rather a thing that was happening to her sight. She had a sudden fear that somehow she'd perforated her eyeball; her fingers went up reflexively to check for leaking blood, slime, humors. She found nothing.

The pinpoints doubled in size, developed angry-looking barbs and curlicues. No longer like tadpoles, more like exotic fish. They began to effloresce at their edges, although at their cores they were still a dank black. They reminded her of the vents that she'd occasionally seen the street warlocks open up in the air. They'd open a door and step in, and it would take them—somewhere else. It would take them into this weird dark space they called the Inside.

They would use the Inside for something that she never quite understood, some kind of prestidigitation that required a spare dimension to function right. Sometimes she'd peer in and see things moving in there, animals maybe, squirming away from her gaze as though they could tell that she was looking at them. The experience would make her feel queasy, dizzy, half on the verge of passing out, and that was exactly how she felt as the blobs in her optical field began to bleed together, coalescing into a palpating inky cloak, threatening to block out the Goodwill entirely.

Pain began to shear into her head. Seeking stability, she reached out and grabbed onto the clothes rack, tightened her fist around the comfort of a cold metal rod.

And then the world began to smell like ground-up batteries, and then the center of the blob burned up, like film melting in a projector: suddenly she could see through it. What she saw on the other side was not the Goodwill. It was the farmhouse, the living room of the farmhouse, the center of her former home. The stone hearth, the fireplace. It was as though she were standing right in the center of the room. Or, not quite: something about the view was a little off, a little wrong: she was looking down on the fire from the wrong height, at an unexpected angle, the way she might see it were she standing on a tall stool. She looked down, at the spot where her feet should be. And there she saw an old sketchbook of hers, in Donald's hands. It was as though she had risen from the pages.

It startled her to see it: she had nearly managed to forget that she'd spent most of a year teaching herself to draw by recording the sights of the farm. Donald rifled through the book and she saw her own old work flit past—images of radishes, of lichens, a wren's nest, the cleavage patterns in a piece of slate—and with each image a memory came shuddering back, and with each memory came pain, more pain, of a different sort than the migrainous pain the vision itself was driving into her skull, but no less real.

You're still there, at the farm, she'd thought, spacily. *You're not free of that place. You left a part of yourself behind.*

And then Donald threw the book into the fire.

No, she thought.

And then she had a seizure.

She doesn't remember it, really. She just remembers her vision going incandescent and her body giving one giant jerk, remembers the cold metal rod springing out of her hand uselessly. And then some unknown segment of time passed, and the next thing she remembers is being splayed on the floor, bleeding from the tongue, with an elderly couple hunched over her, gripping her limbs, holding her steady with a surprising, animal force. They'd urged her to remain lying on the floor; instead she sat up. They'd urged her to stick around for an ambulance; instead she pushed her way through the knot of gawkers and headed out into the street, sucking in gulps of cold winter air. She came home to this apartment and made Victor hold an ice pack against the bruised back of her head for an hour.

You're not free of that place, she thinks again, now, looking at the top photo in the cigar box, which she does not allow herself to touch.

51

Her perfect life, her Great Work: it had a good run. But she can't be sad. She won't allow herself to be sad. She has so much, even without it. When she was young, there was a period where all she wanted for her future was to live longer than her mother had lived—twenty-eight years—and to die without losing her teeth. And now she's thirty-three, and she works at Carnage, an amazing job, a job some people would literally kill her to get, and it's satisfying work, and that's so much. Or it's enough, anyway, most days. To still have satisfying work in her life: that's enough. That's what she tells herself, on mornings like this: *You don't need to want more. You don't need to want anything at all.*

She claps the lid of the box shut, places it back into the drawer of the end table.

It's amazing, she observes, with her hand on the drawer's porcelain knob, just how much you can stuff down inside you. Just how much will fit, if you force it.

"Sorry." A voice—male voice—at the doorway to her bedroom. She's only wearing a long men's undershirt, and violence flashes through her mind, a sudden scene of it, something that could be about to happen to her. But the voice is light and timid and the old fear doesn't last: she knows who this is. It's Victor's hookup from last night, just the latest in a string of guys who come through the apartment and occasionally find their way into her bedroom by accident. Largely by accident. Every once in a great while with some sexual intention. And that doesn't always work out badly, but she gets one look at this guy and she can tell you that this isn't that, even though all this guy is wearing are a tight pair of black boxer briefs of the sort that Victor calls *boy panties*. He's every inch Victor's type: compact, muscular, curly black hair, olive-skinned. Ethnicity tough to peg. For some reason Victor makes a big show out of his refusal to sleep with other Colombian guys, and it'd be a bad guess for this guy anyway, whose features skew a little more Hebraic. Both of his nipples are pierced with tiny steel barbells, giving his chest a look that Ollie thinks of as *perky*.

"Looking for the bathroom?" Ollie says.

"Yes, please?" says the hookup.

"You want the second door on the left," Ollie says. "This is the first door on the left."

Hookup leans out the door again, looks down the hall, leans back in, a smile across his face. Perfect teeth, she notices, again in keeping with Victor's taste. "Thanks!"

"You got it," says Ollie, and she gives a little thumbs-up and then falls back down to the pillow, pressing her face into it, inhaling the metallic stink. A second later she can hear the pipes in the wall shudder into life, the slosh of water falling into the clawfoot's wide basin.

"Isn't he a dear." Another voice at the doorway: Victor. She pulls her head up a second time. His body type is nearly identical to the hookup's and he's wearing the same style of underwear, only patterned with maroon and cream stripes. No nipple studs: Victor's decorative gesture is a crucifix on a slender gold chain.

"He's fine," Ollie croaks. "You think you'll be keeping this one?"

"Oh, no," Victor says. "A young thing like that, his whole life ahead of him? It would be cruel."

"I thought you delighted in cruelty. Didn't you say that once? Something something its exquisite grandeur?"

Victor makes a *tch* sound with his tongue, as though she's misjudged him terribly, and then he comes and gets into bed with her. They go way back, Victor and her, and this is not an uncommon way for them to begin the morning. It's affectionate but not sexual, even though this morning she can smell the musk of fucking on him, and his semihard penis pokes her naked ass as he snuggles up behind her. She grumbles and pushes him back an inch, her palm into his face.

"My sweet," Victor says, and when she goes just a beat too long before responding he props himself on an elbow and asks, brightly, "What are you thinking about?"

What is she thinking about. The same stupid stuff. The farm. The broken circle which used to be Ollie and Donald and Jesse. She could admit this to Victor. He's the one person from her adolescence who she's held on to in adulthood, and so he already knows the whole sad tale. He knows the pre-farm Ollie as well as the post-farm Ollie, just like she knows the pre–Food Network Victor and the post–Food Network Victor. And she's confided in him before on mornings like this one, mornings when she misses the life she made for herself. Sometimes it feels good to miss it out loud, while Victor strokes her hair sympathetically. But sometimes she's not in the mood. Sometimes it feels pathetic to still regret a mistake you made a long time ago. Sometimes you have to front like you're strong. Isn't that the way, she wonders, to actually become strong? Fake it till you make it, like the alcoholics say?

But Victor still awaits her answer. What *else* is she

thinking about, she wonders, trying to remember. She thumbs the scar tissue on her finger, a piece of nervous habit usually, but today it reminds her of knives, which reminds her of Guychardson, which gives her something to offer to Victor, something to get him off the trail of the real answer.

"I'm thinking," she says, "about a knife."

"A knife?"

"A magic knife."

Victor may have ended up turning into a pastry chef instead of a warlock, but he still uses the magic he learned from the street magicians, usually to get himself nudged back into the limelight, with only partial success. He's always nagging her to get back to practicing, too, so she knows this answer will satisfy and intrigue him.

Which it does. His eyes light up immediately.

"It may not be magic," Ollie confesses. "I don't know. But I kinda think maybe."

"Show me," he says.

"Not *my* knife," Ollie says. "It belongs to some guy at work." And she tells him about Guychardson, about the racing.

"You say you've worked with him for a year?" Victor asks, when she's through.

"A year, yeah."

"You've been in the room with this knife for a *year* and you only mention it to me now?"

"It's only twice a week," Ollie protests. "Fridays and Saturdays."

"That's *one hundred times* you and this knife have been together. One hundred opportunities to hold it."

"To *caress* it," she says, mimicking him.

"To *learn something* about it!" he says. "You missed all one hundred?"

"Not everyone has the same hard-on for magic stuff that you have, you know."

"Ut!" Victor says, holding up a hand to halt her. She makes a face, slaps her fist into his palm.

The hookup appears in the hall again, a towel wrapped around his waist. Ollie notices, somewhat grimly, that it's her towel.

Victor eyes the hookup, kisses the air near her ear noisily, and springs out of her bed.

"This conversation," he says from the doorway, pointing at her with two fingers, as though they were the barrel of a gun. "It isn't over."

"Go away," she says. "Both of you."

4

INDULGENCES

Maja sips water from a paper cup and watches Unger use his hammy fingers to punch a number into an obsolete-looking phone.

"Hello," he booms into the chunky black thing. He holds it away from his head and eyes it balefully, as though it is in the process of bewitching him. "Hello. Hello, Martin?"

The tinny squawk of a voice on the other end of the line.

"Martin," Unger says. "Maja Freinander is here. Yes, the Finder. She's expecting to *begin* soon. Are you meeting us?"

Maja eyes the disintegrating file folders on the desk, lets some of their histories drift into her. Visions of libraries begin to unfold.

"No, Martin, no, we're at the *office*," Unger says. "We were—you were supposed to be meeting us here, at the *office*."

A pause. Maja suspects that this piece of information is in no way news to Martin. She lets another library accumulate in her mind.

"Yes, Martin, I under*stand*, it's just"—Unger sighs here—"no matter, nothing to be done. Where are you *now?*"

Unger pins the phone between his ear and his shoulder and rummages in a desk drawer with both hands until he emerges with a chewed-up ballpoint pen and a memo pad.

"And," he says, "is there a place around *there* that we could meet?"

Unger takes his car, and Maja takes hers. She's partially following Unger and partially following her emerging sense of the way. The drive takes half an hour and it leads them through pretty tree-lined roads which occasionally give way to road crossings marked by the presence of commerce. Generic stuff, mostly—drug stores, gas stations—but there are also appearances of a more occasional type of shop that Maja interprets as local oddities. A place called the Doll Barn, for instance. It's actually in a barn.

They end up at a place called Zingers Dairy, an eatery with exterior signage that's done up in a loud scheme of black-and-yellow zigzags.

She follows Unger in. Everyone inside is eating ice cream. Gabbling teens and fattening families. And, among them, one adult-aged male sitting alone. His head is shaved, his chin is dark with two days' worth of growth, his olive T-shirt is grubby, his eyes are hidden by cheap-looking sunglasses. He is bent over a huge banana split sundae, which he's working his way through with clear method and intention, as though eating it is a joyless task but one that he intends to complete efficiently.

"Martin," Unger exclaims. Martin removes his sunglasses and looks up at his father. He lifts his napkin and blots it firmly against his lips. He then turns to look at her, something indolent in the slowness of the motion. He's older than she expected—she can see some gray in the furze of beard growth—but the smile he cracks here has its share of adolescent insouciance in it. It's the smile of someone calculating exactly how much they can get away with. She meets it with a fractional nod, the most minimal of all her available hellos, the one designed to shut down as many possibilities as possible. His smile goes away but she has the sense that he's maybe just saving it for later.

"You must be the Finder," he says, extending his hand. She's wearing her gloves, but to be on the safe side she opts to ignore it anyway, deliberately letting her attention flick to something else in the room. It's a method that she's adopted over the years: if you feign distraction at just the right moment, people usually allow the handshake moment to pass without necessarily concluding anything about you. When she looks back, though, Martin still has his hand out: persistent in a way that implies a certain doggedness. She puts it in a column of things that she'll need to watch out for.

His hand hovers there, in front of her.

She opens her mouth to explain, but Unger cuts her off. "Martin," he says. "She doesn't."

Martin looks at Unger, and then looks back at Maja, lowering his hand. For just a second he has the look that indicates that he's considering whether she's the most stupid person he's ever met. It makes next to no impression on her: this is the exact look that you tend to get when people figure out that you're a person who doesn't shake hands. He blinks it away, resets his face into something benign.

"It's Maja, right?" he says.

"That's right," she says.

"Well, have a seat, Maja," he says. "You can call me Pig."

"Martin," says Unger, lowering his bulk into a chair. "You know how I feel about that revolting name."

Regardless of how Unger feels about it, Maja decides that the nickname suits him. He's not overweight—he has a wiry frame, built out with some muscle—but in his face she can see a mix of appetites, a propensity toward indulgence. It's not only that, though: it's also the particular sort of intelligence in his eyes, cold, a little brutish, something unfinished and raw and wet about it. *Piggish*, yes, that exactly.

Martin shrugs at his father and cuts through a banana with the edge of his spoon.

Maja sits, and in the brief silence that follows the Archive pipes up.

Well, it says, *these people seem totally terrible.*

She waits, and it asks the same question that it has asked her many times before: *Are you sure you want to work with these people? We don't need the money.*

It's important to have money, she thinks back at it.

We have money, it says. *We have quite a lot of money. We could just go home.*

We go home, she replies, *when the job is done.*

Then why do we take half up front? the Archive asks. *We take half up front so we can walk away whenever we want to.*

And how many times have we done that? she replies. *How many times have we left a job before it was over?*

60

We've never done that, the Archive says. *But we could.*

We could, she admits. *If it was impossible to do our job. If we were in danger.*

If we were scared, says the Archive.

I'm not scared, she thinks. *Not of these people. Are you scared?*

No, admits the Archive, after a moment.

That's right, Maja thinks. *These people aren't smarter than us. All we have to do is put up with them until the thing is done and then we take our money and we go and we never think about them again.*

Pig looks up from his sundae, looks her in the face, his expression suddenly all concern. "Do you want some ice cream?" he asks.

Caught momentarily off guard, Maja shrugs, realizing only a moment too late that to show indecision was a mistake.

"Get yourself some. Go ahead, *get some*. A banana split on a hot summer's day? Not much better than that."

The air conditioning, of course, is blasting, so the *hot summer day* is not really perceptible, not as such. *Actually, though, I wouldn't mind some ice cream*, says the Archive. For the moment, though, Maja holds her silence.

"Martin," Unger says, after a pause, "let's not waste any more time."

Pig shows both his palms in a gesture of exasperation. "Jesus, Dad, let her get some ice cream," he says. "It'll take *two minutes*."

Unger draws back into a stony silence. Maja starts working on a way to defer but Pig's already in his pocket; he pulls out a wadded ten-dollar bill.

"Go get yourself some," he says. "On me."

Fine. Maja takes the bill, smiles thinly, and heads up to the counter. On a whiteboard are written the names of twenty-four different flavors. She eyes them with something like wariness. Texas Pecan. Candy Bar Whirl. Jamocha Chip. Moose Tracks. Extreme Moose Tracks.

"What can I get for you?" asks the clerk, a girl with braces, wearing a transparent visor.

"Extreme Moose Tracks," Maja says, just to hear what the words sound like coming out of her mouth.

"Cup or cone?"

"Small cone, please."

The girl processes the answer. "We have Child, Regular, or Double."

This data annoys her. "Double," she says.

Smart, says the Archive.

And in a minute she has her double cone, a terrifying amount of ice cream, and she goes and rejoins the party at the table. Pig regards her with a vague sort of respect as she tilts her head to lick around the edge of the cone: she half expects his giddy grin to return but it stays wherever he's stored it.

In the ice cream she can taste an extensive network of refrigerated storage and, as a back-note, the near-flatline of cow consciousness. But despite that it remains, in its way, enjoyable. She uses her tongue to shape the tip of it into a point.

"May we begin *now*?" Unger says.

"Sure," Pig says. "I want to begin with a question."

Unger looks at Maja. Maja pauses in her ice-cream sculpting and says, "Ask."

"My dad thinks it's in Boston," Pig says. "Is he right?"

"It's not in Boston," she says.

Pig taps the end of his spoon against the hard tabletop, once. Its *clack* coincides with a lull in the noise of the room.

"Three *years* we've been here," he says, quietly, sullenly. He looks at her. He does not look at his father.

"Martin," Unger says.

Pig ignores him, keeps his eyes on her. Absently, he takes both ends of the spoon in his hands and begins to apply pressure.

"You can tell us where it is," he says. "That's what you do."

"That's correct," she says.

"Where is it?"

"New York," she says. "New York City."

"OK," he says. "So we go there."

The spoon's metal bends at its weakest point.

5

FIELDS

Ollie breaks down a beef hindquarter, reduces it to its primal sections. Five major cuts. Remove the flank. Remove the sirloin tip. Remove the loin. Seam out the shank. Separate the round and the rump. This is a sequence she performs daily; several times daily. Sometimes she performs it in her dreams. The steps are ingrained, literally memorized in her body, like a sort of dance. Which means that her attention is free to wander, even though one thing kitchen life has taught her is that you should never really let your attention wander too much, not when you're working with knives.

And yet: her mind is not where it should be, not attending to the task, to the blade in her hand. Instead, she's watching the blade in Guychardson's hand, watching it move. He cuts along a femur, cuts perpendicular to the bottom knuckle. A basic cut, but there's something *off* about the way he does it. It looks fake, like a movie. A movie where, for some reason, they needed to fake the act of butchery, render it in photo-realistic but unconvincing CGI. All the textures are right, but all the physics are wrong. *Why would they do it that way*, she thinks, losing herself in the idea. *When they could just have gotten a real butcher*.

She knows it's not a movie. Guychardson is real. He's right there, standing across from her. She can smell his sweat. She can hear him humming idly even over the choppy black sea of noise she has pouring out of the SoundDock. He's too annoying to not be real.

Still, though, she watches him until she sinks into a light sort of trance. Her hands stop working. She sets her own knife down on the table.

"Guychardson," she says. Or tries to say. Her voice catches, her throat unexpectedly dry. She coughs.

"Guychardson," she says again. He pauses in his work, looks up.

"Let me see your knife," she says.

Guychardson blinks, and then gives a sly smile and pulls the knife out of the knuckle he's cutting through. He holds it out toward her, twists it in the air. The fluorescents glint off its weird double edges, creating some subtle optical effervescence, like something that would manifest at the onset of a drug trip.

"Let me *see* it," she insists, reaching out for it.

"*Non!*" says Guychardson, pulling it back. "See with your eyes, not with your hands."

The tilting plane of the blade sends a splinter of light into her eye. It catches there, dancing in her optical field.

She frowns, blinks: one, two, three times. The glimmer doesn't clear. If anything, it widens slightly.

She looks down. Looks at the cow carcass rendered beneath her. *This is your job*, she thinks, as she looks at spread-open tissue. *This is work. It's normal.* But the light wandering across the webbed mess makes it go weird. Abstracts it into pattern. The gleaming of meat takes on shape, each point of wet light gaining dimensionality, texture, like a set of radiolarians.

"Jesus Christ," she says, blinking fiercely. A fog of pain begins to coalesce around the edges of her perception. "What did you do?"

"I didn't—" she can hear Guychardson say, an uncharacteristic concern creeping into his voice, "—I didn't do *anything*."

The meat surges in her vision, threatening to take on the status of landscape. She pulls away from it.

"I need—" she says. "I need to sit down."

She stumbles away from the worktable, through the front kitchen, out to the floor, eventually coming to rest at the bar, mercifully dark, closed at this hour, although she half-wishes the bartender—Sophia or Tunde or whoever is on tonight—was on duty now to quickly pour her a shot of something, anything.

The roaming bead of light, still not dispelled, settles into the edge of her field of vision and then quivers, once, violently, abruptly expanding, tearing a vertical band through her perception of the world. She grunts and clamps her left hand over her eye, but it doesn't help: the light persists in the darkness, a twisting ribbon of magnesium flare.

She sucks air through her nose: the world smells like ground-up batteries.

I know what this is, she thinks.

What she says is: "Fuck."

She doesn't want to have a seizure at work. The floor in here is polished concrete: it's going to hurt if she bounces her head off it. She considers lying down on the floor but before she gets a chance to do anything, the light gives way to an aperture, a view into something.

She's not inside this time; she's outside. She's standing in the center of the field where they grew cabbages, squash, and beans. The farmhouse is visible over the crest of the slope. She looks down, wondering if she'll spot something that's hers, something like the sketchbook, something that links her to this particular spot. A thing she left behind. And sure enough, half-embedded in the dirt is a cheap LED flashlight that she used to hook to her belt loop, unknowingly dropped here when its clip broke, must have been early last summer, in her final days at the farm. She remembers its orange plastic casing, a tangerine color she admired for its cheerfulness, gone dull now from the sequence of seasons that has passed over it, baked beyond pumpkin, down to a dead beige.

Something troubles her about it. It's wrong that it should be here. If Donald were tending the field properly he should have found it, removed it as part of the process of raking the soil. And the soil around it looks bad: dry and cracked, choked with weeds and stones. A feeling of dread opens in the depths of her gut.

She looks around and the dread turns into a jab of anguish: things are worse than she thought. The entire field is dry, caked. There are a few stunted cabbages pushing up between the thistles, but their leaves are sallow, worm-ravaged. The PVC irrigation tubes that she installed appear to still be in place, but as she looks closer she notes that some have decoupled and some have splintered, suggesting that Donald didn't take the steps, months ago, that would have been necessary to winterize the system.

You don't do this, she thinks. *You don't neglect a healthy field. You don't let it die just because you're a lazy fuck.* It's as if he let a dog starve to death in a locked room because he was too stupid or too stubborn to feed it.

Her mood tilts for a moment, teeters towards guilt. *It's not Donald who's to blame*, she thinks. *It's you. You did this. You stepped away and everything broke.*

Except no. Fuck that. She'll take the blame for stepping outside of the happy little circle of Ollie and Jesse and Donald. She will. But she won't take the blame for this. Just because Donald was *sad* or *depressed* or *whatever* when she left him doesn't give him license to let this die.

This thought leads directly into the next: *Jesse.*

How is Jesse?

How bad is it, without her?

She makes herself stop there, think about it differently. It's not *without her* but rather *with Donald.* How much has her fuckup of a partner fucked up her son? How much *exactly*?

Some cold and rational part of her recognizes that she's engaged in a calculated maneuver here, avoiding feeling guilty by opting to feel angry. The more the guilt threatens to rise, the angrier she has to get.

She recognizes this, but it doesn't stop her from doing

it. She lets the anger rise. She moves across the field like an avenging ghost; she floats over the ridge and descends toward the house, imagining flames streaming out of her hair.

She passes into the house through a window. The ground floor of the house—what in this moment she still thinks of as *her house*—is a vile disorder, appalling. The dining room table is taken up with one of Donald's bows, its string off, halfway through the process of being rewrapped. The kitchen floor is strewn with empty Amazon boxes and air-pillow packing bags. She's almost grateful that it looks so shitty: every out-of-place item is fuel for the anger that she needs.

She whirls into the living room. There's Donald, sprawled on the couch, his hair even longer and more unkempt than the last time she saw him, his feet propped up on a pile of dirty laundry. A new-looking laptop rests on his belly: on the screen she can see some little man, whom Donald is steering through swarming lattices.

She wants to slap the stupid thing across the room. She wants to shake him.

Turn around, she thinks at the back of his head. *You fuck. Turn around and look at me.* But he doesn't.

She wants to tell him to *step the fuck up*. You don't do this. You don't let things go to shit. You have to nurture the things that have been left in your care.

Finally she looks away, lets her attention spin around the room in a wild, dizzying circle. She's still so angry that she feels her spiraling gaze ought to be knocking photos off the wall, cracking the windowpanes.

Wait, she tells herself. *Stop. Find Jesse. Where is Jesse?*

Upstairs. Effortlessly she floats up through the ceiling, rising, disorientingly, into Jesse's bureau, where all she can see are wooden slats, clothes wadded in the darkness. She rises further, emerges through the top of the bureau. It's littered with sticks, stones, a glass beaker, an empty rat cage.

And then, at last, she sees him, sitting cross-legged on the bed, sheets tangled around his waist, his head bowed. He's focused on working something in his hands, interlocked pieces of metal—a tavern puzzle?—so she can't see his face, just the crown of his head.

And what she sees is: he's had a haircut. The long locks of his that she loved: gone. She's surprised at how much it hurts, at how quickly it takes on the shape of a betrayal, seeing him shorn like this. She wonders whether Donald was the one who did it: it looks amateur, like it was cut at home by someone who didn't entirely know what he was doing. She looks at her son's hair: it's patchy, uneven, close to the skull.

Also, it's green.

Green-haired kid: there's a way in which she thinks she could like the change, if only she could find a way through the blockage of hating it. Less metalhead, more punk: maybe not the choice she'd have made but she can see, if she's being reasonable, that it doesn't need to break her heart. It doesn't.

He looks up and looks directly at the spot where she is and her heart jolts. His face is chalky white. For a fraction of a second she thinks that he's *dead*, that she's seeing his *ghost* somehow, and the sudden surge of grief that blasts through her eradicates whatever pleasure she might have taken from being able to look into his eyes again. A rending wail begins

71

to form within her and it doesn't fully subside even when she realizes he isn't dead, isn't a ghost, but has just, for some reason, chosen to cake his face with white greasepaint. A ring of red lipstick carelessly loops his mouth.

He's not going through a punk phase. He's going through a—clown phase? Why the fuck does he look like that?

He peers into the spot where she is and frowns, concentrating.

She flinches.

The makeup has a slightly rotten quality. Blame the August heat, maybe, but he looks *diseased* somehow. If he's a clown, he's the tiniest, sickest clown, a clown that the other clowns might taunt for sport. And why is he a clown anyway?

She realizes that what he looks like, more than anything else, is the Joker. Batman's Joker. The sickest clown of them all. *Why the fuck does he look like that?* she thinks again, helplessly.

A hand drops onto her shoulder. A voice—she recognizes it distantly as Angel's—says, "Hey. Hey, Ollie," and the vision of Jesse splinters up and away, and she's back in Carnage, disoriented and wrenched.

The first thing she does is vomit. She just opens her mouth and her gut gives one solid heave and everything in her issues out directly onto the bar. Tears spring into her eyes, more purgation. As if her body thinks that it can flush out what she's seen.

"Whoa, whoa, whoa," says Angel. He rests a hand between her shoulder blades for a quick second, and then seems to think better of it, moves around behind the bar instead. "Water," he says, and he makes a glass of it happen, sets it down in front of her. She gulps it as he produces a pub towel and wipes down the spattered zinc.

"Bourbon," she says, once she's gotten through about half of the water and ensured that it's going to stay down. Angel flicks her a look like he's maybe not sure that she's sure what she's asking. She gives him the flat look that she usually gives in response to guys giving her that kind of look, and he does what she asked. Neat, with a Coke back, the way she likes it. She finds herself a little surprised that he remembered that; she's only drank with him twice before. She glugs the bourbon down without pausing to taste it. Then she sips the Coke and holds it in her mouth, letting it fizz there until it goes inert, and only then finally swallowing.

"Are you OK?" Angel asks.

"I don't know," she says, and immediately regrets it, because it breaks a rule that she set for herself when she started in this kitchen: *Never look weak.* "Yes. No. I don't know. I should—I should get back to work."

"You should go *home*," says Angel.

Home. Her apartment's in the South Bronx. The thought of sitting on the Pelham Line for half an hour makes her blanch a little, and it must be apparent, more apparent than she wants it to be, because Angel makes a sympathetic noise with his mouth.

"I'll tell you what," he says. He has his key ring out and he's fussing a key off of it. "My place. It's only a couple of blocks from here. I can call the doorman, no problem.

There's a bottle of bourbon there if you, if you decide to, uh, stay on that path. No Coke, sorry. I'm pretty sure you can get Mexican Cokes in the bodega on the corner, though. You know? Real glass bottle?"

He slides the key across the bar toward her. She hesitates. She knows what a man is thinking about, when he gives you a key to his house and invites you to let yourself in and pour yourself a glass of bourbon. She knows there's been an invitation on the table for a while now, and she still hasn't quite figured out what she wants to do about it, and she doesn't want to figure it out right this second because what she wants to be doing right this second is worrying about her son, 150 miles away and looking like the Goddamn *Joker*. But she has to give some kind of answer.

He lifts her hand and puts it on top of the key. He leaves his hand on top of hers when he's done. It feels dry, and warm.

"I don't know," she says, for the third time, cringing to hear the words come out of her mouth. "I'm feeling better. I should just—I could just jump back in there, get back to work."

"You *can't*," Angel says. "We have enough problems with Department of Health as it is, without someone in there, you know, *actively* throwing up." He offers up a smile, which she doesn't reciprocate. He looks at her unconvinced face. "Ollie. You can't. This is me, your boss, telling you *no*."

At the word *boss* he takes his hand off hers. Oh right. 'Cause this isn't just about whether she's going to fuck Angel, some guy, this is about whether she's going to fuck Angel, *her boss*. The biggest possible shit-where-you-eat she can fathom. *Don't*, she tells herself. You just don't. It's not that hard.

She straightens her spine and it cracks. "OK," she says. "If I can't go back to work I'd better just go home."

For just a second, she can see disappointment on his face, and it threatens to become one more Goddamn thing to feel guilty about. But screw it. She can live with his disappointment as an outcome. It's kinda messed up, anyway, that he'd want to fuck her tonight, after having just watched her get sick on the bar. Who *does* that? What kind of guy takes someone else's moment of weakness and molds it into an opportunity?

The kind of guy, she answers herself, who imagines himself as a savior, who wants to have you perform the infamous swoon of gratitude, square into his arms. That's the kind of guy you don't need to feel too guilty about disappointing.

But that look of his is already gone by the time she slides the key back across the counter; he's returned to wearing his normal expression of scrupulous feline cool, all the appetites in it out of sight for the moment.

"Feel better soon," he says.

She goes back into the kitchen, gathers her stuff. Guychardson draws close to her, hovering at the edge of her personal space, a strong whiff of nonverbal apology coming off him, as though he wants to reach out and touch her on the arm but can't quite convince himself that it would be OK. Frankly she's grateful for his restraint. She doesn't want to talk to Guychardson right now. She doesn't want to talk to him, she doesn't want to look at him, and she sure as shit doesn't want to be touched by him. Because he *did something* to her. With that knife. Maybe he regrets it, maybe it wasn't on purpose, maybe maybe maybe. She'll figure it out later. Not right now. She's got enough on her mind to last her all Goddamn night.

6

PATHFINDING

Maja sits in a tower in Boston's financial district, where she speaks to a man in a suit with whom she does not shake hands.

She puts a suitcase full of cash on the desk between them and he does not ask any questions about this, which she appreciates. He simply completes a set of transactions that transforms the cash into an array of numbers in a financial register. She clicks the end of a pen. She likes wealth better once it becomes numbers; there's less sense of it ever having been anywhere, ever having been connected to real things in the world.

Sitting on the desk in the office, in an acrylic box with a mahogany base, is a weathered baseball, an illegible signature across its surface. She can hardly stand to be in the same room with it; there's some kind of meaningful incident radiating off it like heat. The man in the office with his son. The two of them together at a ball game. A flare of enduring happiness. Soon after, the boy is gone; she gets an image of the man in a hospital, wringing a piece of cloth in his hands.

She can't quite figure out what happened to the boy. Some disease, something wrong with his bones, the marrow—? *It doesn't matter*, she tells herself, *stop looking*. She doesn't need the story of what happened in the hospital; she already knows it. Every hospital is alike: they have different forms but serve the same function, and they're all riddled with the passage of the same sad story, the story that she herself lived through when she was eighteen, holding her younger brother's hand. In a way, every object is alike, too. If you look closely enough, every object can always be connected, somehow, to someone's suffering. You have to know when to stop looking.

The man produces a plastic capsule of mints, offers her one. She declines. He taps one into his own hand, but before inserting it into his mouth he pauses and asks, "Can I help you with anything else?"

He can't. She rises to go. He gives her a business card which, the moment she's outside of the tower, she flicks into a garbage can.

With the money out of her hands she can at last let the jet lag catch up to her. She wanders the streets of downtown Boston for maybe a quarter of an hour, carrying the empty suitcase and the rolling garment bag. For a short while she follows a trail set into the pavement, two bricks wide, designed to lead people around this part of the city. She follows it to a cobblestone circle marking the spot where people died. Soldiers firing into a crowd. Almost 250 years ago but she can still feel it.

Boston is interesting: it's young compared to the European towns she's accustomed to, but it's deeply storied. It contains an amount of history that feels disproportionate to the amount of time it has existed. A certain mythic aspect coagulates in its streets. Given more time or less fatigue she could possibly figure out how to enjoy it.

She enters a hotel, one chosen randomly from those available downtown. She books herself a room for a week. She doesn't intend to use it for any longer than just tonight but she's always known that when you deal with unsavory people it's good practice to leave a data trail that points to the wrong place. A safeguard.

A little gift shop adjoins the lobby and she browses in it for a few minutes, finally electing to use a bit of her walkaround cash to buy a book on Colonial Revolutionary Boston. She flips through its pages on the elevator and when she enters her room she tosses it onto her pillow. She turns the air conditioner way up and draws the curtain shut against the late afternoon sun. She takes a hot shower, finally scrubbing away the residue of intercontinental jet travel, and, upon returning to the chill dim room, she immediately burrows down into bed. She uses both fists to gather a hunk of the comforter up into her face; she inhales the familiar bleachy odor. She picks up a distant sense of the bodies—so many—that have been touched by this blanket before, but the strongest association that she always gets from hotel linens is nothing human at all but rather a soothing sense of being repeatedly tumbled and churned by enormous laundry machines, long rows of industrial tourbillions, producing a steady endless roar, like a sea. She's asleep within a moment.

She wakes to darkness and a sensation of dread. The sensation is active, alert, as though it had woken before her and waited, watching her for an hour with living eyes. She scrutinizes it, gives it a name: it's the feeling that she's forgotten something about the job, or, worse, that there was some important piece of information that she never picked up on in the first place. The sense that something has failed to be found.

She thinks about Unger and Pig, lets their faces float before her in the darkness. She remembers what she said to the Archive, back at Zingers: *I'm not scared.*

Are you not, says the Archive to her, now.

No, she's not. There's no reason why she should be. Unger and Pig want something, like all her clients. They have money, they have weapons, and this makes them dangerous, sure, to someone, definitely, but not to her. She's on their side. They want something, and she's willing to find it for them. It doesn't matter that the job involves a gun. Most of her jobs do. All that matters is that she stay on the right end of it. And she always does.

So what is it? What is she missing?

Nothing, she says.

Is it something about the thing itself? The item they want, this blade, this special blade? What makes it worth the money, the time, the trouble?

But clients want all sorts of things, for all kinds of reasons. She once found a particular mannequin torso for a Tokyo nori manufacturer. Trying to speculate too much about motive just clouds the work, mires her in the muck of other people's personalities. She doesn't ask. It keeps things simple. It's likely that the blade is just one more weird thing, in a world full of them.

Except, says the Archive.

Except what?

Well, I don't know, it says. *You're the expert. You tell me.*

Except nothing, she thinks. *Go back to sleep.*

She huddles beneath the comforter again, directs her awareness back to the memory of humming washers and dryers embodied within it, but it's not enough to get her back to sleep. She opens her eyes, rolls over, looks at the clock on the bedside table. Half past three. She gives up, reaches out, turns on the light. The book on Boston is still in the bed, and she picks it up, begins to read a chapter about Paul Revere. The famous midnight ride. The marks he made on silver. Eventually the sun rises and the dread goes away.

She leaves her rental in its downtown garage, instead walks to South Station, where she sits in front of a monitor and blankly watches a video about police dogs until her commuter rail train is announced. She boards, and naps fitfully in the rocking car, until a little over an hour later when the train reaches the end of the line. Plymouth. She disembarks, drags her bag blearily across the platform, blinking against the oppressive August light. She knows that Plymouth is important to the American Story, and everything she knows about this country led her to expect that she'd stumble directly into some kind of tourist village, someplace hawking stuffed Pilgrims or replicas of the famous rock, but all she sees is an empty parking lot and an enormous abandoned department store. In the middle of the lot is a beat-up green town car, and sitting on its hood, cross-legged, is Pig. Something is over his face.

As she draws nearer she can tell what it is. It's a wooden pig mask. It has a lean, tapered snout. Long tangles of braided cord descend from its jawline and the back of its head, forming a kind of bristled mane. The thing has circular eyeholes, ringed with daubs of white paint, and as she approaches she gets the unsettling sensation that she's being peered at, or, worse, peered into. She stops, about twenty paces away.

Pig tilts the mask back so that it rests on his forehead. It casts a shadow on his face but it doesn't hide his grin. "Goood morning," he says.

"Good morning," she replies, evenly. "Nice mask."

"Thanks," Pig says. "Call it my good-luck charm."

"Wonderful," she says, although to be honest she's always hated the notion of luck. "Where'd you get it?" So far she has very deliberately resisted reading it.

Pig looks away, squints up into the sun. "I took it off some dead African," he says, casually.

She's not sure whether he intends for that answer, couched in that casualness, to shock, impress, or intimidate, but in reality it does none of the above: it makes her feel a little irritated and a little bored. She doubts that it's true and she knows that can find out the real answer by giving the object just a little bit of sustained attention, by looking into it for just one moment.

And so she does.

What she gets is a chaotic picture of mud, agitated by boots and heavy rain. Often her reading of objects starts off with her visualizing a moment just like this, but typically what happens next is she gets *more*: she gets the adjacent moments, and she strings them together, and when she's strung enough of them together, she has a story. But she can't do that with this mud: she can't attach it to anything, can't place it on the string of time. It just loops in her head, a meaningless snippet, three seconds of violently churning muck.

Maja frowns. She dips in again. She gets a different image: a helicopter, squatting on a landing pad, black and low-slung and chitinous, its rotors roaring, a group of men striding through kicked-up vortices of trash. She tries to connect one image to the other. She should be able to. She's always been able to. But she can't. The disjunction looms in her mind like a wound, unable to be healed. It's as though the object has been severed from its own past. As though time itself has been cut.

He did something, she thinks, and the dread from last night rushes back into her, pours in, a dank wave. *Pig did something to the mask so that I can't read it.* But that can't be right. She's never seen anyone do anything like that before.

Pig looks away from the sun, turns his eyes back to her, looks over her frown. He maintains the same bland expression, and she can't be sure whether he knows that she has just tried—and failed—to learn something about him. She wishes he would at least put on a satisfied face.

So, says the Archive. *Maybe a little scary after all.*

Yes. The Archive is right. She looks into the blithe face of this man and she feels fear. Not distrust, not middle-of-the-night dread: *fear.*

That means we get to go home, then, yes?

No, thinks Maja.

83

But you said.

I said we got to go home if we were in danger. And we're not in danger. We're just scared. That's different.

She knows what to do, when something has scared her. She has one strategy: she looks into it more deeply. It doesn't matter what the thing is. It doesn't even need to be a thing. The darkness of winter, some monstrous human, it's all the same: she looks into it until she understands it. Just like any thing can be found, any unknown can be figured out, and once you figure it out, it loses its power over you.

I can beat you, she thinks, at Pig and his mask, and all at once her entire face relaxes, breaks into a smile. She notes with some pleasure that, in response, Pig's face gives up a very small flicker of surprise, almost a flinch, before he checks it, transforms it into a smile of his own.

"You ready to do this thing?" he says, breaking the silence.

"When you are," she says.

"All right then," he says. He hops off the hood of the car, takes her bag. "Just point me in the right direction."

"Yes," she says. "That's the idea."

7

DISTRACTION

"Ollie?" Victor calls, from the kitchen, as soon as she keys in.

"Yeah."

"Don't come in here."

"OK," she says. She sloughs off her messenger bag, lets it fall on the couch.

"I'm working on something in here. It's a surprise."

"I said OK."

"Why are you here, anyway? I thought you were at work."

"I was at work," she says. "I got sick."

"Wait, you're *sick*?" Victor sticks his head into the room. His brow gleams with a sheen of sweat; his look is a mixture of irritation and concern.

"I'm not sick," says Ollie. "I *got* sick."

"Wait a second," Victor says, disappearing back into the kitchen.

"Go," she says. "Do whatever it is you're doing. I gotta make a phone call anyway."

And she gets out her phone, and for the first time in a year she dials Donald's number. She knows it's a long shot, trying to reach him on his cell: the farm is nestled into a deep vale not known for its robust cellular coverage. She remembers an argument they had, right before he first got the phone, in which she told him it was stupid to buy a phone you could only use in the loft over the barn or on the crest of the tallest hill on the property, and she remembers a second argument they had about it a month after he'd bought it, when it had already fallen into disuse. Maybe it's different now, she tells herself: maybe cellular waves or whatever they are, invisible lines of force, are everywhere now, maybe they penetrate into the insides of everything. But maybe not.

Sure enough, dialing him yields only twenty seconds of dead silence and then a busy signal. She recognizes this as a category of error but isn't sure what precisely it means. She hangs up.

She shifts on the couch. She taps her phone against her kneecap, once, twice, three times, and then she stands up again, paces from the couch to her bedroom door. Taped to the door is something she tore out of a magazine, a super-saturated photograph of a human heart.

She stares at it until she realizes she's holding her breath. She forces herself to exhale, and then she lifts her phone and dials the number for the farm's landline. She's extra reluctant to call the farm this way, because there's the chance that Jesse could answer, and she doesn't know what she'd say to him; there's a part of her that believes that if she heard his voice, even his voice saying just one word, just *hello*, then whatever has been holding her together this year would snap, and she would, at long last, go completely to pieces.

But Jesse doesn't answer. And Donald doesn't answer. Instead, after five rings, she hears the heavy clunk of tape heads engaging. Oh right: the landline is still connected to an answering machine. She remembers it, a slab of plastic slowly warping in its dirty little corner, terrifically obsolete.

"You have reached Illuminated Farms," a wobbly version of her voice says into her ear. She recoils at hearing this, startled at imagining her voice emerging from a machine, speaking to an empty, dusty sunroom every time someone calls the landline. And, of course, maybe the room's not empty. Maybe Jesse is there. She tries to imagine what that must feel like, hearing a recording of your mom's voice, a year after she's moved out. Trying to imagine it makes her feel like she's been punched in the chest.

She does not leave a message. She hangs up, stares down the heart taped to the door. It's a lovely muscle but it's got no sense.

She forces herself to lie down on the couch again. She flips through things on her phone, considers texting Ulysses. She considers this sometimes, when she's feeling low, and she usually rejects the impulse, exactly as she does now. Eventually Victor enters, balling up an apron in his hands. She lifts her head and he comes and sits on the couch, providing her with a lap to lower back down into. He puts his hand in her hair in the way that she finds comfortable.

"Now, tell me again, *what* happened?" he says, once they're situated. "You threw up?"

"Yes, Victor, for the tenth time."

His hand pauses in her hair. "But you're not sick."

"No. It was from—I don't know, I guess you would say *stress*."

"What stress?" His hand begins to move again, rubbing tension out of her scalp.

"Shit is all fucked."

"Tell me."

"You remember that vision I had at Christmastime?"

"The seizure."

"The vision. The seizure. Whatever. Just—you remember."

"Of course."

"Well, yeah, I did *that* again."

She tells him the whole thing. Guychardson's knife: the way that the more she looked at it the more it seemed to destabilize her reality. Throwing up. The new vision. Jesse with green hair and clown makeup.

"So, in conclusion," she says, "shit is fucked."

"It's a little bit fucked," Victor concedes. "But, wait. No. You know what this is? It's a phase. Kids go through phases. They do stuff that's difficult for adults to make sense of. That's the whole point of half of what they do. He's just been listening to some ICP, now he's doing a little mini-Juggalo act."

"I don't know what those words mean," Ollie says.

"You're hopeless, my dear. The point is that it's not serious. The situation is under control."

"It doesn't *feel* under control."

"It's going to pass. Phases do end, you know, that's why we call them phases."

"Sounds like bullshit," Ollie says.

Victor seems to weigh this. "Hey," he says. "If it's bullshit you should at least take it as well-meaning bullshit. It is bullshit with a purpose and a function."

"Which is?"

"Which is to make you feel better, my darling."

"Not everyone *wants* to feel *better* all the time, Victor. You ever consider that?"

"I have not," Victor says.

"Well, maybe you should."

Victor looks down into her face, pursing his lips as though the idea is distasteful. "I never really understood whatever great *merit* there is to be found in wallowing endlessly in the swamp of one's own feelings all day, especially when the ready alternative—to feel better—allows one to, actually, you know, *feel better*."

"You want me to feel better?" she snaps. "Fine. But you're not going to be able to make that happen by pointing at my problem with your magic wand and saying, '*Hey, that problem, it doesn't exist any more.*'"

"Remind me," Victor says, "of exactly what your problem is."

"My problem is—my *problem* is—"

"Explain it to me this way," Victor says, delivering her from her spluttering. "Tell me what bothers you the *most*."

Ollie thinks for a moment. She wants to say something about the clown makeup again, she wants to convey just how disturbing her son looked caked with cheap greasepaint, but she pauses. She considers the question put before her: is that really what bothered her the most? Is that really why she feels so gutted right now? And she realizes that it isn't, not really.

"I just wish," she says, "I just wish they hadn't cut his hair."

"It's hair," Victor says. "Hair gets cut."

Oh, right. Hair gets cut. That's part of what it means, to go away, to be gone for so long. It means time passes without you. Hair grows, and it gets cut, and it grows again, and none of it has fuck-all to do with you. You get no say.

It hurts. Tears spring into Ollie's eyes; she blinks them away, furious that her body would betray her in this way, reveal the extent of her humiliation. She bites her lip.

Victor sees her reaction, and he knows he's partly responsible, and his face softens a little.

"I'm sorry," he says. "Listen," he says, then, "I'm sorry that I'm being an asshole. I just don't know what to do. Tell me what to *do*."

"Fucking—distract me," she says, angrily. "Give me something to think about instead of my fucking problem." As she says this, she realizes that this is effectively the strategy she's taken with herself over the last year. She has served herself a long sequence of distractions, each one enabling her to forget for a little while longer.

"Actually," Victor says, brightening, "I know *exactly* what will serve this purpose. I was going to wait and show you when it was truly ready, but, what the hell."

She raises her eyebrows, faintly optimistic. It's Victor

90

who's talking, so she's expecting this is a buildup to some tasty concoction, a summertime treat of some variety or another. An emergency dessert: deploy in event of shitty day. She envisions a flash-frozen spiral of watermelon, something you could plunk in a tumbler of clear liquor. Who is she to say no? She has no interest in playing the role of gloomy saint, of being wrapped so deeply in the cowl of her woes that she misses out on the world, phenomenal, before her.

"Up!" says Victor, and they both rise. She heads into the kitchen; he follows along. "Voilà," he says, once she's all the way in the room.

There's no dessert in here. There's nothing simmering on the stove, no remnants of production spread out on the steel prep table. The immersion blender and the infuser and the blowtorch are all racked in their usual slots. But then she sees what Victor wants her to see.

It's about the size and shape of a wrinkled napkin, and it hangs in the air between the refrigerator and the sink: a tiny cut in space, palpitating gently at its edges. A little vent, opening onto a weird darkness, a darkness that seems more tactile than optical. She recognizes it immediately. It's a portal to the Inside.

"Holy shit," she says.

"You know what that is," Victor says, quietly, a half question.

"Of course I fucking know what that is. I'm just—surprised to see it here in our kitchen."

Victor drapes his arms over her shoulders. "This is the part where you tell me how *amazing* I am, and how you're *very impressed* with me," he says, into her ear, ever the pupil, ever in search of the next pat on the head. Opening a portal, even a tiny one like this, is tricky as hell and this is the first time she's ever seen anyone do it who wasn't a street warlock. So, yeah, she *is* very impressed. But she's also a little alarmed. She knew that Victor still tinkered with magic; she knew he would use it every now and then to prod his career along, to try to stay on top of the game. But it's been years since she's seen him do anything more than some little charm. She didn't know that he was dabbling in major stuff like this.

Victor releases her, approaches the portal. He waggles his eyebrows and says, in a goofy voice, "Hey, Rocky, watch me pull a rabbit out of my hat," some reference that she doesn't catch. And he plunges his hand in. Just as she'd remembered, nothing comes out the other side.

"Oh my God," Ollie says. Upon seeing this, some of her old teenage enthusiasm for magic rushes back, wiping away her adult concerns for the moment. "Let me try." The street warlocks would never let her enter the doors they'd open; she was always left to wonder what it felt like, in there. Now that she has the opportunity she's eager to seize it.

"Be careful," Victor says, pulling his hand back out. "Remember that there are things *living* in there."

"I remember them," she says. Shadowy fishlike things, moving about, always just beyond the threshold of where she could see. She lines up her face with the hole, looks in, tries to catch a glimpse of one.

"They used to creep me out, she says, "but—do you think they're dangerous? I mean—the street warlocks used to go in there and *walk around*, right?"

"True," Victor says. "But never for very long. And I do remember them saying that you had to *be careful*."

"Well," Ollie says. "I'm great at that."

She pokes three fingers into it, to see if they feel weird once they're on the other side. They do, a bit; they encounter a sort of wet resistance, as though she is sticking her fingers into a pudding that is exactly the temperature of the air. She sticks her entire forearm in.

"You look like you're helping a cow give birth," Victor says.

"Nice," Ollie says. She reaches in further, going in past the elbow, until the aperture tightens around her bicep like a rubber ring and she can go no further.

"Can you make it wider?" she asks, flexing her fingers. She can feel little vectors of invisible force radiating from her fingertips: as though every gesture she makes is magnified. She's starting to get it: what it would be like to go through. She can feel that you could *do things* in there that you can't do out here. She's not quite sure what kinds of things, exactly, but she knows that being able to do them would make you powerful. At the thought her heart begins to beat a little bit harder.

"That's as wide as I can open it on my own," Victor says, watching her. "But I think I could get it wider if I had a tool."

"A tool like a wand?"

"A tool like a dagger."

"Ah," Ollie says. She slides her arm back out of it; it feels like she's peeling off an opera glove. "A tool like Guychardson's knife."

"It doesn't have to be *his* knife."

"No?"

"No. I mean, if there's some other magic knife out there that triggers clairvoyant visions and makes people barf, that one would do just as well."

She smirks, despite herself, then frowns.

"I don't know, Victor, I don't think he's exactly in the habit of *loaning it out.*"

"I can be very persuasive," Victor says sweetly. "Just invite him out. Invite him to tomorrow night's thing."

"What thing?" Ollie says.

Victor sighs, showing his annoyance at yet another piece of evidence that Ollie can't be bothered with keeping her finger on whatever pulse it is that Victor cares about. "Tomorrow," he says acidly. "Industry night at Ovid?"

"Oh right," Ollie says. She remembers now; she actually heard about this one. "You *know* I hate those types of things. I'm not going."

Victor's acid tone shifts straight to pleading: "You should *go*. And invite this Guychardson fellow."

"Tomorrow's Sunday. I only work with him Fridays and Saturdays."

"It's the modern age, my dear—text him. You have his number in your phone?"

"I don't know. Maybe?"

"Check."

"Yeah, OK," she says, not really thinking about whether she'll do it or not. She slides her hand into the portal again. This time it comes into contact with something firm yet spongy, a sort of reactive tissue—it clutches at her with what feel like a hundred tiny sucking mouths. Her heart leaps and she yanks her hand back.

"Shit," she says, looking at her fingers to make sure they haven't been compromised in some way, even though there is no pain. "Shit. Fuck. Shit."

"What happened?" Victor asks.

"Something touched me," she says. "One of the things in there touched me."

They look at the portal and watch together as it undergoes one powerful pulsation.

"Did it just get wider?" Ollie says.

"It did," Victor says.

"Are you sure?"

"I'm not sure. But you saw it."

"I'm not sure I saw it."

"You saw it. You were the one who asked if *I* saw it."

"We both saw it."

"Maybe—" Victor concludes, "maybe it's time we make it go away."

"You can do that, right?"

"What do you think I am," Victor says, "stupid? Of course I can do that."

He reaches out and claps his hands once, sharply.

Nothing happens.

"Huh," Victor says.

"Fuck," Ollie says.

Something slides out of the portal and hits the floor.

8

TRIANGLE

Maja and Pig drive south from Plymouth, heading toward New York. For the first part of the drive, as they pass through Massachusetts, Maja struggles against the temptation to try reading him again, to double-check that he's really done whatever strange thing that he's done to his history. She wants to, but the shock that it gave her left her with a sort of negative conditioning: she's afraid to reach into him because she doesn't want to get the same shock a second time. She oscillates, for a while, between wanting to and not wanting to: this keeps her on edge for maybe an hour. But after she's gone that hour, without looking, it seems like she's made her decision, and the question stops being interesting for her. If she needs to revisit it later, she will.

For now she looks out the window: watches the green landscape of Connecticut flicker past. As they draw near one of the state's cities they pass an exit with a sign for Albertus Magnus College, which makes her smile.

"Albertus Magnus," she says, breaking the long silence that's risen up between them.

"Huh?" Pig says.

"Albertus Magnus," she says again, pointing through the windshield. "Some people think he was a magician, you know."

"Oh yeah?" Pig says.

"An alchemist," she says. "He may have believed in the occult properties of stones. There's a rumor that he discovered the philosopher's stone and passed it on to Thomas Aquinas."

"Magic stones, huh?" Pig says. He affects boredom but she can detect an edge of interest in his voice. "Do you buy it?"

"Do I buy it?" she repeats, seeking clarification.

"Yeah. Do you think a stone can be magic?"

"Yes," she says, without hesitating. "Anything can be magic."

"Really," Pig says. "Anything."

"Well," Maja says, "think about it. How do magicians make an ordinary thing magical?"

"They wave their hands over it or some shit," Pig says.

"That's one way of doing it," Maja says, smiling a bit in spite of herself. "But really it's even simpler than that. You make an ordinary thing magical just by paying attention to it. And humans can pay attention to all kinds of objects. So any kind of object could, theoretically, be magical."

Pig's eyes flick away from the road, range over her face for a second. She feels pleased, like she's gotten him to reveal something, although she's not sure what, exactly.

"Well, that's your whole thing, right?" Pig says.

"What is?" Maja asks.

"Paying attention to stuff," Pig says. "I mean, that's what you do, right? That's how my dad described it to me, anyway: you pay attention to like *layers* in things that other people don't see?"

"Something like that," Maja says.

"So everything's a little bit magical to you, then?"

She considers this. "Yes."

"OK, then, let me ask you something else."

"OK," Maja says. "Sure."

"How is it that you're not crazy?"

What makes you so sure that we're not crazy, says the Archive. Maja, playing it more cautiously, replies, "Pardon me?"

Pig frowns slightly, adjusts his hands on the steering wheel. "Well," he says. "Things talk to you. They talk to you and tell you what they're all about." Maja considers, for a moment, whether to engage this line of questioning. But it's nothing. It's no more than she would explain to any other client. So why not. "What they're all about, yes."

"Which includes where they are."

"Where they are, where they've been," Maja says.

"Where they've been. You mean, like—in the past."

She hesitates on this, bites her lip. Pig's mask, with its glitchy history, still doesn't sit well with her, and his curiosity about that aspect of her talent sharpens her suspicion slightly, makes her regret having alluded to the past, even casually. But she proceeds.

"Yes," she says. "Like in the past."

"And it can be something that's up close or far away," Pig says.

"Yes."

"So, OK," he says. "If you've got everything in the whole world talking to you—I mean, I'm no expert, but that's a lot of Goddamn things, am I right?"

"You're"—at this she has to actually crack a smile—"you're not wrong."

"So if they're all talking to you simultaneously—how is it that you don't just go nuts?"

"Ah," Maja says, understanding finally. "That was a problem," she says. "Originally. When I was a teenager, and was just figuring out how it worked." She frowns, wanting to take what she's just said and refine it for accuracy. She's still not eager to open up to Pig, but her distaste for imprecision works to override this. "The problem wasn't the things," she clarifies. "Most things just—they're peaceful. They sit there quietly, like they're waiting. Waiting to be asked something. And when I ask, they answer. But otherwise they tend to be quiet. It's not like you put it, it's not like they're all talking simultaneously. But people—it's different with people."

"So, wait," Pig says. "Your thing works on people, too?"

"Of course," Maja says. "A person is really just a special category of thing. But—less quiet. That's what was hardest, back then."

She remembers puberty, remembers the queasiness she would feel in the physical presence of other humans, the way she would feel sprayed with the constant broadcast of their shames, their secrets. Even the mundane glimpses she would get of other people's lives left her feeling uneasy: she did not want her head crammed with visions of people chewing up breakfast meats or adjusting a bra or sitting on a toilet.

"So how'd you manage it?" Pig asks.

"I swam," Maja says. "A lot of laps."

Being at the natatorium, alone in water, seemed to mute her awareness of a world filled with other people. She would occasionally catch a glimpse of a swimmer in an adjacent lane but the water would just seem to wash away any sense of them as a particular human. After her swims her usual routine would be to change into her sweat suit and jog a mile to the library, her tangled hair freezing in the dark. In the library she would sit in the remotest carrel she could find and she would read biographies, which she experienced as a manageable way to learn about others, without having to submit to the overwhelming experience of actually being around them. But she doesn't tell Pig about the library. That's a thing that she wants to stay hers, and hers alone.

Remembering that time reminds her, also, of Eivind, her brother, three years younger, who similarly shied away from others, adults and youths alike, electing to spend his afternoons walking along the roads that ran along their town's shoreline. In the evenings when they would both return home they would retire to their individual rooms: occasionally, she would look in on him and find him scratching out complicated labyrinths on graph paper, or poring over some English-language rule books for role-playing games. For a while it struck her as odd, his interest in these games, as she never saw him play them with friends. Nor did he ever ask her to play with him. Eventually she figured out that it was something about these systems themselves that satisfied him. To him, the systems were ways to conceive of a world that ran according to rules, according to procedures that he could grasp and make function. Once she realized that, she could understand the appeal.

That was the thing about their relationship. They spent little time together—it was not uncommon for them to go a day without even exchanging a word—and yet she felt like she understood him. She felt as though they were close, although it was a strange closeness, a closeness that manifested itself in distance. They each recognized the tendency towards solitude in the other, and each respected this tendency, gave it room to survive. They gave one another space as a gift.

She understood this as love. And to be loved that way—it brought her a happiness that she has not felt since. She revisits the emotion in memory, some days, as though to confirm that it was real, and she can almost feel it again, but not quite: the emotion in remembrance is like an orchid, viewed through frosted glass. But she feels grateful to have been loved that way, even if it was only for a short while, and even if everything would have been different had they been *normal close*, close in a more traditional way. If they'd been normal close, if they hadn't allowed one another quite so much distance, then maybe she would have felt alarm earlier, the night that he didn't come home; maybe she would have tried earlier to reach their father on the boat; maybe she would have called the number for her mother that she never normally used; maybe she would have understood that his absence was an emergency instead of only understanding this in the morning, when it was far too late. Actually, no, maybe the emergency would never even have happened: if they'd been normal close she would have had more opportunities to protect him, the way an older sibling is supposed to. No one would have approached the two of them if they'd been together, inseparable. What happened only happened because he was alone, because he was being loved only from afar.

"And the gloves?" Pig says.

"What's that?" Maja says, blinking herself back to the conversation.

"The gloves," Pig says. "You wear gloves. That's part of it, right?"

"Yes," Maja says. "That's part of it."

They arrive in the city, starting by driving straight down into midtown Manhattan, into the glut of cabs choking the streets. She probes the grid, beginning to feel for any trace of the blade. After an hour or so she's amassed enough little hitches, enough tugs in the right direction, that she's able to have Pig turn around, head back to the Heights.

"No, wait," she says, after they've gone north for a while. "East."

And so they leave Manhattan, heading over the Washington Bridge—and then the tugs lead her south again, down Grand Concourse. She frowns as they make the turn. Something's wrong. She feels pulled in separate directions and she can't figure out why.

By this point, she's tired and thirsty and she has a pattern of snags in her mental map that are adding up to a dull headache and nothing more.

"Pull over," she says eventually, and she gets out of the town car, stands there for a second on a Brooklyn street corner, breathing the smell of hot garbage on the August air, squinting into the light bouncing off the window of a dry-cleaning place, as though the glare might trigger some epiphany.

She balls her fists and presses them into her face for a hard second. She feels angry. She is angry at whoever has the blade, angry at the idea that this person might be keeping it from her, her specifically, even though she knows there is no way that this could be accurate. She is angry at the idea that this person is deliberately preventing her from doing her job, even though she knows that this is not accurate either. She doesn't care about what is accurate; she just needs a way to focus her displeasure. She tries to envision the person laughing at her. Without knowing anything about the person, this is difficult: all she has is the knowledge that he or she is out there, somewhere. But she tries anyway, tries to form this raw sensation into something that she could treat as a nemesis, some shape with a face.

She gets a blurry sense, vague eyeholes hovering in a field of mist. *You're not smarter than me*, she thinks at it, angrily. *I'm smarter than you.*

And it works. She pulls the answer away, just as if she had pried it directly out of someone's hands.

She gets back in the car, slams the door. Pig looks up at her. There is something boyish about the expectation in his face; she can see then, maybe for the first time, just how badly he wants to find the thing.

"It moves," she says.

"It moves?"

"The blade," Maja says. "It moves around. I was looking for something in a single place, staying put. But it doesn't stay put. It changes location."

"Someone's—wielding it?" Pig asks.

"Moving it. Carrying it."

"As a security measure?"

"I can't answer that."

Pig frowns. "Does this," he starts, before breaking off. She waits while he compiles a sentence in his mind. "This is new information," is what he eventually settles on. "How much does it *change* what we're doing here?"

"Mildly," Maja says.

"How much is *mildly*?"

"What are you really asking here?" she says, impatient with this line of questioning.

"Can you still find it?" Pig says, slowly.

"Yes," she says. "We just have to do it a little differently. I'm going to stop trying to pinpoint where the blade is *right now*. Instead I'm going to figure out where it's *been*. I'll be—looking for the pattern of its movements instead of for the thing itself."

"But you'll still be able to *find* the thing itself."

"Eventually," she says. "But yes."

"Yes," Pig says, as if double-checking.

"Yes."

"OK, then," Pig says, and he grins a little bit; she allows herself to grin back in return. "So what do you need from me?"

• • •

She needs supplies. They stop at a Duane Reade and Pig purchases everything she points at: hand wipes, pens, highlighters, yogurt, a bag of almonds. A packet containing a pouch of tuna, some crackers, and a selection of spreads. A road atlas of Westchester County and Metropolitan New York.

All he buys for himself are three cellophane bags full of sour gummy worms.

She's not sure how he continues to function; she hasn't seen him eat anything but candy since they left Massachusetts, about nine hours ago now. She wonders if he's going to hit a steak house in the middle of the night, wolf down a plate of red meat. But for now she sets the question aside.

What she needs next is a room with a desk, someplace where she could sit and concentrate. And so they drive into New Jersey, thinking it best to stay some distance from the thing they're looking for. They stop at a Best Western motel and Pig saunters inside to the registration desk. She gets out of the car, walks to the furthest edge of the parking lot, stares into a tiny copse of ornamental pines. After the long day spent driving around in the city, it's soothing to lay her eyes on something, anything, that hasn't been built by human hands. She exhales, then twists at the waist, cracking her spine.

Pig rents two rooms, a suite separated by an adjoining door. Once she's alone in her room she sits at the desk, turns on its tiny brass lamp. She peels off her gloves, uses the hand wipes. She eats the crackers and tuna and then turns her attention to the atlas. She spends a long time with it. She finds the pages that correspond to the places through which they drove, and she uses the pen to trace over certain streets. She marks specific points with heavy dashes, indicating certainty, certainty that the blade has crossed through those points. She works slowly, takes her time. She moves back and forth through the atlas for an hour, returning repeatedly to a few specific pages to ornament them more intensely, entangling them in dense thickets of ink. Eventually the process slows, as though she's depleted some reserve inside her. She sits for a minute to be sure, and then turns back to the beginning of the section, so that she can examine all the boroughs at a larger scale. After a moment she draws a slash across it at a very particular angle. To this slash she adds two more. Together they form a triangle.

She knocks on Pig's door, enters. He's lying on the bed, over the covers, his boots still on, his head propped up with a pillow folded in half. He's watching television with the volume turned all the way down to zero, eating worm after worm as televisual color plays across his face. He looks bland, harmless, almost goofy. But she knows it's an error to think of him that way.

"Three points," she says, handing him the atlas, indicating the triangle with the tip of her pen. "The knife primarily moves between these three points."

He reaches out and traces the triangle with his finger. Two of the points are in Brooklyn, the third in Manhattan.

"What are these places?" he asks.

"I don't know," she says.

"So tomorrow we find out?" Pig says.

"Yes."

She sleeps soundly, for the first time since arriving in America. She sleeps and she dreams, dreams of the Archive, and, as it often does, in dreams, it opens up to reveal the face of Eivind, her brother.

9

THING

"Oh my God," Victor says. "Kill it."

But neither of them make a move to do this. Instead they both take two steps backward.

The thing is a fat worm, about two feet long. Its body is composed of hundreds of transparent nubs, terminating in tiny little grasping suckers. Behind this seething tissue Ollie can see weird rudimentary organs clenching and pumping, a loop of slime being crudely circulated from one end of its body to the other. The worm contracts and contorts, smacks itself wetly against the baseboard.

"It's going *behind the stove*," Ollie says, trying to intuit some order in its chaotic twisting. "Don't let it get back there!"

"OK, OK," says Victor. He takes a step toward it, half-crouched, hands splayed open, like he's an alligator wrangler.

"Jesus Christ, don't *touch it*," Ollie says.

Victor reels around to look at her, helpless, baffled in the face of these competing injunctions.

"We have *tools* for this," she says, grabbing the handle of the nearest drawer. She jerks on it hard, too hard by half thanks to her fight-or-flight response: she's left holding an empty drawer, swinging out behind her, while all the utensils spill across the floor in a cacophonous tide. The worm lashes back from the clanging mess, whips itself complicatedly into the legs of a bar stool.

"Tongs," Ollie says, pointing at them with her foot.

"On it," Victor says, scooping them up. He takes one step toward the stool and pauses there, considering his angle of approach.

"Don't *touch* it," Ollie says again, because she can't think of what else might constitute good advice in this situation.

The worm uncoils, releasing the stool legs from its grasp, and throbs once, propelling itself toward Victor's feet. Victor takes this opportunity: he darts in, gets the tongs around the worm's midsection, and lifts it up to eye level. It writhes in the air. Ollie shrieks. Victor blanches.

"Now what?" he yells.

"The sink," Ollie says, gesturing at it with both hands. Big motor movements seem to be about all her body wants to produce in this situation. "Get it in the sink."

Victor lunges toward the sink and drops the worm in there, drops the tongs in as well, just for good measure. He steps way back and Ollie cautiously steps forward, taking his place.

"Kill it," Victor says.

"Just wait a second," Ollie says, leaning forward, trying to get a better look at the thing. It contracts and expands gently in its crude confinement, as though gathering strength, and then thrashes outward, whacking the side of the sink, which makes about the same sound as it would if you had just hit the steel soundly with a rubber mallet. Both of them jump.

Ollie reaches out and peels a cleaver off from the magnetic strip mounted on the wall.

"Kill it," Victor says again, a little more pleadingly this time.

"Just a *second*," Ollie says. "You ever think that our first response to this thing maybe shouldn't just be *kill it*? We don't even know—"

She has to pause here, because the list of what they don't know is so lengthy that she can't even select an option that would meaningfully fill in the blank.

The worm coils and then, as Ollie watches, it slowly extends one of its tips into the air, as if sniffing, although it doesn't appear to have *nostrils*, as such. She can't even say for certain that she's looking at its *head*: it seems to have a total lack of sense organs. She has barely completed making this observation before it is rendered obsolete: a thin seam opens up along this risen end. The seam ripples and opens, revealing rows of needlelike teeth, and the worm *hisses*.

"Yeah, nope," Ollie says, and she terminates this development right fucking now by bringing down the cleaver and lopping off the hissing part. The body twists reflexively a few times, black fluid spuming from the wound and splashing across the sink's stainless surface. And then it stops.

"OK," Ollie says, still gripping the cleaver. She wants very badly to wash her hands but she's afraid to put her fingers in the sink.

"We still have a problem," Victor says, pointing at the portal, which still hangs in the center of the room. Maybe it's just the extra adrenaline talking but it seems to have taken on a baleful aspect, like an accusing eye.

"You *forgot*," Ollie says, pointing the cleaver at him accusingly.

"Forgot *what*?"

"You forgot the first fucking rule of this shit: don't make something manifest if you don't know how to banish it."

"I *knew* how to banish it," says Victor.

"You *thought* you knew, *maybe*," Ollie yells. "But you were *wrong*."

"Fine, you want me to say 'I was wrong'? Will that *gratify* you?"

"A little bit!"

"OK, *fine*: I was wrong. But are you going to stand around *enjoying being right* or are you going to *help* me get this thing closed before it shits another snake into our kitchen?"

For the moment, she puts aside the fact that she's supposed to be finished with doing magic, and instead she thinks: *banishing ritual*. She's done banishing rituals hundreds of times; it's one of the first things you learn when you're learning magic. You gather your will, focus it, channel it towards the disruption of whatever craziness you summoned up. Normally it's easy, like disturbing a reflection by dragging your fingers through still water. But this one doesn't look like it's going to be easy. So when it's not easy, you reach for something that can help, something that can amplify your willpower. Wands, holy symbols, objects with deep personal significance, whatever—

"Tools," she says. Victor shows no signs of hearing her: he's staring abjectly into the portal. She claps her hands together to break his trance and regain his attention. "Victor! Tools! Magical implements. What do you have?"

"Bells? Sacred bells?" he says, after a moment.

"Awesome. Get them."

"What do *you* have?" he asks her.

She considers the question for a second, tries to remember where any of her old magic shit might be. After a grudging moment—*don't do this*, says the part of her brain that's afraid to look at the past—she realizes that she might have something that will work. She bolts out of the kitchen, nearly colliding with Victor in the doorway.

She skids down the hall, finally coming to a stop in front of the closet. She yanks out the lumpy sack that contains Victor's old air mattress and chucks it out of the way, letting it thud onto the floor. Behind it lies a beat-up cardboard box, the final repository of the occult claptrap that she collected in what seems like some former life. Objects with significance. She pulls it toward her and blows coils of dust off the top of the box with one sharp huff.

"OK, here," she says, bringing the box to Victor. He's working hurriedly to untangle a string of tiny bells that he retrieved from somewhere. Behind him, the rift undulates

113

calmly. "There's got to be something in here that will work," she says.

"Open it up," Victor says. She hesitates, then reluctantly plants the box on the thin strip of counter between the sink and the rangetop. She braces herself for just a second, and then she opens it, for the first time in years.

She sees a silver cup, a loop of prayer beads, a lump of wax. She sees an acrylic box that contains two human teeth: one of her own baby teeth and one tooth that fell out of her mother's head in those final bad weeks.

She digs down a layer and comes upon a dirty zip-top bag that contains things that she kept because they connect her to Jesse. Just a few things that he handled. A red plastic kazoo from one of his birthday parties; arcade tokens, from the day she took him to Coney Island. She remembers him standing before a machine, oversize mallet in hand, pounding down cartoon totems as they popped up through holes; remembers thinking that he looked exactly like a tiny wrathful god.

Seeing all this stuff delivers a whomp, straight to her chest, just as she feared. She tries to ignore it, tries to remain focused on the problem at hand—the rift in her Goddamn kitchen—instead of the larger, more amorphous problem of how to reconcile herself to every fucking thing in her fucked-up past. She fumbles with the bag, gets it open, gets the kazoo in her hand, holds it aloft with something like a gesture of triumph.

"That?" Victor says.

"This," Ollie says.

"Not exactly the first thing one thinks of when thinking of a magical instrument."

"Trust me," Ollie says.

"Why the fuck not," Victor says, and he reaches out to take it. She almost hands it off but then she hesitates; something about the idea of Victor playing Jesse's kazoo bothers her. If anybody is going to use it for a magical purpose it should be her.

"I got this," she says.

She puts the kazoo between her lips and blows.

A forgotten force moves from her belly up to her head, out through her face. She projects herself out into the air and tangles with the impossible shape of the rift. Everything that's happening is invisible and intangible but it reminds her of physical grappling. Wrestling; rough fucking. The application of force and the response to force. It reminds her of Ulysses and it reminds her of Donald. And—she has to admit—it feels good. Scary good.

She sucks breath and then buzzes on the kazoo again. It shrieks. The rift quivers. Victor starts jangling the string of bells finally but that doesn't really matter; he's not a factor in this ritual anymore, if he ever was. He's like someone who's been nudged out of a threesome: it's all between her and the rift now.

She concentrates; she frowns. She can sense the many ways in which the rift is trying to fight her but she knows just as many ways to smack it back into behaving. She knows exactly what she's doing.

And the moment that she knows that, with certainty,

it's over. She's won: the rift collapses down into a single delicate tendril of smoke. She steps forward and whiffs it away with her hand.

"Jesus fuck," Victor says.

"How about we not do that again," Ollie says, breathing hard.

"Yeah, OK," Victor says.

"OK," Ollie says. Except. Except there's a part of her that's still exhilarating from the experience, like a kid who just got off a roller coaster, and all that part wants is to do it again and do it again right now. That part of her is already calculating how it could be done better, how *next time* she could control the experience more effectively, maybe by using the right tool at the outset instead of bringing it in later—

She looks down at the kazoo, to see if it could serve this purpose, but then she sees that the ritual took something out of it. It's been desaturated somehow, its red gone grayish. She bends it gently between her fingers to test its plasticity and it crumbles like an old rubber band.

Nothing comes without its cost, one of the oldest rules there is. But she can't say it doesn't hurt, to have one more piece of the past disappear like that.

She looks up, her exhilaration forgotten, and she considers holding Victor accountable for this loss, thinks about confronting him with the pieces of the kazoo, waving them in his face. It would feel good to have someone to blame, to be able to convert the sadness to anger. But, stung and sad, she can't muster up the feeling that there would be any point. So she stands there, still, while Victor paces around the kitchen for a minute, looking jumpy as hell.

Finally he glances into the sink. "Ew," he says. "What are we going to do with this?"

Oh yeah: that severed worm. "Do you think it's wrong to just throw it in the garbage?" Ollie says, after thinking about it for a second.

"I don't know. It feels wrong. Maybe. Yes."

"You think it's dangerous?" Ollie asks. "I mean—it's, what, it's an *interdimensional monster*. It seems like maybe that's dangerous."

"It's dead," Victor says.

"Right, but—for all we know it could be doing harm just by being here, as a thing that fundamentally doesn't *belong* in this world? Like, is this thing doing damage to the *fabric of reality* by being here, in our kitchen?"

"No? Hopefully not?"

"I'm just saying," Ollie says, "it seems wrong to just throw it in the garbage unless we're sure."

"I don't know how we can be sure."

"Maybe we can—keep an eye on it for a while."

"What, just leave it there in the sink?"

"I don't *know*, Victor, I'm just trying to—"

"Wait a second."

Victor rummages around in the cabinet under the sink and finds a paper lunch-bag, flaps it open. With his other hand he gets the tongs and lifts the two pieces of worm, drops them in the bag one at a time. One corner grows a little sodden, from leakage. He rolls the bag closed and opens the freezer.

"Really?" Ollie says. "No."

"Do you have a better idea?"

"I'm not saying I have a better idea. I'm just saying I don't like the idea of there being a *dead thing* in our freezer."

"Have you *looked* in our freezer lately?" Victor says. "'Cause it looks like fucking Pat LaFrieda's Meat Purveyors in there."

"A dead thing that isn't food, I mean."

Victor shrugs. "I owned a snake when I was a teenager," he says. "Used to feed it mice. You know where you store dead mice?" He nods at the freezer.

"OK, fine," Ollie says. She bites her lip uneasily as he packs it in there. "I just want to go on record as saying that there was almost certainly some better solution."

"The only other thing I could think of was to cook it and eat it," Victor says, wrinkling up his nose a little.

"Right," Ollie says. "'Cause there's no way that *that* could have been a total disaster."

"Hey," Victor says, "for all we know it could be delicious. Char-grill it, hit it with some unagi sauce, serve over rice? Yummy."

"Enough," Ollie says. She looks up at the kitchen clock. "Shouldn't you be on your way out anyway? Aren't you working tonight?"

Victor looks up at the clock, then checks it against his watch. "Fuck," he says, finally. "Yep. I gotta go."

They head up the hall together. In the doorway, Victor lingers for a moment. "You know," he says, "you looked awesome back there. You were like *on fire*."

"Well," she says, after a moment, "thanks."

"I never really understood," he says, "why you stopped."

"What do you mean?" she says, unsure as to whether

she really wants to have this conversation. "Why I stopped what?"

"All of it," he says. "Magic. I don't understand why you stopped doing magic. You're really *good* at it. You could have been one of the greats."

She thinks for a minute. And then finally, she says, "It's stupid to want to be *one of the greats* at magic. Magic is supposed to just be a means to an end. A way of getting what you want. And when you get what you want, you should stop."

"So that's you, then?" Victor says, an edge of irritation in his voice. "The woman who got everything she wanted?"

"Sure," she says, affecting a theatrical blitheness. "I have a good job and an affordable apartment and a roommate who is a tiny little bundle of naked ambitions, and who hardly ever violates space-time in order to pursue those ambitions"—she gives him a smile with some venom in it; he looks demurely away—"what more, in my wildest dreams, could I possibly want?"

But the thought crosses her mind, before she can stop it: *My kid. My Goddamn kid.*

"No, you're right," Victor says, looking her straight in the face. "I can't think of a solitary thing."

Once Victor's gone she goes into the bathroom, washes her hands finally. From there she splashes hot water on her face, glares at her reflection. She's too exhausted to brush her own teeth. It's been a long day. She's still wearing the clothes that she got sick in. She strips them off, drops them to the floor.

It's only like eight o'clock; way too early to go to sleep, but she climbs into bed with her phone nevertheless. She flips glassily between a couple of different news stories but can't coherently assemble them into anything that matters to her life in any way.

She keeps thinking about the Inside. What it would be like if you could get in there, what you could do. She's still not exactly sure what it would mean, to have the power that that space promises, but she has a gut feeling that you could use it to get things, that you could use it to get anything you wanted.

If those things—those worms—whatever they are—didn't kill you first, she thinks. *They're dangerous.*

But maybe, just maybe, says a little voice from deep within, they wouldn't be as dangerous if you had the right tool. Something to give you more control over the experience. A tool. Something you could use to protect yourself. A weapon.

Something like a magic knife.

No, the reasonable part of herself thinks, trying to stuff that thought back down before it can gain momentum. But her body is already acting independently, poking at her phone, checking to see whether Guychardson's number is in there. She scrolls through her contacts and is a little surprised to find him. She taps his name and some options pop up.

Without really thinking about it, she starts a message to him: Hey it's Ollie. You going to industry night at Ovid tomorrow? My roommate Victor and I are going, maybe see you there?

And then she hits send. She stares at the screen as it

goes, frowning slightly, as though she's not quite convinced that what she's seeing happen is entirely real.

Well, OK, she thinks, finally. *There's that, then*. She falls asleep while waiting for a response. The phone cradled loosely in her open hand.

10

ATTEMPT

When Maja was eighteen years old, Eivind, her brother, had been found in a graveyard in the foothills near town, dragged into a shallow gravel ditch, unconscious, blunt force trauma about the head, skull fractured in two places. It was the worst violence her town had seen since the war.

Journalists came to the house, where she was alone, and interviewed her. One team spent the entire day outside on the tiny square of gravel lawn, waiting for her face to appear at the window. One team met her father at the pier, attempting to catch a shot of his face as he got off the boat, hoping to see what a grieving fisherman looks like.

She spent the better part of the following two days in the hospital, at her brother's bedside. It was awful to look at him but at least it was quiet, at least there was no one there to ask her questions, to ask her how it felt to have a brother who was a victim, as though the answer to that was not the most obvious thing in the world.

Besides: she thought she could learn something from

looking at him. She thought that if she saw his wounds she could understand them. She could learn their history, figure out how they came into the world. And if she could figure that out, she could figure out who had caused them, and why. But the wounds were covered in sterile pads and so all she could see was his face, which was horribly still, and the history of his face was, of course, the history of his fifteen years on earth, and the tangle of memories and impressions that came from looking at his face shared so much confusing overlap with her own memories of those years. The same home, the same parents, the same streets. She was afraid that if she looked into his face for too long she would lose sight of which experiences were his and which were hers. She only wanted to see the wounds, going so far as to ask a nurse whether the dressing could be removed, just for a minute, a request which was firmly denied, and accompanied by a look she'd become familiar with, the look that told her that she was acting strangely.

On the second day she realized that she was going to need to touch him. Touching people was worse, for her, than just being around them or seeing them. The flow of information was steadier, more intense—too intense. After a few bad experiences she'd instituted a complete ban on touching others or being touched by them.

This ban was not especially difficult to implement, once she'd really decided on it: she kept her distance from strangers as a matter of course, had few friends, and came from a family in which no one was prone to physical affection. But sitting by Eivind's bedside she found herself wanting to know as much as possible about what had happened to him, and by morning on the second day she knew that touching him was going to be the best way to achieve that goal. And so when she was alone with him she let her fingers rest on his forehead, and she let his knowledge flow into her.

The first thing she looked for was his memory of the morning of the assault. Walking among graves, his heavy 35mm camera bouncing against his chest. Bending low to inspect some particular engraved name, then pausing, framing the name in the camera's viewfinder, taking a photograph. And then: the peculiar surge of light that accompanies a concussive blow.

She jerked her hand away. She felt a rush of blood enter her face, constrict her throat, push tears into her eyes. She paused. She exhaled, hard, and when she was ready she touched his forehead again.

He was crouched over when the second blow landed: all he could see was stones, grass, dirt, the dangling camera. But after the second blow he managed to get up, start running. The graveyard sawing crazily as he barreled forward, panicked. The sounds of someone in pursuit.

At some point he stopped and turned, to face his pursuer, and as she watched these memories she pleaded with him not to stop, not to turn, instead to keep on running. But even as she begged him silently to do the one thing that she knew he would not, did not do, she also wanted him to stop, to turn, to look. There was a part of her that needed him to make this bad decision, that needed him to pause and take the blow that was coming. To get a square look at the person who was dealing it. And he did, almost as though he knew

that she would want him to. Almost as if he was accommo-
dating her wish.

She saw what she needed to see. She saw the face of the
other boy. Older than Eivind, but not by much. Younger
than her, but not by much. She guessed seventeen. Denim
jacket, lank hair, a spray of pimples across the bridge of his
narrow nose.

She saw the baseball bat in the boy's hand. Her lips
went thin. It was just a toy. Some fucking American toy.

"Stop," she heard Eivind say.

The boy raised the bat again, swung it into Eivind's
face.

She took her hand away. At this point she knew what
she had the ability to do. She could find the boy. And if she
couldn't find the boy—humans still being hard for her, at
this time—she could certainly find the bat.

She did not have a plan for what she would do when she
found it. But she knew that once she left the hospital, the first
thing she would do would be to begin looking, and she had
no doubt that once she began, she would be successful.

She felt no need to rush. It was more important to stay
here in the hospital, with Eivind. So for another day she
stayed there, periodically touching his hands or his shoulder
or his bruised face, and she learned more and more of what
he had seen in his life—not just the assault but all sorts of
things. The things he took photos of. The images in his
rule books, the maps he drew for himself. The way that she
looked through his eyes. She came to understand the way in
which, for the only time in her life, she was beloved.

She took more and more of him in. Normally this was

not a thing she would have done. She understood that it was invasive, that she was well beyond any limit that either of them might have set under ordinary conditions. She watched as he pined after a girl, a classmate, watched as he timidly kissed that girl on the eve of her move to another town, watched him cry into his pillow that night. She read the letters he wrote to her. She looked at the things that he looked at on the computer when no one else was around: jagged pictures of women, their breasts out, grainy and alone in ordinary rooms.

She was holding his hand when his brain functions failed, when he went into cardiac arrest and died. Triage nurses, arriving in response to some squalling machine, tried to pull her away, but she held on ferociously, swinging wildly out with her other hand. All the swimming had made her strong, for when it mattered.

In the moments it took her brother to die he was able to send her a transmission of exquisite richness. He gave her everything: a complete repository of everything he had seen or thought or felt, compressed into a single packet, faceted, internally reflective, like a diamond. And *edged* like a diamond: it entered her mind, shearing as it went, until it had cleaved out a space for itself. A space where she could store him, in his entirety. An archive.

When the transmission was complete and her brother was dead she allowed herself to be yanked away; she vividly remembers a furious technician striking her a glancing blow across the face, although even later that day, at home, showering off the stink of the hospital, she found the memory impossible, tainted with a whiff of the unreal.

* * *

She awakens. By eight she's back in the car with Pig, stoically enduring the sluggish flow of morning traffic like any other pair of commuters. For breakfast they each have coffee and a doughnut.

Once the traffic thins out, finding the points of the triangle is easy. The first one they find is a three-story building in Brooklyn, Bedford-Stuyvesant. Pig looks out the window at it.

"Here?" he says, skepticism in his voice.

It doesn't look like much, it's true. Three stories, brown paint over brick. The building's upper edge is adorned with a row of plastic satellite dishes; the windows are occupied by boxy air conditioners and exhaust fan units. The ground floor is a retail place that primarily appears to sell Mylar balloons. But the other entrance—a plain unmarked door—is registering in her mind with almost psychedelic intensity. She can detect hundreds of teeming currents of energy, each one a path that the blade has taken, each slightly different, but all of them pass through the frame of that doorway. When she closes her eyes she sees the traces as luminescent lines of force, threading together: the doorway glows in her mind like an afterimage that won't fade. She frowns: she's not used to the traces of an object burning this brightly. The blade is not merely coveted, desirable, precious, it's something more. It's powerful.

"Is it in there right now?" Pig asks.

She concentrates, tries to sort the paths in a way that would allow her to detect whether the knife went in and didn't go back out. But there's too many flows, radiating too intensely: she can't manage to sort them into a chronology.

"I don't know," she says.

She turns away from the door, looks Pig in the face, watches the warring impulses playing out there. She can see the part of him that wants to go for it, the part that thinks a 33 percent chance of success is close enough to warrant making a move. He's wanted this blade his whole life, as near as she can tell, and he's never had a 33 percent chance of success before, and she can see that it's making him go a little crazy. She can see that it's tempting him to get up, right this second, get out of the car, retrieve his Beretta M9A1 9mm pistol out of the trunk, and commence a forward assault, forcing his way through the door and upstairs, into the unknown. The moment grows tense, as though some taut figure were hovering in the air of the car.

Is this guy really that stupid, asks the Archive.

He wants what he wants, replies Maja.

Yeah, I can see that, says the Archive. *But that doesn't excuse bad strategy.*

We've seen bad extraction strategies before, Maja replies.

Sure, says the Archive. *But they're always embarrassing.*

It's none of our business, Maja thinks. *We just find what the clients want us to find. After that they can do whatever stupid thing they want. We can always just walk away.* It's a canned line, the one she always uses, although knowing what she knows now—how powerful this object is—makes her feel a little uncertain about its truth.

Pig releases a held breath and something dissipates. His sense has won out over his appetite, at least for now.

They stick with the original plan, visiting the remaining two points of the triangle. The first one they hit is the other Brooklyn one: a Caribbean restaurant, Café Soulouque. Tiny, twenty feet of storefront hidden behind a metal grille. Again its entryway is alive with intensities, the traces of passage. Pig gets out of the car, toes the lock that holds the grille shut, crouches down to inspect its long shank. Maja gets out, too, just to stretch. She leans back and looks at the vinyl awning, which bears multiple occurrences of what she quickly determines to be the Haitian coat of arms: a palm tree, cannons, flags, bayonets. Pig walks down the street a bit, past a minuscule income tax place, checks out a chain-link gate, locked with a loop of cable. Behind it a broken concrete path leads to a side door, presumably the entrance to some kind of service corridor.

He takes the chain-link in one hand and gives the gate an exploratory rattle. "Does the knife ever go through here?" he asks. "In addition to the front door?"

"Yes," she answers.

Pig nods, then takes the lock cable up in his hand, and pauses, calculating something.

And then they both get back in the car, drive back over to Manhattan, and find the final point: another restaurant. This one's in a busy downtown district, so they don't park, but they drive around the block three times to examine the door, a tall piece of heavy smoked glass, recessed between a pair of dark marble pillars, seething with evidence. From the street you can just make out the single etched word CARNAGE.

. . .

"Restaurants," Pig says. "A couple of fucking *restaurants*."

It's ten p.m. They've returned to the Caribbean place, figuring it was the easiest site to make an initial extraction attempt.

Pig works a Butter Rum Life Saver off the roll and pops it into his mouth, gnashes it up between his teeth. "I mean," he says, "just look at this place."

Maja puts her book down, looks out the window of the car. Café Soulouque doesn't have any posted hours but it gives every sign of closing soon. One of the workers, maybe the bartender, has exited the building. He leans in the door-way, relaxing in the cooling night, wiping his hands on a rag before running them over the surface of his bald head. Maja inspects him in her mind to see if he's holding the knife on his person and gets nothing other than a busy fizz of residue.

"Honestly?" Pig continues. "I expected that it was going to be in a *vault* or something. Maybe—*maybe*—a museum. Point is, someplace defensible, fortified. And instead we're going to find it in some little mud-person shithole?"

Maja looks up from her book again and waits for more. Typically, her clients turn inward during the final prepara-tory stages before an extraction attempt: they concentrate, grow quiet, sometimes they even descend into a kind of so-lemnity, as though they are reflecting on what it will mean to get what they want. But Pig has grown increasingly chatty: either he's nervous or else it's just that his sugar intake is finally beginning to express itself as surplus energy. Or both.

"Unbelievable," Pig says.

Maja says nothing. Maybe earlier in the day she would

131

have made the effort to mirror his astonishment, but in truth, even then, she felt no surprise. The things she finds are never where anyone expects them to be. If they were where you expected them to be, you wouldn't need to hire her in the first place.

"I'm not complaining," Pig says. "Don't get me wrong. Tactically, it's a huge win for us."

For you, Maja thinks.

"I mean," Pig says, "I was ready to fight a private security force, hell, a Goddamn *army*. But this place—it's just run by a couple of fuckers. Degenerates."

Pig looks out of the car at the bartender. Maja looks over at him as well. Bits and pieces of his life begin to trickle in. An image of him in a market, buying prawns, then a later image of him sitting at a table in a hot apartment, in his undershirt, eating the prawns, drinking from a wet bottle of beer. Putting down his fork to sift through a pile of junk mail.

She snaps her attention away from him and looks through the restaurant's window instead. She can dimly see only one pair of remaining diners, a man and a woman, a couple maybe. They've finished their meal and are draining the last of their drinks. The man stands, hands off some cash to the waiter; from their body language it looks like the two of them are laughing, sharing some joke.

"Things have learnt to walk that ought to crawl," Pig says, absently. "I can take them no problem." He looks over at her. "I need you to do something for me."

"What?" Maja says, blinking. "No. I got you here. That's what I do, and I've done it."

"It's that side gate," he says, continuing as though he hasn't heard. "The service entrance. That's the only thing. My plan is to just go through the front and I think I can secure the scene pretty quickly. But somebody could get out through that side gate. I need someone there."

"We've been over this," Maja says. Her eyes flit to the front of the restaurant: the couple is leaving. The bald bartender follows them out onto the street, he's produced a long metal rod which he begins to insert into the grill mounting. "You pay me to get you here," she continues. "But I don't hurt people."

"I'm not asking you to *hurt* anyone," he says, a sneer in his voice. "Just keep an eye on the gate for me. You can do that, right? That's what you're *for*, isn't it? *Looking* at shit?"

She compresses her lips, not wanting to dignify these questions with an answer, even accidentally.

"Well," he says, opening his door, "consider it."

He slams the door, then goes around and pops the trunk. She can hear him opening one of the gun cases.

She watches him walk purposefully across the street and press his pistol into the jaw of the bartender. The metal pole clatters to the pavement. Pig marches the bartender back through the door, back into the restaurant.

Maja looks away. She picks up her book and turns it around in her hands, runs her finger over the spine. She does not open it. She plants her thumb over the bar code on the back of the book as though she's pressing a button.

Here we go, says the Archive.

Yes, she thinks, simply. She closes her eyes. She allows her mind to drift back, further and further, twenty thousand years, a silent time, before the city was here, when everything was just bedrock covered with ice.

From Café Soulouque she hears a pop and a certain quantity of information is subtracted from the air.

Commotion from inside. A raised voice, barely audible from this distance. She looks up, watches a jogger trot past the storefront, wearing earbuds, noticing nothing.

A second pop.

Almost over now, she thinks. She lets her mind drift back to the ice sheet, grinds her anxiety down with a vision of the implacable calm of the long-ago glacier. It reminds her of home. Home. She allows herself to envision the trip back, long hours on the airplane, yes, but then the part that she enjoys: walking into her cottage, turning on the lights, drawing a bath. She imagines the entire routine, the layout of the bathroom, the items on the shelf. A jar of lotion, a bottle of perfume, each in its proper place.

She hears the rattle of something, someone, hitting chain-link. She doesn't want to open her eyes, doesn't want to obey Pig's imperative, but reflex wins out: she looks. She sees a young man climbing over the gate. She tries not to focus on the frantic desperation that she reads in his motions.

He clears the top of the fence and lands in a crouch, which permits her a view some sort of satchel slung across his back. Maybe the blade is in there?

She looks into the satchel and finds a box, and there's something inside it, so she looks deeper, and the outline of a blade begins to take form, and at that very second her mind fills with white light, as though a pressure nozzle were blasting high-intensity data into her skull. She makes a sharp noise. She rears backward, slamming her head into the passenger-side window, and the onslaught of light begins to stutter, and she can see that it is made up of images, a thick coalescence of images, too many to parse. They begin to speed up again, to blur back into an overwhelming torrent, and to stop the intake she bites her tongue as hard as she can, until she tastes blood.

She spits into her gloved hand, then slaps the glob of crimson slime away with one quick motion.

Her vision clears, and she sees Pig, clambering over the fence after the young man. He has the pistol in one hand still, so his progress is slow, clumsy; he ends up kind of rolling over the top of the fence, landing on his shoulders and neck instead of on his feet. But he rights himself quickly. He staggers out into the middle of the street, raises the pistol, and fires once after the fleeing man. But the distance is too great.

"Fuck," shouts Pig. He lifts the gun a second time.

This really is getting stupid now, says the Archive.

True. Maja will allow her clients to do just about anything they want to do, as long as she can still walk away, but opening fire in a public street in one of the busiest cities on the globe might be the kind of action that will expand to implicate her. She rolls down the window.

"Get in the car," she calls.

He wheels around, looks at her uncomprehendingly, his eyes wild, his mouth distorted with frustration.

"Put down the gun," she says, firmly, "and get in the car."

Something shuts down in his face and a tense focus replaces the wildness. He does what she asks.

"That was him, wasn't it?" Pig says, jamming the key into the ignition. "Not the other two. Him."

"Yes," Maja says, her mouth still thick with blood.

Pig starts the car and pulls away from the curb wildly. An oncoming van hits its brakes hard to avoid colliding with them.

"Calm down," Maja says. "Drive better."

"Calm *down*?" Pig cries, reversing savagely. "We're going to *lose him* and you—"

"No," Maja says. "Listen to me. We're not going to lose him."

"But he's already—"

"I've seen him," Maja says. "So it doesn't matter where he goes. Not anymore. Wherever he goes, I can find him."

11

OVID

The evening is hot and the cavernous space of OVID is crowded: there's a four-person-deep throng between Ollie and the bar. This is the kind of scene that she likes to think of herself as hating—who wants to spend all day in a restaurant, around restaurant people, and then go out to a *different* restaurant and get drunk with *different* restaurant people? She's said these exact words to Victor a million times. But tonight she has to admit that being here serves as a real respite after the last couple of days. If you just give yourself over to being bumped and jostled, it can become a kind of peace, like being tumbled by the sea. There are times when an elbow jammed into your back is exactly what you need to jog you out of whatever you're thinking about, to wreck your internal narrative, to strip away your worrying details and leave you an anonymous member of a mass. Sure, she may be a little taller and a little older than the average resident of this room but the stink of a workday on her skin gets subsumed just fine by the same stink coming up off everybody else. And as she presses her way along the edge of the impromptu dance floor, trying not to get clocked in the face by people who are flailing to the terrible EDM blasting over the sound system, she has to acknowledge that she actually does get the point of industry night—it isn't really to be around other restaurant people, it's to be *away from the public*, to be in a room where you *aren't* called upon to serve as anything: where you can just be a body, animal among the bodies of others.

She makes it to the bar eventually and gets a vodka tonic. She has a sip, and follows that with a deeper sip, a sip that could probably be considered a full-on gulp. She turns away from the bar, fights against the crowd for a minute, holding her drink up at eye level so it doesn't get knocked around too bad. She keeps an eye on faces, on the lookout for Victor or Guychardson. She sharpens her perceptions, scans the room, starts to wonder whether she was stupid to expect to find them here. And then she stops, having gotten no more than eight feet from the bar, and standing there she carefully tilts her glass into her mouth and drains the rest of her drink, and enjoys the realization that it doesn't matter. Maybe she'll find them, maybe she won't. The total number of fucks she needs to give the matter is zero.

Back to the bar. A second vodka tonic ends up in her hand. Cold and perfect. And quickly finished.

OVID's one of those joints where the back end basically just opens into the kitchen, and there's another glut of people there, watching a pair of burly chefs. One is frying up pieces of battered Feta, the other is anointing the resultant bite-size wedges with quick scribbles of honey and dispensing them to the hungry audience. Behind those dudes she can see the head chef here—famous guy, what's his name, something Greek, Mastrokopoulous maybe, she feels like she should know this for certain. He's grilling up massive heaps of octopus. It smells delicious—he's getting generous with the oil and lemon juice and the grilled meat is aromatic enough to begin with—but the sight causes her to remember yesterday's weird being, which she'd been assiduously working, tonight, to forget. She looks away, but her gaze falls instead on Misterpoppodokous's assistant, a guy with his arms elbow-deep in a big plastic vat of salty water. He's vigorously massaging tentacles in there. She watches them writhe around in turbulent motion.

She'd been ready for a bite but suddenly she feels a little queasy. She closes her eyes for a moment to still the swimmy feeling. Without the visual, she can go back to enjoying the smell. And it does smell delicious. She wonders whether she and Victor should have cooked that thing after all.

A hand lands on her shoulder and squeezes. Speak of the devil: it's Victor. He's saying something, but she can't hear him over the dance music.

"What?" she shouts. He turns and looks at her, grinning.

"They're letting people up on the roof," he yells toward her ear, and he points to the service ladder, mounted to the wall between the restroom doors. Victor tugs on her sleeve, intending to draw her down that way.

"I don't know," she mumbles. Between the drink in her system and the fading nausea she's not entirely sure it's a good idea for her to be up on a ladder, or up on a roof for that matter.

"Don't let your life be boring," Victor hollers. "How

long has it been since you've been up on a motherfucking *roof*?"

She has to yield the point: she can't remember the last time. But she can remember how it felt. In a vague sort of way she can remember that being up there and looking out over the city made everything feel right with the world. To-night she could use a way back to that feeling, and so she nods once and goes along.

She leads the way up the ladder, climbs about twenty feet. Once she's almost reached the ceiling, her head almost at the level of the propped-open trapdoor, she pauses, twists around to look out over the heads of the people at the bar, over the churn of the dance floor. She looks all the way back to the front of the house, her eye drawn by the glowing glass spheres garlanded there in a constellation around the doors. And then she sees Guychardson come in. She frowns: even from this distance she can see that something is wrong. His face is pale and slick; the orange LED light gives it an infernal cast. She watches him for a long second, waiting for him to come the rest of the way into the restaurant, but he just stands there, gazing about restlessly, his head yanking from one position to another, as though it's being pulled by a string.

"Guychardson's here," she shouts down to Victor.

"Who?" Victor yells back.

Ollie sighs. She considers clambering back down to greet Guychardson, but reversing the flow of people coming up behind her seems logistically impossible. Instead she thrusts one arm out, away from the ladder's rungs, to wave at him unsteadily. After a moment his head snaps in her direction, and he gives a tiny jerk of recognition, and then begins to make his way through the crowd, toward her, moving bodies gently with the back of his hand.

Once she sees this, she ascends through the trapdoor and emerges onto the roof. It's quieter out there, but only just: being outside cuts the high-end and mid from the sound system inside, but there's still plenty of bass booming out, giving everything a swamped, underwater quality, as though the floods have come and reclaimed Manhattan, as predicted, as though the stone cornices and planes of mirrored glass she can see from up here are all actually at the bottom of the Atlantic.

Young people in fashionable street wear have gathered at the edge of the roof in a thick cluster, firing bottle rockets out into the night. She's not sure how long they'll be able to get away with that at two a.m., especially post-9/11 two a.m., but for now everybody seems to be having a great time. The rockets scream and pop and the crowd cheers and the young people trade fist bumps and kisses.

"So cute at that age," Victor says, and he sips his drink, something electric blue, like toilet-bowl cleaner. Ollie has no clear idea how Victor managed to climb a ladder with a drink in his hand without spilling any, without even dislodging the curlicue of lemon rind perched on the edge of his glass. Maybe he used magic. A little jealous, she reaches out to take the glass from him.

"Ut!" he says, slapping her hand away. "Get your own."

She looks around up here for a bar or even an unclaimed drink on a ledge somewhere, but to no avail. What she does eventually see is Guychardson, climbing up through the trapdoor. He doesn't look any better up close. If anything, he looks worse: his face is sweaty, his eyes are glazed, his breathing shallow. She's seen some people look pretty rough after August shifts in hot kitchens—she's sure she doesn't exactly look zestfully clean after her own double—but he looks like he's just spent a day enduring combat operations in some godforsaken jungle.

All the same, she promised Victor an introduction, so: "Guychardson, this is my roommate, Victor; Victor, this is Guychardson."

Victor smiles and puts out his hand; Guychardson shakes it, but only distractedly, as though he can't quite remember what the convention is supposed to establish.

"Are you OK?" Ollie asks him, after an awkward pause.

"No," Guychardson says.

"No?" Ollie repeats, a little surprised to hear this as the answer.

"I need your help," he says.

"What's up?"

"I am—*freaking* out," Guychardson says.

"Why?"

"Somebody shot at me."

Ollie blinks. "Wait, what?"

"I was at work," Guychardson says. "And right as we were closing, a man came in. He fired shots. I think he killed—" A bottle rocket goes off, tearing apart some of his answer. When the rocket pops, he flinches and stops speaking entirely.

Ollie finds that she has clapped her hand over her mouth. She lets it drop now, and she says, "Jesus Christ. Are you OK?"

"I ran," Guychardson says, slowly. "I came here. I knew you were here and so I came."

Ollie blinks. "Why though?" she says. "I mean—what am I—you think I can help somehow?"

"I know what this is about," Guychardson says.

"What *what* is about?"

"I know why this man came. I've been expecting him to come. Him, or someone like him."

"I don't understand."

"I have something very valuable," Guychardson says. "A blade. You know the one I am talking about. You have admired it."

"I'm not sure I'd say I've exactly—" Ollie begins, but then all at once she can't see the point of disagreeing in this situation. *Why lie?*, is the way she phrases it to herself. "Yeah. OK. I've admired it."

Guychardson says nothing in response. Instead, he goes down into a crouch and removes his canvas backpack. She and Victor watch as Guychardson rummages for a moment and then pulls out his lacquered box, the one that he keeps the knife in. She feels a sudden impulse to reach out, to take it from his hands, but he hasn't offered it to her, and so she holds this desire in check.

"I need to go away for a while," he says. "Back to Haiti," he says.

Ollie opens her mouth, then shuts it again.

"I don't think this man will stop," Guychardson says, slowly. "This man has come because he wants the blade, and if I stay here, he will come after me. So I have to go."

Ollie says nothing.

"I will leave tomorrow," he says. His voice is firm; he sounds like he's had this plan in mind for a while. "I have to go home first. I'll need to get my passport; I'll need to destroy a few documents."

"Is it safe?" Ollie says. "I mean—does this guy know where you live?"

"I don't know," Guychardson says. "I don't need to be there for long. I can stay somewhere else tonight. But yes, there is a chance that this man knows where I live. And so it is better for me not to bring the blade there. Just in case. It is important—very important—that this man not take the blade from me. *That is the most important thing.* Do you understand?"

"I think so. Do you need me to—" And now she does put her hands out, offering to receive.

Guychardson looks at her for a long moment, as though he's assessing her.

"You can keep it safe," he says. "For one night."

It is not quite a question, but she answers, without having to think about it. "Yes," she says. The word comes out with unexpected solemnity, as though she's at a wedding, making a vow.

"I believe you," he says. He presses it toward her, and she takes it.

"I will come to work tomorrow," he says, looking her in the face. "Before I go to the airport. I will come to work and retrieve this knife from you and, after that, you will not see me again."

"Guychardson," she says, "listen, you have to tell me what this is *about*. I know that the knife is magic—" At this

Guychardson winces, as though she's blurted out a secret. She supposes she has. She tries to back up: "I'm just saying, I have experience with this kind of thing; you can let me know what's going on."

He seems to consider it for a moment, but then he shakes his head, a pained expression contorting his features. "It is better," he says, "if I explain that to you another time."

"OK," she says, although as she says it she feels a heavy sort of certainty that this other, better time will never actually arrive.

Guychardson looks away from her. He looks around the roof, then at the surrounding buildings. He shrinks down into himself a little, as though the night had suddenly turned cold.

"I have to go," he says.

"Wait," Ollie says.

"Hang on to the knife," says Guychardson. "Bring it to work tomorrow. I will see you then."

"OK," Ollie says, although in actuality a sort of squirming dread has awoken inside her. "Just—just tell me you're going to be safe."

Guychardson tells her no such thing. He turns to Victor. "It was nice to have met you," he says.

"Likewise," says Victor, a little quietly.

Guychardson looks at Ollie and gives her a crooked little smile, and then he turns and heads back down through the trapdoor. She stands there and looks helplessly at the lid of the box.

Victor pipes up: "He's cute, you know. It's too bad he's crazy."

"Shut up, Victor," Ollie responds.

They stand there in silence for all of about three seconds.

"Cheer up, kiddo," Victor says. "The world may be full of violence and strife but on the upside we have a new toy to play with."

"Shut *up*, Victor," she says again, with a little more vehemence.

"But we got what we *wanted*," he says, a pout in his voice.

She doesn't bother to respond. She's still looking at the trapdoor through which Guychardson disappeared.

"Maybe we should go," Victor says, after a minute, more solemnly.

"Yeah," she says, "maybe we should." Another shriek as another bottle rocket streaks out into the night: she jumps. She yanks her head and catches the last second of its trajectory: a spiral, twisting in on itself until, *bang*, it's gone.

12

ADVANCES

"He's moving around," Maja says. Her eyes are closed. Her fingers rest lightly on her forehead. She holds the young man in her mind, envisioning him as a bead of light, drifting through a luminous net of mismatched grids.

"Don't lose him," says Pig, steering the car around the same block for the third time. They've been driving aimlessly for half an hour, unwilling to leave Brooklyn but also afraid to stop moving, knowing that they aren't that far from the double homicide they left behind them.

"I'm not going to lose him," she says. "You need to remember that I'm actually good at this."

"Yeah?" Pig replies. "Well, *you* need to remember that you need to tell *me* what the fuck is happening."

"I *told* you what is happening," she says. "He's moving around."

"Right, but—*moving around* like what? Like *fleeing the city?*"

"I don't think so. He doesn't seem to be heading toward an airport."

"Bus station? Train?"

"Possibly," she says. "He's crossed back over to Manhattan. But unless he's prepared to flee with only what he's carrying—"

"We could follow him over there," Pig says. "Go to Port Authority, head him off?"

Maja opens her eyes, thins her lips, shakes her head *no*. "If he does decide to get on a bus, you aren't going to be able to stop him," she says. "An enormous bus terminal is very visible, very public; it's the last place in the world you'd want to attempt an engagement."

"I just don't want him to get away."

"But that's what I keep *telling you*," Maja says. "He can't *get* away. If he gets on a bus, we follow him. In fact, you *want* him to get on a bus. It puts you at an advantage. It will be easier to engage him literally anywhere a bus might go than it will be to engage him in the middle of New York City."

As they near the base of the Williamsburg Bridge, Pig pulls the car over into an open spot on the side of the street, kills the engine. "All right, fine," Pig says. "He can't get away. I get it. But I don't just want to sit here." He snaps his hand out toward the windshield, a way of condemning the street beyond it. "I want to drive. That's my job. I drive the car, I fuck up the people who get in my way: that's what I do. But you know what *your* job is? Your job is to get me closer to this guy. Your job is to tell me where the fuck I should be going. So why don't you do that before I get tired

148

of talking to you." She becomes aware of his presence, a big man, sweating in the August heat, filling the car with the stink of his anxiety, his impatience, his rage.

So what it will look like, between them, when he finally *does* get tired of talking to her? She understands that it could happen, and she understands that she must plan for it, prepare: the same thing she does with any other uncertainty. She assesses his capability for sudden violence, what she might use to respond to it. She's not helpless, in a fight: she's done some defense training, and all her swimming has made her strong, but she's not sure she could win on force alone. She may need something else, some point of leverage to work with. A thing to look for, later. For now she answers his question, so as not to keep him waiting.

"We go back to the apartment building," she says. "The one we visited this morning."

"His place," Pig says.

"He'll need to sleep," Maja says.

"He could sleep on a bus," Pig grumbles.

"I'm doing my job. I believe at this junction, you do yours."

Pig turns away from her, stares out the window at the pilings of the bridge, at the towers of Manhattan beyond the water. And then, without another word, he turns the key in the ignition, and they pull back into the street, joining the flow of the traffic, sparse here, at this hour.

She's tracked things to all sorts of places. Storage garages. Corporate boardrooms. The vented hilltops beneath which landfills are hidden. Institutional basements heaped with uncataloged mess, a richness of things haphazardly piled there in wood-grain-print file boxes. Not every job ends up outside the door of someone's home. But some do.

They are parked across the street from the young man's apartment, and they are waiting, and, as she does at times like this, she is remembering the first time she waited outside someone's home, remembering the ugly house with the orange shutters. The house with the bat in its yard, the bat that had killed her brother.

Some of her clients, caught up in the excitement of being this close to having what they want, like to describe what it is they are doing at times like this by using the word *stakeout*. The word pleases her with its Americanness, *stakeout*, the way it uses great action in the service of describing something that is actually very boring. She would only ever say that she waits.

If you'd been watching her that first time, outside the house where the boy who murdered her brother lived, you would have seen little more than a teenage girl with a red bicycle standing at the edge of a yard, looking down at a bat for a long time. Eventually you would have seen her walk across the street, park her bicycle, sit on top of a low stone wall. She took off her backpack, unwrapped a cheese sandwich that she had packed for herself, and began to eat it. She worked slowly through it until all she had left was one tiny dry corner of bread that she held between her thumb and forefinger. She flicked this into the road, then looked at it for a long moment. Inside herself, she was wondering if someone would ever be able to connect that little fragment back to her, if anyone would ever be able to tell that she'd been here. Not one car had gone by in the entire time she had been eating her sandwich.

Nevertheless, she moved her bike behind the stone wall, so it couldn't be seen from the road, just in case. She lingered there for a while, sitting in the grass, hidden from view, looking at the lichens and the grasses growing between the stones. She admired their simple forms, which contained nothing beyond a record of the singular urge to push on. Straightforward in a way that she could aspire to. A few cars did eventually roll by but she felt certain that they could not see her.

She waited. There was still the opportunity to go home, to resolve this some other way, and as she waited she contemplated this opportunity. But she did not leave.

She could feel when the boy was coming, and then she heard the tread of his footsteps on the road, but still she waited, until she heard him turn onto the garden path that led to the door. And then she rose from behind the stone wall and for the first time she saw him with her own eyes. He was not facing her but he had the long hair, the denim jacket, that she recognized from Eivind's memories. He had headphones on and keys jangling in his hand; he was humming, half-singing, as he climbed the three steps leading to the door. She walked briskly across the street, stepped over the low garden wall to enter the yard, reached down and lifted the bat, and continued on, heading in a diagonal toward the brick path, falling directly into the space behind the boy as he stood on the stoop, looking for his key.

Her swimming had made her strong. For when it mattered.

"He's coming," she says, when she's sure. It's almost three in the morning.

Pig, wearing his mask, stirs in his seat. She suspects he might have fallen asleep, off-loaded the burden of being attentive to her.

"He'll be coming from the west," she continues. "He's maybe two blocks away."

"OK, then," Pig says, gathering himself up. The gun reappears in his hand.

She watches the corner. "There," she says, as the young man comes into view.

Pig's knuckles tighten on the door handle. "Wait a second," she says. "Something is different."

"What's different," he says, lifting up the mask to get a better look at her.

"The blade," she says. She can tell right away that he's not carrying it. She extends her awareness across the street so that she can rifle into his satchel with her mind, just to be sure, but it isn't really necessary: if the blade were this close she'd know. She remembers the way it felt as it passed her, outside Café Soulouque, the way it seemed to warp the very fabric of the street, as though it were immensely dense. When she sees the young man now, she detects none of that accompanying immensity, and its absence glares. Now he's just some furtive guy, not a king in exile.

"What *about* the blade," Pig says.

"It's gone," she says. "He's stashed it somewhere or handed it off."

"You're *kidding* me," Pig snaps. His eyes widen, craziness in them. "No. We waited out here all night and we *lost* it?"

"We haven't *lost* anything," she says, hurriedly. "I can track everywhere he's been. And I've been close enough to the blade at this point that I could—"

"You know what?" Pig says. "I think there's a different way to handle this. I can *make* this shitbag tell me."

"You don't need to do that," Maja says. "It isn't necessary—"

Necessary or not, Pig is out of the car, and heading across the street, toward the young man, pulling his mask down over his face as he goes. She knows what is going to happen next. This isn't going to be an interrogation, regardless of Pig's intentions. It's going to be an execution. And there's no reason to watch an execution. They all go the same way, more or less. Sometimes you need to know when to stop looking.

But she doesn't stop looking. Not this time. Sometimes it's important to look, to remember exactly what you are complicit in. She sees the young man look up, his nerves clearly on alert. She sees him break into a run, and she sees Pig drop into a kneeling stance in the middle of the street and fire off a shot.

The young man, caught in the back by the bullet, goes sprawling down, and she loses sight of him as he falls behind a row of cars. His howl of pain rises. It all happens exactly as she thought it would.

Well, that's good, says the Archive. *I know how you hate surprises.*

Quiet, she says.

Still horrible, though, says the Archive.

Quiet, she says again.

I was just trying to distract you. So you didn't have to sit here and listen to this guy screaming, says the Archive. *But whatever*. And then it goes quiet, just like she'd wanted.

She sits there, alone, listening to the young man's screams, reading the desperation in the air, watching as Pig rises from his firing position and advances.

Watching this, she remembers what it was like, for her, that first time, as she was completing her own terrible advance. Standing on that garden path, outside that ugly house, staring at the back of a singing boy, holding a bat in her hands, paused there, waiting for the impulse that would impel her into action. As though it could come from anywhere other than inside.

13

CLEAVING

Ollie and Victor are on the subway, heading home from OVID.

"Just let me hold it."

"No."

"Just for a second."

"No."

"Just let me *look* at it."

"No."

"I'm not going to *do* anything, I just want to—"

"Jesus Christ, Victor, *no*, OK? It's not yours to mess with and even if it was I wouldn't want you waving it around right now."

"I wouldn't be *waving it around*, just—"

"This thing is *dangerous*, Victor, do you not get that? Did you miss that part of the conversation earlier? People are"—she lowers the volume on her voice here—"people are getting *shot* over this thing."

"We don't know that," Victor says. "He could have

been wrong. He talked about it like it was some big conspiracy but ordinary people *do* sometimes just try to rob restaurants. I mean, not ordinary people, exactly. Criminals. But, you know, criminals without overriding mystical interests."

Ollie stares flatly at him.

"I'm just saying," Victor says. "You don't know."

"I don't know. I don't care. I'm going to do exactly what I said I was going to do. I'm going to bring it *home*. I'm going to keep it *safe*. I'm going to bring it to *work* tomorrow and give it back to the person it *belongs to*. And that is it. That is the end of the story."

Victor opens his mouth.

"Ask yourself," Ollie interjects. "Before you say anything, ask yourself, *is what I am about to say a thing that Ollie will want to hear?* And if the answer is *no*, I would urge you to reconsider the wisdom of *saying it* as a course of action."

Victor closes his mouth again. He turns away, sullen. His silence gives her the time and the space to think, which turns out in actual practice to be the time and the space to worry: about the safety of her friend, and the safety of her kid, and the safety of herself. After a minute of that shit she finds herself tempted to reopen the conversation, to find a way to get Victor wheedling at her again, just to buy herself a few minutes where she doesn't have to worry.

"Hey, Victor," she says.

But, deep in his sulk, he doesn't reply, and she's left alone, with a knife in her bag and terrible visions in her head: clowns and murderous thugs, corpses and worms.

• • •

They get home. It's nearly three a.m., but their apartment still retains the day's accumulated heat. Victor, groaning, heads off to the shower, whereas Ollie decides that the choice move is to drink some more. She heads into the kitchen, sets her bag down on the counter, and opens the freezer, her mind on a bottle of chilled vodka that she knows is back there somewhere.

She stops and stares.

At first she's not exactly sure what she's looking at: a weird clump of black foam? For a second she thinks maybe it's one of Victor's desserts gone wrong: her irritation at him flares up all over again. But then she sees the wet shreds of brown paper flecked through the mass and she realizes, with a sinking feeling, that the bag that she and Victor put in the freezer last night has burst, and that whatever she is looking at right now is the stuff that has burst out.

"Victor," she says, but her voice can't find its force; she's trying to call out to him but it comes out softer than if she was simply speaking.

She looks closer at the clump. It's made up of little spheroids, webbed together, each one about the size of a Concord grape. She doesn't dare touch them but they give off the distinct impression of being unpleasantly sticky; their surface—their skin?—looks like it's been swabbed with tar. And they're *warm*: despite having been in the freezer all day, they're radiating enough heat to have set everything else in the freezer to thawing, enough heat that she can feel it lap out wetly at her face.

She winces, closes the freezer, presses one hand into the freezer door's surface just to make sure it stays shut.

They're alive, she tells herself, even though she wants very badly not to believe this. *If they're generating that kind of heat, they must be alive.*

"Victor," she says again, still not anywhere near loud enough for him to hear over the noise of the shower.

Finally she forces herself into motion, walks down to the bathroom. Knocks. Sticks her head in.

"Victor," she says.

"What," he says, from behind the shower curtain.

"We have a problem."

They don't let the things touch their exposed flesh. They use gloves. They use tongs. They use a silicon scraper. They get all the spheroids out of the freezer and onto a serving platter, and then they bring them over to the prep table so they can get a look at them under the intensity of some good light.

They don't find the body of the worm, just some tattered bits of skin mixed in with the shredded paper.

"So—these things hatched out of it?" Ollie says, prodding one experimentally with a spoon.

"But they couldn't *fit* in it," Victor says, puzzled. He pulls off the yellow dishwasher's gloves and ruffles his wet hair. "They're *bigger* than it. The worm fit in the bag. But these things *didn't* fit in the bag. So—"

"So they're growing," Ollie says, grimly. "They're alive, and they're growing."

"They're eggs," Victor says.

"Fuck me," says Ollie, although she'd been expending substantial mental effort to avoid reaching exactly that conclusion. She looks at the heap on the platter and imagines it as a clump of black caviar, grotesquely magnified. Once the resemblance is seen, it can't be unseen.

"So we cut the thing's head off . . . and it basically exploded into a hundred copies of itself," Victor says. "Is that what we're looking at?"

"I don't know," Ollie says.

It would be a nasty trick, if it were true. They both lean in, look a little closer at one egg, imagining a tiny worm coiled within it, building itself.

"We have to get rid of these," Victor says.

"No shit, but how?" Ollie says. "We can't exactly just flush them down the toilet unless you want alligators in the sewers times a million."

"We destroy them," Victor says. "We stick them in the blender."

"I don't like it," Ollie says. "We turn them into slurry, sure, but then what? We don't know how this stuff makes copies of itself. I don't want to grind up a hundred of them only to find out in the morning that we made a thousand more."

"Blowtorch," Victor says, after a moment.

"Maybe," Ollie says.

"They couldn't come back from a burning."

"We can't be sure."

"Rising from the ashes?" Victor says, incredulous. "I'd like to see that."

"I wouldn't," Ollie says.

That shuts Victor up for a moment. She takes the opportunity to get out the bottle of vodka and set them both up with a heavy pour, no mixers. She drinks. Victor drinks. She drinks again.

She slams her glass down on the table. "We send them back."

Victor grasps what she means immediately. "You think?" he says.

"Yeah. We open up the portal again, we shove 'em back to where they came from, we banish the portal, we call it a done deal. Can you open it?"

"I can open it," Victor says, "but I don't think I can banish it. Not if it's like it was before."

"I can banish it," Ollie says.

"You're sure?" Victor asks. He gives her a look that she can read. It says, *Maybe we could use the knife.* She gives him a look back that says, *Don't even ask.*

"I'm sure," she says, perhaps showing more confidence than she feels.

"OK," Victor says. "Go, team."

They high-five sloppily across the table, and begin to prepare. She retrieves her beat-up little reliquary of occult stuff out of the hall closet while Victor lights four bundles of herbs, one for each corner of the kitchen. When she gets back he's begun to enact a sequence of murmurings and hand-wavings; as an assist she pulls a dry-erase marker out of the utility drawer, uses it to draw out an arcane symbol on the floor's white vinyl, placing him at the center. When she's done she leans up against the wall, and waits.

She can feel when it begins to happen. The air in the kitchen takes on a kind of structure, an architecture, as though the room were a nexus point, the square formed by the intersection of two vast corridors, extending out in four directions, infinitely.

"There," Victor says, and sure enough she can see the space before him wrinkle, like it's wilting. She feels a neuralgic throb pulse through her skull. She smells the odor of ground-up batteries, which she remembers as the precursor to some Bad Shit. An uneasy sensation, not yet panic, begins to rise inside her. *Hold it together*, she tells herself.

She sets her vodka down on the counter and lifts the platter of weird goop. She looks down at it: maybe it's just her imagination, but the protoplasmic mass seems to have come awake somehow, it seems to be seething, expanding.

"Hurry," she says.

"I'm trying," Victor says. He's opened a rift that's about two inches high, not wide enough unless they're going to stick the eggs through one at a time. His face contorts with exertion and all at once the rift doubles in size. It seems to take on mass, a kind of doughy weight; it begins to sag.

"OK, that's plenty," she says. Victor groans, his face clenched. She can't tell whether he's heard her or not, but in either case he doesn't seem to be able to stop the runaway growth of the shape. It elongates, drooping with sudden, scary rapidity, unzipping the world as it goes.

Well, all right. She steps forward. She tilts the platter into the void. The eggs, sticky, cling, creeping toward the edge at snail speed. *Damn it*, she thinks; she tilts the platter more steeply and gives it a good shake but to no avail. She considers just chucking the whole thing in there and being done with it; can't come up with a good reason why not. So she does.

By this point the portal's lower lip has touched the floor: it is puddling there, into a weird little heap that is also a hole. The vinyl of the floor's surface seems to be reacting unhappily to these twisted physics; she can smell it changing form internally, as though it were being curdled.

She's pretty sure that no good will come of it if she lets this thing burn down into the apartment beneath. So it's time to banish. She turns to the counter, looks at the carton containing her old stuff. All those things from the past. She reaches for it, then hesitates. Next to it sits her bag, and inside it, Guychardson's lacquered box. She can feel the knife. The ongoing ritual has awakened it, somehow, or awakened her to an awareness of it. She can feel arcane power radiating out of it, pouring through it, like fields around a powerful magnet.

And like a magnet it draws her hand. She opens the bag, takes out the box, flips the lid, and looks at the knife. It births within her the unshakable conviction that its handle would fit perfectly in her grip.

Leave it alone, she thinks, but she's already reaching out for it.

She grasps it, and she whirls, and she is graced with a sudden understanding: the understanding of how exactly to carve the rift. She can see it as clearly as if she had a butcher's chart in the air before her. She moves. She lunges forward, slashing a diagonal through the portal, bisecting it. Each half wobbles and flickers and she swings back, cleaves again, this time drawing the knife in a line from ceiling to floor, leaving four quadrants hanging in the air, just for a moment, and then they sputter and are gone.

Victor breaks from whatever trance he'd been in, rears

back, gaping at her in what might be awe, as though she were some primal force made manifest. She rises from her crouch and he turns away from her, rubbing at his face with his fists. But even once his eyes are no longer on her she has a sense that she's still being watched. Her skin prickles. She can't quite shake the feeling until she's returned the knife to the box, and even then it persists, tickling at the edge of her perception.

Victor coughs, wipes his mouth with his hand. "Well," he says.

"Yeah," she says.

He tries to look over her shoulder, get a glimpse of the knife, but she's already closed the case and latched it.

"So all that stuff," he says.

"All what stuff?"

"All that stuff you said about how we're not going to look at the knife, we're not going to touch the knife, the knife doesn't belong to us, the knife is dangerous?"

"Oh, that stuff."

"Yeah," he says. "What happened to all that stuff?"

"I don't know," Ollie says.

For a minute, both of them look at the box in silence.

"It's hard, isn't it, being good all the time," Victor finally says, softly.

Ollie frowns, then gives one curt nod.

"You should give yourself a break from it more often," Victor says.

To this, Ollie says nothing.

"Well," Victor says, after an interval. "Can I just say that I'm wide awake now?"

"Yeah," Ollie says. "I hear you."

"I'm kind of wanting to get out of here," he says, stubbing out the herb bundles on the edge of the sink and trying to fan away some of the pallor that's accumulated in the room. "You want to go grab a booth at the diner? Bad coffee? Lumberjack Special?"

She has to work tomorrow, and that's going to suck if she stays up all night, but she doesn't really want to be here right now either. She uses the toe of her sneaker to poke at the little melted crater that the rift left where it touched the floor. "Yeah," she says. "Let's go."

While Victor changes back into street clothes she goes and hides the knife under her bed. It's not exactly an impregnable fortress, but it'll do for the night.

At the diner. The two of them bathed in neon. She sips at the aforementioned bad coffee, stares groggily at the laminated menu.

"Eggs," Victor says.

"Ugh," Ollie says.

She ends up straying from the menu, eyeing instead the desserts revolving in their tower.

"Pie," she says.

"No," Victor says. "I eat pie for my job. And good pie, too, not shit made from Sysco fruit out of a *can*."

"Pie," Ollie says again, almost growling the word.

Victor grimaces, then seems all at once to succumb to the inevitability of pie. "Fine," he says.

"Two orders of apple pie," Ollie says to the waitress.

164

"Ice cream with that?"

"Yes, please."

Victor shakes his head once she's gone. "Apple pie," he says.

"American as," Ollie says.

"Actually," Victor says, "that reminds me."

"Reminds you of what."

"Reminds me of Rufus. You remember Rufus?"

At this, she has to give up a smirk. "Sure," she says, "I remember Rufus." Rufus was the oldest street warlock they ever knew, probably, although his actual age was tough to figure out. At first glance you might say sixty, if you were judging from his sun-blasted, grizzled face, the broken blood vessels in his nose, or the decade's worth of tangle in his beard. But if you were judging from his quickness, the litheness of his movements, or the mirth in his laughter, you'd guess two, maybe three decades younger. But the important thing about Rufus is that Rufus was crazy, and Ollie says as much.

"Crazy?" Victor says. "Yes. But."

"No but," Ollie says. "Rufus was crazy, period."

"Yes. Period, but."

Ollie sighs. "But what."

"But do you remember: he was always talking about American history?"

Ollie casts back. "Yeahhh," she says. "The—oh, God, how did he put it?—the occult underpinnings of America? America as a—something, a vessel?"

"A Hermetic vessel?" Victor says. "I don't know. Who can remember. But I *do* remember that somewhere in that mix of crazy shit he also talked about these special blades? That were key to the whole thing somehow?"

"What did he call them," Ollie says. She thinks for a second. "World Knives?"

"Something like that," Victor says. "Knives that could cut through space and time."

"Whatever *that* means," Ollie says. "That doesn't mean anything."

Victor ignores this. "Rufus said that the World Knives might still be around."

"If I recall correctly," Ollie says, drily, "he also used to say that one of the World Knives used to belong to *George Washington*."

"Was *stolen by* George Washington," Victor adds. "During the—the Siege of Boston?"

"Who knows," Ollie says.

"You know," Victor says, "I think Rufus still works as a third-shift parking lot attendant," Victor says. He sucks down the last of his coffee. "You up for an adventure? You want to roll on down and find him, see what he has to say on the topic?"

"No I'm not *up for an adventure*. We've had far too much adventure already. I want *less* adventure."

"It could be interesting, to see what he might say."

"If he's going to say that Guychardson—a tiny Haitian man, let's recall—somehow ended up with a knife that once belonged to George Washington and changed the destiny of U.S. history, I'm pretty sure I don't want to hear it."

"But that would be *amazing*," Victor says.

"It *would* be amazing," Ollie says, "if it weren't so obviously insane. Guychardson works in a kitchen. He doesn't know George Washington. He doesn't know anybody who ever *knew* George Washington."

"Maybe," Victor says, "maybe somebody in his *family* knew somebody in George Washington's family?"

"Unlikely," Ollie says.

"But you don't know."

"I'll ask him," Ollie says. "I'll ask him exactly that. *Does anybody in your family know anybody in George Washington's family?* I'll ask him tomorrow."

Victor issues the correction: "Later today."

Ollie looks out the window. Blue predawn light has begun to collect in the streets.

"Ugh," she says, pressing both hands into her face.

"Cheer up," Victor says, as the waitress returns. "There's pie!"

14

KILLING

It turns out it's not that hard to kill someone. Guns, like Pig uses, make it easy, of course. But even without a gun it's still not as hard as maybe it should be. You just have to hit a thing and keep hitting it until it stops moving. Then you hit it some more. As a series of physical motions it's no harder than any other kind of repetitive work. Like digging a hole or chipping at ice. Emotionally it's a little more challenging, but the trick is just to ignore everything that tells you that the thing you're hitting is a person. The noises that it makes, the way its face looks, the fact that it has a face to begin with. You just decide not to listen, not to look. It's a decision you can make, like any other.

As Pig drives them back toward Jersey, Maja remembers making that decision: remembers being eighteen, standing there, over the destroyed thing that used to be a boy, the bat in her hand. Looking at the ugly house's orange shutters so that she wouldn't have to witness what she'd done. But the Archive was waking in her then, for the first time, and it undid that decision, because it wanted to look. That was the first thing she learned about it. Her brother was an observer, a photographer, and so it was with the Archive: always after some way to make a moment into record. She could feel its hunger inside her skull. And so, as a kindness, she looked down, eyes open, fed it, gave it something to see.

Well, it said. The first thing it ever said to her. *I guess this means I've been avenged.*

A minute passed. *We'd better go*, it said, then. She was shaking. The Archive guided her through what she had to do. She got back to her bike. She balanced the bat across the handlebars. She rode down the hill. She kept her face neutral so that in case anyone passed her she would look calm, unremarkable. And before they'd reached the shore her feelings matched her face. It was because she knew exactly what was going to happen next.

She knew that she would leave her bike by the road in order to clamber out onto a jetty that the Archive cherished as a favorite point. She knew that she would throw the bat into the water. She knew that it would never be found and she knew that she would never be caught.

The two crimes—the murder of her brother and the murder she'd committed—were so close to being identical that the police would be forced to consider them as the work of a single assailant, which would leave them unable to consider revenge for the first killing as a motive in the second. And as long as that first, faulty assumption held—and she believed, correctly, that it always would—she would never be considered a suspect; the flawed logic would never allow for it.

Even if they had some reason to suspect her, she still knew, as she stood there, as the bat left her hands and fell into the choppy black waves, that she was safe. There were no witnesses. She'd left nothing behind save the crumb in the road. Maybe a hair or a flake of skin, but the idea that the police officers of Hammerfest, groping through the infinite world of things, guided only by their ordinary perception, would be able to find such a mote—? It was laughable.

And so she learned that this part, the part where you get away with it, was easy, too.

And it always has been. She's had five jobs that ended in the death of at least one person, and not one of her clients has ever been arrested. Ultimately she's no more worried about it now, with Pig, than she's ever been. She reads up on forensic science, every now and again; she's watched the press enshrine the practice, as though it were the gesturing of some conjuror, summoning evidence out of the aether. But the crudeness, the limited utility of the actual findings, does nothing but make her smirk: compared to what she can do, at the height of her powers, police officers are nothing but bumblers, helplessly believing that they are the architects of the labyrinth within which they stumble.

Pig drives them across the bridge into Jersey. She can feel a camera mounted above them take a photograph of their license plate, store it within some dense array. She can imagine, theoretically, some scrupulous cop gathering the casings left behind at the restaurant and the apartment, linking those casings through a ballistics analysis, finding witnesses of one murder or the other to interview, piecing together observations of the town car, gleaning the license plate number, querying it against the database, learning of their comings and goings across this bridge—

And yet she also knows full well that, no matter how much she might look, she will never find such a cop.

15

HELLO

Ollie finally gets into bed right as the sun begins coming up and she sleeps uneasily, with turbulent dreams, until around nine, at which point she wakes in a panic, certain that the box under her bed is gone.

She pulls herself up, crouches down on the floor to look. It isn't gone. It hasn't even been moved: it's in exactly the spot where she shoved it, drunk, just six hours ago.

"Christ," she mutters, half-relieved but mostly irritated at her own nerves.

She gets back into bed, pulls the sheet up over her face to block out the light, tries to let herself go under again. But after an hour of trying to force her way back into sleep, she has to admit that she's getting nowhere.

She pulls the box out from under the bed, sits it in her lap, rests the palms of her hands on its surface, and thinks about how glad she'll be to rid herself of it later today, when Guychardson comes and picks it up from her.

It's not that she's worried about being attacked. Guychardson seemed serious about the existence of some psychopath out there, willing to kill in order to get this knife, but now that it's daytime and she's sober, that whole line of thinking seems a bit like paranoia. She believes that people got shot but there have to be other explanations. Victor was right: it could have been petty robbery gone wrong, or somebody else's crime of passion, with Guychardson just a guy who was in the wrong place at the wrong time. True, being close to the knife does make her feel like someone's eyes are on her, even now, even with it safely in its box, but that could just be her imagination stirring up feelings. Just because you feel like you're being watched doesn't prove that there's a watcher.

No. What she's afraid of is that she'll want to use it again. She used it last night to banish Victor's spell, but she knows that it could be used the opposite way, too: not to close a portal to another world but to open one. That was what Victor wanted it for in the first place, and after having felt it in her hand she feels certain that it could serve that function.

She carries the box out into the hallway, past Victor's room, his door ajar. She looks in on him: he's in his bed, soundly asleep.

In the kitchen she starts a pot of coffee. She sits on a bar stool and listens to the coffeepot drip and looks at the spot where they opened up the Inside last night. Even now that the portal's gone, the air doesn't look quite right: its emptiness seems fake, labored, like it's hanging together only with effort. If she weren't so tired she'd rise from her stool and wave her hand through the space just to make sure that she can.

The Inside is dangerous. Things live there. Things with crazy reproductive systems. Things that she really doesn't want to see loose in the world. She gets that now. But now that they've opened the Inside twice, she's learned something else about it, too. She knows that the space itself is a source of power. She knows that you could use that power. She's not quite sure how, but she knows that when she put her hand in there it gave her access to something, and she knows that if you stepped all the way in you would have access to—something more.

She remembers Rufus, his talk about the World Knives: they could cut through space and time.

What does that mean? she thinks, same as she thought last night. *That doesn't mean anything.*

Except maybe it does. Maybe it's just that she hasn't had any coffee yet, and she's allowing her groggy mind to run away with itself, but she thinks maybe she gets it now. She thinks that maybe it means that if you got in there, with the knife in your hand, as a tool, you could work space-time as though it were material. You could carve it, sculpt it, make holes in it.

So—what would that mean? *Just think it through*, she tells herself. Go on ahead. Push the intuition to its extremity. It would mean—that you could get whatever you wanted?

No. It's more. More than even that. It would mean that you could change history. You could fix the mistakes of the past. You could cheat the world more effectively than ever.

She thinks about her son.

She taps her fingertip on the surface of the box. She

wants to see the knife again, in the light of day. She wants to see if it still fits in her hand as well it did last night. To see if it would feel good, to wield it again.

Hello, bad ideas, she thinks to herself. She pushes the box away with the heel of her hand, frowns, gets up and pours a cup of coffee before the pot's even done brewing, just to have something else to put in her hands.

She heads in to Carnage a little early, just on the chance that Guychardson will be there, waiting for her. But no dice.

She sits on the loading dock, smokes a Marlboro, starts a text: I'm at Carnage. But then she looks at this, thinks for a moment, reads it through the lens of paranoia. She imagines Guychardson's phone in the wrong hands. Maybe it's not just one psychopath after this knife but instead some shadowy cabal. And if there's a shadowy cabal, then there's nothing stopping them, in her imagination at least, from using any number of surveillance tricks that Ollie half-remembers from bad techno-thriller television: like maybe they cloned Guychardson's phone, or something? Isn't that a thing people can do? She doesn't know.

In any case, she revises: I'm here. Come any time.

She waits for a minute, watching the screen for a response, but none comes. So she gets to work. She carries carcasses off trucks. She heaps meat into a dumbwaiter; she hits the button that sends it down into the basement. She cuts things into pieces, using just her regular knives, resisting any temptation to try out the special knife. A day like any other day, at least as much as she can make it so.

The repetition of work helps: she pushes her body to do the things it ordinarily does, and at a certain point everything else—her exhaustion, her fear—just falls away.

Angel sticks his head in when he arrives. "Feeling better?" he asks.

"Um," she says, "sure?" She blinks. It takes her a minute to remember even why he might be asking this question: throwing up at the bar seems like a distant memory, even though it was only yesterday.

"You're still not looking a hundred percent," Angel says, approaching her. "I mean—that's bad to say, isn't it? *Believe* me, I'm not saying you're not gorgeous, it's just that—"

"I haven't been sleeping well," she says, ignoring about fifty percent of what he's saying.

"But you're OK to—"

"Yes."

"You're sure."

"Yes."

"Great!" he says, breaking into a broad, goofy smile. She smiles back, with sincerity: despite the fact that Angel's interest in her makes everything a little bit weird between them, she does, ultimately, *like* him. She is able to think of him as a fundamentally decent person in a world that has often felt all too short of them. Then he gazes into her face for a second too long, his expression shifting into one of open yearning, and she feels something like pity well up inside her. Embarrassment. She breaks the eye contact, goes back to looking at the work in front of her.

"Just—let me know if you need anything," he says, a little hesitantly.

She contemplates this offer for a second. "Hey," she says, as he turns to leave.

"Yeah?"

"Just a question. Have you heard from Guychardson today?"

"He doesn't work today—"

"No, I know. I was just wondering if you'd heard from him, is all."

Angel shrugs. "No."

"OK," she says. "I'm kinda—he was supposed to be dropping by today, so—"

"So—"

"So if you see him, tell him I'm here, and I have—the thing."

"The thing," Angel says. He looks at her like she might be trying to incompetently orchestrate a drug deal.

"Sorry," she says, grimacing. "How about just tell him I'm here."

"I will—definitely do that."

"OK, good."

He leaves, and she gets back to work. But as the day winds along she begins to reconsider his offer. She starts to wonder whether she shouldn't talk to him, explain what's going on with Guychardson, enlist his help.

Because Angel could help. If she brought him into the loop on this situation he could maybe protect Guychardson. The idea isn't totally implausible. He has money. He has resources. She remembers what he said yesterday, when she threw up. He has an apartment and it's nearby, just a few blocks away. It has a doorman. It might not be Witness Protection, but in terms of a place to hide it's got to be better than wherever Guychardson normally lays his head. She could ask. *Can we use your place?* It's a simple question. She could use her fucking legs and go into the kitchen right now and ask.

But she hesitates. She hesitates because asking means going behind Guychardson's back. She doesn't want to do that; she just wants everyone on the same page. But she can't get Guychardson on the Goddamn page because he isn't here. Where the fuck is he?

She goes out to the dock, lights a cigarette, checks her phone. Her shift's almost over, and he still hasn't returned her text from this morning.

WHERE ARE YOU, she texts. Afterward she can't think of anything else to do, other than send it to him a second time, an impulse she resists, but just barely.

At the end of her shift she stays on. She eats the family meal; she sticks around and helps the chefs work their way through the service. Carnage is as popular as it's ever been, its star still rising, and they're extra busy since it's summer, with long warm nights keeping people out later. The volume of customers easily warrants an extra pair of hands, even on a Monday night. But through it all she can feel Angel watching her, as though he knows that she's not really staying just to help out. She can't guess how he's interpreting her weird behavior but she's pretty sure that whatever motive he's reading into it is wrong. But she's also too worried now to care. Guychardson hasn't appeared, and she's starting to doubt that he will. All her texts—she sends a third to let him know that she's staying late—remain unanswered.

And so, as the dinner service winds down, she makes

a decision. She's hot, exhausted, worried, maybe more than worried now, actually: maybe scared. She needs to bring someone else in on this. She no longer cares about going behind Guychardson's back: it's time to talk to Angel. She's not sure exactly what she hopes Angel will *do*, at this point—they can't give Guychardson a place to lie low if they don't know where he *is*—but there must be *something* that the two of them could come up with together. Angel knows where Guychardson lives: he must, right? He must have an address in a file somewhere; maybe the two of them could get in a cab and go over there together, just to see. Maybe they'll find Guychardson safely at home, in front of a TV, drinking beers.

She waits until almost everyone else is gone, lurking in the corners of the kitchen, waiting for Angel and Jon to finish counting out the take, trying to look busy even once the cleanup has finished and there's nothing left to do. The chefs, ever territorial, eye her suspiciously as they depart, one by one.

She drops her elbows onto the stainless steel of one of the prep tables: *boom*. She makes a cradle for her head with her hands and drops her face into it. So fucking tired.

Finally Jon and Angel emerge from the office, joking with one another about something. She's always been impressed by the way the two of them have managed to make it look easy, maintaining a friendship, a real camaraderie, through all the stresses of keeping this restaurant alive. Hearing them laugh almost gets a smile to rise up through her fear and fatigue. But before it does they notice her standing there, and they can tell something's up, and they stop laughing.

"Hey, Ollie," Jon says, tentatively. "Everything OK?"

"Sure," she lies. It comes out with less authority than she'd hoped for so she tries again, more force in it this time. "Yes," she says. "I just—I just needed to talk to Angel about something."

Jon looks at Angel. Angel returns a helplessly bemused face. Both of them look at her. Jon's look has a touch of concern in it, as though he's trying to figure out what, exactly, he's missed. Angel's look, by contrast, is fake-casual, the kind of casual that's working overtime to mask the excitement behind it. Excitement, hell—it might even be a kind of benign terror: it's the look of someone who's trying to hide both the fact that he thinks he's going to get something he really wants, and the fact that he has no fucking idea whatsoever as to how to deal with that.

"Well," Jon says, shifting his glance from one of them to the other, "I guess I'm off then."

"So," Angel says, once Jon goes.

"Yeah," Ollie says. She's trying to figure out where to start. It probably makes sense to say *I have to talk to you about Guychardson* but she's starting to think it might be necessary instead to lead with *I think you have the wrong idea about why I'm here.* It might be just the fatigue, but neither assortment of words seems quite at the ready: instead she just lets her mouth hang open dumbly.

Angel takes advantage of the gap. He snaps his fingers as though he were just remembering something. "One more thing—gotta flush out the keg lines," he says. "Why don't you come down to the basement with me?"

"Uh," Ollie says, jolting. "I need to talk to you."

"So I keep hearing," Angel says. "Come down to the

basement with me and we'll talk." He puts his hand on her shoulders and revolves her, points her in the direction of the basement door. As she starts walking, she shrugs, hoping to shake him and give off a *don't touch me* vibe, and he lifts his hands for a second—she's grateful—although then one of them finds its way to her again, lands on the small of her back, steering her. It's only the lightest, gentlest touch, but it gives her the creeps, and with it comes the sudden feeling that she shouldn't be going down there without a knife in her hand. Her station is only five feet away. Guychardson's knife, in its lacquered box, is there.

But by this point she's halfway through the door leading down into the basement. She pauses. "Hey," she says, half-turning to face Angel.

"It's OK," he says.

"I don't want to give you the wrong idea," she mumbles.

"Ollie," Angel says. He laughs. "It's me. It's Angel. We're just going downstairs to talk. OK?"

"OK," Ollie says, and she begins to descend the stairs, with Angel behind her.

They're halfway down when they hear a noise, a bang. Something being slammed open, kicked against a wall. Loud. Angel pauses, turns, looks back up the steps.

"What was that?" Ollie says.

"Could be Jon?" Angel says, but he doesn't sound sure. More sounds; heavy footfalls. Unmistakably someone moving around in the kitchen. Ollie's mind goes suddenly to the knife, still at her station.

"Hello?" Angel calls, taking a step away from her, heading back up toward the kitchen.

"Wait," Ollie says, dropping her voice to a hush. She reaches out, clutches his shoulder; this time it's his turn to shrug her away.

"Jon?" Another step.

"Jesus Christ, Angel, get back here," Ollie hisses. But he doesn't listen. He climbs another step and then he's standing in the doorway. From the darkness of the stairwell she sees him only as silhouette.

"Hello?" he says.

Gunshot. Angel jerks, stumbles backward; his foot makes a wide circle in space and she thinks for one hopeful second that maybe the whole thing is a trick, a joke, he's OK, he's going to take one wobbly step backward and then another, and another, and then he'll be back there by her side and they'll go down to the basement and make out and talk and come up with a plan that will fix everything, that will keep everyone safe, forever and ever. And then he falls.

He falls past her, almost colliding with her, and she screams. She tries not to, but she screams. It takes her maybe two seconds to stop doing it and start cursing herself instead. So stupid. So fucking stupid. She screamed for two seconds and now whoever is in here knows exactly where she is. And if she knows one thing, she knows this: whoever shot Angel will also shoot her, without hesitation.

So she runs. She turns away from the light spilling through the kitchen doorway and runs down into the wet darkness of the basement, where there's still a chance she might be safe. At the base of the stairs Angel lies in a heap; she has to will herself to leap over his fallen body. *See if he's OK*, says one hopeful voice in the midst of the blazing panic

183

that's seized her brain, but she knows he's not OK, and so she runs; she runs all the way to the end of the tunnel, until there's nowhere left to go.

She slaps her palms against the cool dank brick; she digs her fingers into the rough mortar, as though her fear might have somehow enabled her with the power to rip apart a wall, to tear a passage through stone. But it hasn't.

She's going to die down here. She feels certain of it. And a regret blossoms up within her, like blood in water— she regrets that she won't see Jesse again, before she dies. That he will continue to grow up without a mother. That there is *no point yet to come* at which she will have worked her shit out enough to see him again, no future in which she and Donald have mutually worked their shit out enough to give their son the basic gift of two fucking parents. Down here, waiting to die, she suddenly understands that whatever existed between them could have been untangled with a little attention, a little effort. It wouldn't have been that hard. And she's going to die, knowing that.

No. No she's not. She turns, looks back up the length of the tunnel, past Angel's body, and there it is: the dumbwaiter. If she makes it to the dumbwaiter she can get out.

She runs. As she runs past the stairs, she takes one frightened sideward glance and sees the shooter, beginning to descend, she sees the shape of a weapon in his hand, and that's all she has time to make out. She does not stop, she keeps running, she hears him shout *Hey* but she does not stop. She reaches the dumbwaiter and climbs in, curling up in order to fit. She grabs the control box, dangling from its length of heavy cable, holds it in her hands, and waits.

She doesn't punch the button right away. The last thing she wants is to emerge into the kitchen while the shooter is still up there. She has to let him get closer, down into the basement. And then, when it's time, she'll go.

She can hear him come down another step. "Come on now," he says, his voice carrying an accent that she can't quite identify. "You want to cooperate."

No I don't, she thinks.

He comes down another step, and pauses. *Closer*, she thinks. *Come closer, you fuck.*

She hears him mutter something, profanity she guesses, although it doesn't sound like English. And then he descends three more steps, coming, finally, into view. He reaches Angel's body, prods it with his boot. He takes aim at Angel's skull with his pistol and fires a bullet into it.

Ollie must cry out because the shooter whips his head up and spots her. OK, now. She punches the button and the dumbwaiter lurches awake. For one horrible second she's afraid that the shooter is going to turn and run back up the stairs—he hadn't gotten as deep into the basement as she'd hoped—but instead he rushes at her, trying to catch her before she vanishes up the shaft. The gap through which he is visible closes as she ascends; she lowers her head, trying to get a good look at him as he charges closer, but she ends up with little more than an impression of menace.

It feels like it takes a long time to get up to the kitchen. The dumbwaiter is slow but it's never in her whole life seemed this fucking slow. She sniffles. She touches her face and finds it wet with leakage, snot and tears that she hadn't even realized were coming out of her.

At long last, she reaches the top of the shaft and she tumbles out into the kitchen, breathing hard. She has, what, seconds maybe, before the shooter comes back up from the basement. She uses these seconds. She crosses the kitchen swiftly, with determination. She reaches out toward a rack without breaking stride, without even really turning her eyes away from the basement door. Her fingers brush the handle of a cast-iron skillet and grasp. She slides the pan out as she advances, feels its heft in her hand.

This, she thinks. *This will do.*

She presses herself against the wall, at the door's edge. She brings the pan up to her shoulder. The sound of clambering footsteps, boot-shod, grows louder, but she makes herself wait: *until you see the whites of his eyes*, she thinks, the phrase swimming up from somewhere.

She tries to calm her breathing; she tries not to shake.

She sees the shooter's fingers grip at the jamb.

And the moment she sees his profile emerge from the doorway, she swings.

During the month Ollie worked on Ulysses's homestead she helped him to kill pigs, and he thought it was important to learn all the ways in which this could be done, and one method, which he'd learned from his dad, was killing them with a blow to the skull from a sledgehammer. And when she feels the pan hit the shooter's face, when she feels the recoil drive into the palms of her hands, into her arms, that is what she remembers. It feels exactly the same.

The shooter groans tremendously and goes over backward, down the stairs, into the darkness. She stands there for a second, breathing hard, tempted to follow him down there, finish the job, straddle his chest and pound his head with the pan until he stops kicking. But she's not stupid. He still has his gun and in any battle between a frying pan and a gun, the gun's going to win. So she releases the pan, lets it clang to the floor: with its utility expended it's just extra weight. Her hands, now free, wipe frantically at her eyes: once she can see the way, she hurries to her station, gets Guychardson's box up under her arm, grabs her messenger bag, leaves everything else. She heads to the service entrance, notices the broken lock, pushes her way out into the night, and she runs.

She wants to call the cops but first she just needs to get the fuck *away*.

She rounds the corner and nearly collides with a dark-haired woman, middle aged, just standing there in the middle of the sidewalk.

She knows she should say to this woman *You need to get out of here*. She knows she should say *There is a shooter in the building, get to safety*. But something about the way the woman just stands there, agog, staring at Ollie's miserable wet face like the worst kind of tourist—it still manages, even in the thick of every other Goddamn thing, to just rub Ollie wrong.

"Don't fucking look at me," Ollie has time to spit out, before she shoulders past the woman and keeps running, down the street, around the corner, away, anywhere, away.

16

PROFESSIONALS

"Don't fucking look at me," says the woman to Maja, and then she flees. She has the knife, in a box shoved up under one arm. Maja does not pursue, does not engage. Instead she turns, watches the service door that Pig forced his way into, waits for him to reemerge.

He finally does, a minute later, with a pub towel clutched to his face. Even from a distance Maja can see that it's stained with blood.

"You drive," Pig says, his voice muffled. He flings her the keys, and she snatches them out of the air.

She doesn't know what's happened, but OK: she opens the car door, gets in the driver's seat. It takes her a few seconds to find the right key and jam it in the ignition, but she does it while Pig fumbles at the door, trying to open it without dropping the towel from his left hand or the pistol from his right.

In the time that it takes him to stuff the pistol in his waistband and get in, Maja looks at the recent history of Pig's gun.

She sees a bullet being fired and she sees the outcome: blood gushing from a man's chest. She sees a second bullet and she sees the spatter pattern blown out of a skull. So there's a body. She retrieves a fresh set of black gloves from her purse and she dons them. If she has to be a getaway driver fleeing the scene of a homicide she at least doesn't want to leave incriminating prints all over the steering wheel while she's doing it.

The desire—the need—to wear her gloves isn't just a way to reduce the traces of herself she'll leave behind. It's also a way to reduce the amount of Pig's person that she'll pick up through her palms. Even with her gloves on, she can tell that the wheel is tacky with sugars, the residue of treats. And she absorbs an awareness of other things, too, things below the sticky surface: to take hold of this wheel, to sit in his seat and steer his car, is to feel herself in his position, to literally take on his point of view. Even with the gloves on, she begins to apprehend his appetites, to feel his stunted furies. She begins to understand the way this city looks to him: fallen, overrun with subhumans, a world soiled by the hands of inferior beings. She sees the empire that he envisions as his birthright, purged, clean. The continent that he hopes to leave to his descendants, horrifyingly purified, rising into being upon unfathomable tiers of suffering. She presses down on the gas, pulls the car out into the street, attempts to blink these visions away.

There's no time to consider them anyway. Instead they have to run. The woman with the blade is going to be calling the cops any second now, if she hasn't already, and police are going to be all over this block.

She makes a turn.

Pig tilts his head back as they drive, keeps the stained towel pinched to his face. When he hears the sirens, he drops it into his lap, hoping to look normal, just another passenger in the flow of nighttime Manhattan traffic, as inconspicuous as anyone.

Maja sneaks a look at him. She can't help but speak her immediate observation aloud: "You've broken your nose."

"No shit, Sherlock," he whispers savagely, as two police cruisers shriek by in the opposing lane. He works hard to keep a neutral expression on his face, but she can feel fear pouring off him like an odor. The fear of being spotted, of being caught, of getting this close to having what he wants and then fucking it up.

Once they're safely past the police, Pig reaches up abruptly and does a thing to his nose with his hands; he makes a stifled cry of pain as he does it. Then he stretches into the backseat and retrieves his satchel, roots around in it until he has his mask back out. He lowers it down, over his face, and then he's quiet again.

He does not ask to be taken to a hospital, and she does not offer. In the absence of any other instruction, she heads back to the motel in New Jersey. There's nothing they can do to get any closer to the blade, not tonight: the woman who has it is going to be talking to police for who knows how long. Hours, probably. And so their only move, right now, is to wait until morning. Pig seems to understand this, or, in any case, he has fallen into a sullen silence that she reads as understanding.

Four now, says the Archive again. Four bodies, up from three.

Yes, Maja thinks.

That's a lot.

It could be more, Maja replies. *There have been times when it's been more. You know that. Remember Osaka. The whole boardroom.*

I haven't forgotten, the Archive says. *But still.*

But still what.

But still, four is a lot for a job that's ongoing. Where the client still doesn't have what he wants.

Yes, that's true.

Because it means there are more to come.

More to come: at least one more, anyway: the woman. The running woman. Maja has seen people run like this before. They always do one of two things: either they keep running, or they stop somewhere to hide. It makes no difference which of these options the woman with the knife will take in the morning, Maja tells herself: either way, she will be found.

And once she's found, she will be shot, the Archive offers.

Yes, thank you. I understand. At least then it will be over. The killings don't matter. All that matters is that the job ends.

All that matters is that the job ends: this is what she tells herself, when things get ugly. Once it's over, she can go home, where things are orderly, and she can collect the other half of her fee, and then after that there will be a long period in which she will not have to do anything. All she will need to do is remain quiet, and the record of her passage through this city will fade, and time will pass, and it will bury whatever traces connect her to these crimes, and with it, her memory of the crimes themselves will be effaced.

She can feel the camera on the bridge take a photo-graph of their license plate as they cross back into Jersey.

Pig doesn't speak again until they're back at the motel. She follows him into his room, waiting to talk with him about tomorrow's strategy. He heads into his bathroom, and she pauses in the doorway there. Over his shoulder she can see him in the mirror; she watches him as he inspects his swol-len face.

He catches her looking. He looks into her eyes in the mirror. She holds the stare.

"You saw her," he says, after a minute.

"Who?" Maja asks, although she knows who.

"That woman. The woman who did this."

"Yes," Maja says, flatly.

"Well," Pig says. "Let me just tell you."

Maja waits.

"I'm going to enjoy killing that woman," Pig says.

The killings don't matter, she tells herself again, but to hear Pig say this with such obvious relish pulls distaste out into her face. She quickly relinquishes the expression, but not so quickly that Pig fails to notice.

"You think that's wrong?" Pig says, watching her reflec-tion closely.

"Not wrong, exactly," Maja says.

"Not wrong, exactly," Pig says, with a sneer in his voice. "*Regrettable*, maybe?" He wheels around, comes toward her, contempt beginning to contort his swollen face. She keeps meeting his gaze but simultaneously she considers what objects in the room behind her might work as a weapon. She remembers a pen on the desk, the coffeepot's glass carafe.

"I know people like you," Pig says. "With your *moral codes*. Let me guess what you're thinking: the loss of life, in pursuit of a goal: always so *regrettable*. Best *avoided where possible*."

Maja considers a set of conciliatory things she could say. Noises that might soothe this man. Making those noises would be the safest thing to do. All the same, she's tired of being frightened of Pig. He's not going to shoot her. He's not going to shoot her, because he needs her. Deep down, she knows this, and she knows that he knows this as well. And so she says exactly what she's thinking.

"It's not regrettable to kill people," she says. "It is wrong."

Pig looks like he might spit. "Listen to you," he says.

"It shouldn't be so surprising a thing," Maja says, "to hear me say this. It is wrong to kill people. As a—how did you put it?—as a *moral code*, it is neither elaborate nor unusual. It is, ultimately, very simple."

"Still though," Pig says. "I bet it's *real* nice, to be in possession of a moral code that allows you to feel bad when somebody dies but that's still flexible enough that you can pal around with killers when there's enough money involved."

Maja composes a line of thought in her head, and then gives one slow, deliberate blink, and begins to speak, as calmly as though she were reading from a document. "You have—or, rather, your *father* has—employed me to find and retrieve something for you. That is all. Any moral judgments I make regarding the activities that you should undertake in the process fall outside of the scope of any obligations concerning my employment. I may choose to either issue these judgments or withhold them. Whether the motivating forces behind my moral code appear hypocritical to you is of no concern whatsoever, from a contractual perspective. However. If, for reasons that I could not possibly begin to fathom, it has become important to you that we redefine my contractual obligations in a manner that requires me to present the appearance of moral consistency, or to offer you a regular opportunity for moral absolution, then please, by all means, get on the phone to your father and convey this to him, promptly, so that, from there, we can discuss the consequent adjustment to my fee. I ask only that you be alert to two facts: one, that this adjustment will be substantial, and two, that should your father and I fail to reach an agreement, I will not hesitate to walk away from this job."

Pig regards her.

She reaches behind her without looking and lifts the phone handset, offers it out toward him.

"Go ahead," she says.

At this, he cracks a smile.

"You know what, Finder, you're hard-core," he says, shaking his head infinitesimally. "But you're all right. Within the, uh, *the scope of the contractual obligations of your employment*, you're all right. If I may say so."

"You may say so," Maja says, after a moment.

"OK, good," Pig says. "I'm saying so."

She hangs up the phone.

17

MONARCHS

The police take Ollie in until morning. They put her in a grubby room where two separate detectives bring her two separate paper cups of equally bad coffee and ask her essentially the same set of questions. They move her to a cubicle where she answers more questions from a guy who tries to use his computer to make a face of the suspect. Were his eyes closer together or further apart? Did he have more of a square chin or more of a rounded chin? Her answers all effectively amount to: It was dark. I couldn't see. I don't know.

She doesn't talk to anyone about the knife, in its box, inside her bag.

At some point they give her a brochure from the Witness Aid Services Unit and leave her in a plastic seat in a hallway. She flips the brochure open, stares at its information without exactly reading it. Counseling, support groups, shelters, orders of protection. She has no idea which of these she might need. The only thing she can really think of that she needs for sure is sleep. No one's attending to her but no one's told her she can leave, either. She curls up as best she can in the hard shell of the chair, holds her messenger bag against her belly, and falls in and out of fitful dreams.

When she wakes up there's like thirty notifications on her phone. Texts, e-mails, Facebook messages. She blinks at them groggily, tries to untangle what's happening. It seems that the murders at Carnage made the papers: front page of the *Post*, first page of the Metro section in the *Times*. Everybody wants to know where she is, whether she's OK. Messages from Victor, messages from Jon, messages from Carnage people she didn't even realize had her phone number: random cooks, servers, even one of the dishwashers. There's a message from Ulysses: SAW WHAT HAPPENED. WHAT THE FUCK. CHECKING TO MAKE SURE YOU'RE SAFE. This followed by another one: I'M COMING DOWN. WHERE ARE YOU?

There's nothing from Donald. Not that she expected anything: it's been a year since he's been in touch. To the best of her knowledge he doesn't even look at her Facebook page so he might not be seeing what people are posting there. Unless some mutual acquaintance of theirs forwarded him the *Times* article, he might not even know. But still. She remembers the early conversations they'd had in the first years of their relationship, the way he could calm her down, just using words like they were their own form of magic. She remembers the way he could seem to reach into her skull and help her to untangle the snarled emotions she'd jammed away in there. She could use that deftness today. She misses it, even though she tries not to, even though she works hard to forget that it ever was a thing.

There is also no word from Guychardson. She looks at the last text she sent him. Still unanswered. She gets an awful feeling in her gut.

She begins the process of replying to everyone. She texts Victor back first, just the words I'M OK. WITH THE COPS. She texts Ulysses with the precinct name. She texts Jon, asks him to let everybody else in the Carnage network know that she's alive, just so she doesn't have to deal with reaching out to every last person. She thinks for a second and then sends Jon another text: SORRY ABOUT ANGEL. It feels like such a worthless thing to say, but you have to say something. He replies with like a million questions, which are basically the same questions that the cops asked, and for now she just ignores them all.

One of the detectives she talked to earlier comes down the hallway. "Hey," he says, "you're up."

"Listen," she blurts at him. "This guy? The—what, the suspect? The shooter? I think he might also have shot somebody else. Maybe Sunday night, late. A guy, Haitian guy. My friend. Guychardson."

A phone call is made. A third detective gets called in; she ends up back in the same grubby interview room.

"Wait a second," she says, before he can begin in on the questions. "I just need to make sure of what's happening. I just need to ask—is he dead?" She can hear her voice begin to get unhinged, but she keeps speaking. "You're a homicide cop, like the others, but you're not the *same* cop, that means, I mean, that has to mean he's dead, doesn't it? Just tell me. Fucking tell me."

The third detective looks away, seems to take a moment to summon something from some reserve, and then turns back to her. "Yes," he says, "your friend was shot and killed early Monday morning outside of his apartment, in Brooklyn."

"Jesus Christ," says Ollie. "Jesus fucking Christ."

And right there at the table, she cries. Once she starts it feels like she might not be able to stop. The cop looks down at his own hands in a practiced way while waiting for her to finish; after what seems like a long time he gets up and heads out, eventually returning with a box of tissues that he found somewhere. She clutches it, turns it in her hands, as though it were a piece that had fallen out of her life. As though if she revolved it in just the right way she could snap it back into its original position, return it to its place in the original configuration, and then the whole thing would miraculously start working again, as though nothing had ever happened, and everything would be OK.

Instead she's in the police station for two more hours of questioning. By the time they're done with her she feels completely hollowed out. She rises from the chair, rubs her temples, rolls her shoulders. Checks her phone. Loads more messages from everyone, but there's one specific one she's hoping for, and she finds it. It's Ulysses again: IN THE LOBBY. COME FIND ME.

And she walks through a set of doors and there he is. She still doesn't know exactly how she'd describe the nature of their relationship but right at this moment she's simply grateful to have someone in her life who is large, solid, someone who can serve, literally, as support. She walks into him the way one would walk into a wall. He manages to turn it into something that might pass for an embrace by getting his arms up and around her.

"I'm so glad you're safe," he says.

She clenches her eyes shut.

"I'm so glad you're safe," he says again, lower, murmuring it into her ear. She doesn't feel safe. She pushes into him harder, as though the way to safety might somehow involve moving *through* him, breaching the boundary that keeps them apart and distinct, winding up inside one another.

They stand like this for a minute, pressed together, half-embraced, until finally Ulysses says, "Um, cops kind of freak me out. Do you want to get out of here?"

Yes. Yes she does.

"Do you want to go home?" Ulysses asks her, once she's situated in the front of his big old Buick.

"I don't know," she says. "No. I don't know. I don't think I'm safe. That guy's still out there, still here, in the city somewhere."

"You think he might be after you? You specifically? People online are saying botched robbery—"

"Probably it is, yeah. But I don't think it's just, like, a *random* robbery. This guy wasn't just trying to grab cash from the till. He was after something specific. And the fucked up thing is that I have it."

"You have what?"

"The thing the guy was after."

"Yeah, I get it, but what *is* it?"

"It's a knife."

"A knife? You think this guy shot Angel over a *knife*?"

"Angel and Guychardson."

"Wait: Guychardson?"

"You know him. Haitian guy?"

"Short?"

"Yeah."

"That guy got shot?"

"He's dead."

"Jesus Christ."

"Yeah. Maybe some other dudes, too; I'm not totally sure."

"Over a *knife*?"

"I think so. It's a special knife, I think."

"What's so special about it?"

Ollie thinks about this for a minute. How to explain it. Ulysses doesn't really believe in magic. She remembers exactly when she told him that she was a practitioner: a warm night, last summer, when she was living with him at his homestead. The two of them had gone through half a box of wine and she had begun to feel big confessional feelings; she had admitted that part of how she'd captured his eye in the first place was by committing a tiny act of sorcery. It had felt incredibly shameful, to say it out loud—to essentially admit that she had manipulated him, against his will, without his consent—but he'd just snorted, as though she'd told him that she'd first chosen him because she thought they had compatible zodiac signs. After that she didn't bring it up much with him. And yet she's not sure she has any better explanation.

"It's magic," she says.

Ulysses just lets that hang there.

"Look," Ollie says, "You don't have to believe that it's magic. Just—just think of it as something that's like *super valuable*. What's the most valuable thing you can think of?"

"Me personally?" says Ulysses.

"You personally."

Without missing a beat, Ulysses responds, "A John Deere 5M series utility tractor."

"OK, cool," Ollie says. "So just imagine this knife as a very tiny, very valuable tractor with unique properties."

"Magic tractor," Ulysses says, trying out the idea.

"Yes," Ollie says.

"Unique properties."

"Special powers," Ollie says.

"So what can it do?"

At this, Ollie frowns, because she still isn't exactly sure. "It can cut through space and time," she offers, finally.

Ulysses frowns back in return. "What does that mean?"

"I have no fucking idea. But it's what everyone keeps saying."

"OK," Ulysses says, after a minute. "You wanted a strategy. Here's a strategy: I drive you to the river, you throw the Goddamn thing in there, and we're done with it."

"No," Ollie says.

"Why *not*?"

"Guychardson thought that it was valuable. He thought it was valuable enough to risk his *life* over."

"Sure, but—he's fucking *dead* now."

"Right, but that doesn't mean he was *wrong*. And if

this thing is so important that people are willing to kill over it, it just seems like maybe we should hang onto it until we know more."

Ulysses considers this. "So, all right, this guy, this killer, you think he knows where you live? You think he might show up at your place?"

"Maybe." She thinks. Fear begins to crawl over her as she adds up what she knows. "Guychardson got shot outside of his apartment, so this guy knew where Guychardson lived. That could mean that he has access to the Carnage personnel records or something. Definitely fucking possible."

"OK, so—let's get you way the hell away."

"Yeah," Ollie says. "Yeah. Let's do that."

"How 'bout my place?"

She thinks about Ulysses's homestead, out in the middle of Goddamn nowhere, nothing if not way the hell away. She could go. There's nothing really stopping her: she's learned from her phone that Carnage is closed for the time being; no one seems exactly sure when it's going to reopen but probably not for another couple of days at least. So she could go. A couple of days spent hiding out might be enough time to make a long-term plan. A couple of days might be enough time for the cops to catch the guy. She tries very hard to believe in the probability of that outcome.

"Yeah," she says. "Let's do that."

"You want to swing by your place, grab some clothes or something? A toothbrush?"

"Fuck it," Ollie says. "I can get that stuff on the road. I think it's safer just to go."

Safer just to go: this causes Victor's name to pop up, an

alert in her mind. If the apartment's not safe, then he's not safe.

"I gotta call my roommate," she says, fishing her phone out of her pocket for the thousandth time today.

"Go for it," says Ulysses.

She dials. Victor answers.

"Ollie," he says. "Are you OK?"

"Yeah," she says. "I mean, I think so. This whole situation is pretty fucked."

"No kidding," Victor says. "Where are you?"

"I'm with Ulysses—we're driving around Manhattan. I think we should—come get you? Maybe?"

"What? Why?"

"'Cause there's some maniac running around shooting my friends, that's why. And—this is going to sound crazy, but I think he's after that knife."

"It's not a knife," Victor says.

This gives Ollie pause. "What do you mean?" she says.

"It's not a knife," Victor says again. "It's a piece of a sword."

She considers this, imagines it as the tip of a sword, embedded in a handle. It explains the weird dual edge and the lack of a bolster. And she thinks suddenly back to Rufus, and his crazy theories, and she remembers that World *Knives* wasn't the phrase that he used, it was *swords*: World Swords.

"How do you know that?" she asks, carefully.

"Well," Victor says. "Let me back up a minute. Guess where I went this morning?"

"I have no idea," Ollie says.

"Well, with everything so royally fucked, as it is, it would be uncharitable to force you to guess, so I'll just tell you. I did what we *should* have done Sunday morning: I went to Manhattan, and found the parking lot where our old friend Rufus works, if *working* is the word you would use to describe someone who sits in a glass box reading Hermetic manuals all night. Regardless: I caught him at the end of his shift and I told him if he came to our apartment and told me everything he knew about magic blades that I'd make him the best breakfast he'd ever had. I told him I make an amazing popover. So let me just say it's been a pretty interesting morning."

Ollie blinks. "Wait, is he there now?"

"He's here; he has popover in his beard; the whole thing really is magnificently disgusting."

"Did he have information about the knife, or the sword, or whatever the fuck it is? What did he tell you?" Ollie asks.

Victor pauses. "To some degree I'd have to say it resists summary," he says.

"Jesus Christ, Victor, I'm running for my life here, you think you could just give me a straight answer?"

"Straight's not exactly my forte, my dear, but—wait—Rufus, don't, we don't *grab* in this household. Ollie, I am gathering that he has an interest in speaking with you directly. His hands are impossibly filthy so I'm just going to put you on speaker"—scuffling sounds—"and set the phone down right here, juuust out of reach. Can you hear us?"

"I can hear you," Ollie says. "Hello? Rufus?"

"Monarchs!" Rufus exclaims. "Royals!"

"Hi, Rufus," Ollie says. "Can you slow down a second? Which royals?"

"Warlock-Kings and Witch-Queens! Impossible monarchs of the oldest Europe! Europe before Europe! Time as tissue!"

"OK," Ollie says. She pinches the bridge of her nose. "I need a verb. Can you give me a verb?"

"The Swords," Rufus intones. "The World Swords. They forged the Swords to enact their will."

"All right," says Ollie. "So they use the Swords to get what they want—but what in the fuck do a bunch of old world kings want?"

"Ollie," Victor interjects, "they're kings. What do you think they want? They want to rule. They made the Swords so that they could rule the world."

"Look," Ollie says. "I'm sure there's something to be gained from this history lesson but mostly I just need to know one thing: Should I chuck this thing in the river or not?"

"No!" Rufus exclaims. "Water won't lose it. The primal Sword was sunk before—then found! Every schoolchild knows! The lake. The lake in the story."

Ollie's scalp prickles suddenly. "What story," she says.

"Think monarchs," Victor says.

"I'm thinking monarchs," Ollie says.

"Think monarchs with swords," he continues. "Monarchs with special magic swords that allow them to enact their will over an entire country—?"

"Motherfuck me," Ollie says, "you're talking about King *Arthur*?"

"Bingo," says Victor.

18

M●VING

The woman is moving. The woman and someone else. Maja can feel it happening, even in her sleep, like something snagging on silk, tugging. She stirs, wakes, sits up, presses her fingers into the corners of her eyes to remove the specks of morning grit.

She probes at the roof of her mouth with her tongue. Dry: she hasn't been drinking enough water these last few days. In the bathroom, running the sink, she works a hole into the polyethylene wrapping of the single-use cup the motel has provided, but when the vision of a petrochemical refinery begins to loom in her mind she just sticks her head under the tap instead. Swishes, spits, takes another swig and this time swallows. The faint taste of minerals in her mouth. Images of layered stone deep within the mountains to the north: a suitable basis on which to found a morning. A point from which she can work.

She sits at the desk, spreads out the maps, tries to align

her sense of the woman's movements with the rendering that's there in front of her. She puts her finger on a highway, considers it, moves her finger to a different one.

The Archive looks at the names of towns, notes the ones that it finds funny.

Once she's reached a point of suitable certainty, she lets herself into Pig's room. He's still asleep, his breathing labored through his bruised and broken nose. He'd brought ice with him to bed last night, and now a clear plastic bag filled with water rests on his pillow, beached there, distended, like a jellyfish on a shoreline.

"Wake up," Maja says. Pig doesn't stir. "Wake up," she says again, a little more loudly.

"Fuck," Pig says. "What time is it?"

"It's not early," she says.

Pig groans, rolls over in the bed, pushes the bag of water away with the edge of his hand.

"They're moving," Maja says.

"They," Pig repeats.

"The woman. The knife. Someone else traveling with her, I can't quite get it. A man. A friend."

"A bodyguard," Pig offers.

"I don't know. Possibly."

"Where are they headed?"

"North."

"That's all you can give me? 'North'?"

"I'm not a fortune-teller," she says. "I can't give you the future." The future appears to her as it always does, shapeless, inchoate, terrifying in its inability to be known by the precise location of its things. "But," she continues, setting these thoughts aside, "I can tell you what's happening now, and what's happening now is they're headed north."

"OK," says Pig. "North." He pushes himself upright, throws his bare legs over the edge of the bed, gathers the sheet around his waist. He's not wearing a shirt and she examines his tattoos. On one shoulder, three heavy black bars, arrayed in a configuration that resembles a trident. On his other shoulder, a cross in a circle, again made from heavy, dark lines. Across his chest, a wild pig, in profile, head lowered, tusks up. Taken together as icons they create a sinister effect, the suggestion of coercive force.

With any other client, she'd take this opportunity: read the tattoos, learn more about where he got them, when, why. She begins to do it, but the tattoos, like everything else about him, are clouded by a halo of noise, a history that's been reworked somehow, cut up, spliced back together. She gets a vague sense of them as images on flags, being waved by hateful crowds—but the image is jumbled, low-quality, like video footage she might see on a news broadcast, shot chaotically in the midst of a scuffle.

She could ask him. She's not in the habit of using conversation as a way to learn about people's backgrounds; she's never had to do it so she's never really developed the skills that are necessary. All the same, she recognizes that it is a thing that is humanly possible to do.

Pig touches his nose gingerly, winces.

"All right," he says, blinking himself the rest of the way awake. "They're moving. Do we know mode of transport? Plane, train, what?"

"They're on the road, I think," Maja says. "They're

moving fast, but not as fast as a plane would take them. And it seems to only be the two of them, so probably they're in a car. I'd feel more people if they were on a train or a bus."

"On the road, in a car," Pig says. "So we can catch up with them."

"They can't drive forever," Maja says. "They'll have to stop somewhere."

"And anywhere they stop will be better than here," Pig says, experimentally, as though checking the veracity of the observation.

"I would say yes," Maja says. "Most places that aren't this city will confer advantage to us. Fewer people, lower density, less surveillance."

"Not as many cops."

"Not as many cops."

"OK," Pig says. He smiles, showing teeth.

19

LIVING

"So—so—so wait a second," Ollie says. "Are you saying I have a piece of King Arthur's *sword*? *Excalibur*?" She can feel the incredulous expression on Ulysses's face without even having to turn to look at him.

"That's—no—that's not exactly it," Victor says. "Rufus says Excalibur is still where it should be. Where you'd expect it to be. Like, in Britain. But—there's more than one."

"OK," Ollie says, her head whirling. "How many are there?"

"It's complicated," Victor says. "My laptop is open and I open a new tab every time Rufus says something and I have like twenty tabs open now. There's this list he showed me, on this message board, it proposes there are five, maybe?"

"Five!" Rufus barks. "Unstable number, inverted pentagram, superimposition upon the globe."

"So, listen, Arthur has the first one, the one Rufus calls the primal one, which, as you know, he uses to rule Britain. And France—it's like an arms race back in those days; England has one so France needs one—so you have Charlemagne. Charlemagne *fronts* like a Christian, which is genius, 'cause to hear Rufus tell it it sounds like he's actually the head of this enormous magical death cult—whatever—anyway, he's got a sword, Joyeuse, which is basically the French equivalent of Excalibur. That's the second one."

"French," Ollie mutters. She thinks back to the accent of the guy who shot Guychardson. It could have been French. She wrenches her attention back to Victor, who is continuing on, saying something about various wars between France and England—

"—anyway, at some point they get tired of fighting with one another, and instead they start looking outward across the globe. They start making more of these swords. Queen Elizabeth apparently gives the third one to the British East India Company in 1600, which they use to establish company rule over the Indian subcontinent. And then King James makes the fourth one, in 1606, when Britain establishes colonies here, in America. To help them rule us. And part of how we were able to break free is that during the Revolutionary War we get the sword and destroy it. At the Siege of Boston. You remember that part."

"What happens to the other ones?" Ollie asks.

"OK, so Excalibur—it seems like the Royal Family still has it, somewhere. The American sword is destroyed in 1775 or 1776. The British East India sword is supposedly destroyed, 1857. Shit with Joyeuse is a little more complicated. The French monarchy hangs onto it for like a thousand years, but then it's stolen and replaced by a fake in, uhh, 1792, during the French Revolution. The original ends up with Napoleon; he gets his hands on it in 1795, uses it to great success during the Napoleonic Wars—it gets broken at some point, nobody's clear when exactly. It does seem like the individual shards float around for a while—one ends up with Napoleon III—Napoleon's nephew—who tries to use it to set up a puppet emperor in Mexico. That fails, but then he uses it to start carving into Asia, basically setting up French Indochina. Looks like that one's finally destroyed as recently as 1954."

"OK," Ollie says. "So the one that I have—"

"Well," Victor says. "I left something out."

"Tell me," Ollie says.

Big sigh from Victor. "There's this fifth one."

"The fifth one," Ollie says.

"It's also French," Victor says. "They make it so they can rule Haiti."

Ollie blinks. *Fuck*, she thinks. "Haiti," she says, for confirmation.

"Yeah," Victor says, quietly. "In 1665."

"Blood and sugar," Rufus mutters. "Sugar and blood."

"And that one—"

"The Internet says it's destroyed, 1803. During the Haitian Revolution. But that could mean—"

"Shards," Ollie says. "I get it."

"Scattered shards," Victor says.

"Each piece hidden," Rufus says. "Passed from mothers to daughters. Passed from fathers to sons. Separate threads. Draw them together, though, and—make a knot!"

"But even a shard," Victor says, "would be—"

Ollie completes the thought: "Worth killing someone over."

"I was going to go with *extremely powerful*."

"Powerful enough to change the course of history," Ollie says.

"Maybe. Possibly. So, in conclusion, worth killing someone over, sure."

"Worth killing a bunch of people over."

"Pretty much, yes," Victor says, uncomfortably.

"So what this basically means," she says, "is that I'm going to die."

She can feel Ulysses flick a look over at her.

"Maybe not!" Victor says.

"I'm going to get shot," she says, miserably, "and I'm going to die."

"I don't know," Victor says. "I mean—you're doing the right thing."

"Running? Is that what you think is the *right thing* in this situation?"

"Absolutely," Victor says. "This guy, this shooter—he doesn't know shit about you."

"He knows where I work."

"He knows where you *work*," says Victor. "That's nothing. So that's the one place you don't go for a while."

"It's closed anyway," Ollie says.

"So what else? He doesn't know your name. He doesn't know where you live. He doesn't know where you're going. Did he see your face?"

Ollie considers the question. "No," she says.

"OK. So he doesn't know what you look like. He doesn't

216

even know if you have the knife, the shard, whatever. So *if* this guy is looking for you—big if—he's essentially fucked. The trail is cold. And we know that there's definitely cops looking for him. This guy is probably running the fuck away from you just as fast as he can."

These words work. At least a little.

"So," she says, "your advice, for now, is just: hold on to the shard and keep running."

"Hold on to the shard. Keep running. Stay alive."

Keep running, stay alive. She can do that. They're already out past Yonkers, passing the exits to White Plains. The further she gets away from the city, the safer she feels. And as she clears some threshold, makes it some particular distance from the site of the shooting, she suddenly releases a breath that had been lodged in her and feels herself hit by a surge of gratitude. Gratitude about surviving, gratitude that she's still here, in the world, experiencing things. She looks out the window, and for the first time in what feels like a long time, she takes pleasure in what she sees. She looks at the trees and the shrubs and the sun and the clouds and the buildings and they seem like occasion for joy. She looks over at Ulysses, his graying beard, his strong hands on the steering wheel, and she thinks to herself: *He's hot*. She's thought this every time she's seen him for the past year. But today is different. Today she doesn't just think it, she doesn't just make it as an observation: she *feels* it. She's riding in a car on an August day with a hot guy, and she's alive, and it feels good. She feels giddy, intoxicated.

She blinks, opens her mouth, and without premeditation, blurts out these words: "I want to have sex with you."

Ulysses looks away from the road, looks her over, incredulous.

"Yeah," he says, once it seems like he's assessed the sincerity in her face. "OK. Let's get back to my place."

"No," Ollie says. She slaps the dashboard. "I've been through a thing today. I might be fucking *marked for death*. No more waiting. I'm seizing the moment. I want to have sex with you *now*."

"Um," he says. "We're in the middle of the Saw Mill Parkway."

"Ulysses," Ollie says, firmly. He snaps to attention. "Do you want to have sex with me?"

He opens his mouth as if he's about to embark on some disquisition, then closes it again. "Yes," he says, finally.

"OK, then," Ollie says. "If there's one thing that I know about you, it is that you are a resourceful person. *Make it happen.*"

"I—" Ulysses tries.

"Fucking find a way," Ollie says, irritation creeping into her voice. Ulysses nods, a little solemnly, as though he were agreeing to go into battle. He flips on his turn signal and heads for the exit.

In the end they find a high school parking lot near Tarrytown. It's August, so no one is there. She gets into the backseat and pulls off her filthy pants, slides off her underwear and holds them in a ball in her fist. Ulysses stands

218

by the back door, his hand on the roof of the car, and he looks down at her, then looks nervously over his shoulder. He's hot, even now, in his moments of awkwardness. *Hot enough to be a bad decision*, she thinks, not for the first time in this life.

"Come on," she says, to Ulysses.

He unbuckles his belt. He unbuttons his jeans.

"It's OK," she says. "Come on."

"Are you—are you sure about this," he says, in a near whisper, as he climbs in, on top of her. At this, she has to smirk, just a little: for the last year Ulysses has been making it perfectly clear, with varying degrees of explicitness, just how much he'd like to sleep with her again, and now, here she is, literally spread out in front of him, and he's hesitating and stammering. It's a little bit touching, although honestly it's more concerning: what she needs, right now, is to feel him wanting her, to feel his desire come across with enough force to take her out of this day, out of this moment, and when she sees him this way, uncertain, she starts to worry that he might not be capable of providing that. Maybe not anymore, not like he used to. He's holding there, his body poised above hers, like he's at the apex of a push-up, looking foolish.

"Yes," she says, irritably. "I'm sure." She's not, not really—she's never really known how to be sure, entirely sure, about sex, but the answer gets him to lower down, to finally lie fully upon her, and that feels good, as good as anything can, today.

He tries to kiss her but she stops him; she pushes the heel of her hand up into his mouth. She doesn't want to be kissed right now. He moves down, lets his mouth move over her collarbone, over the tops of her breasts: no. She doesn't want that either. She wants straight fucking: the kind that is the most likely to get her to forget everything that's happening, even if just for a moment. She knows he's capable. She cups the back of his skull in one hand and lets her other hand move down to his hip; she tries to pull him up into position. But instead he slides away, lets his hands run down over her ribs, through the ratty fabric of her T-shirt. He presses his face between her legs and inhales.

OK, she thinks, as he puts his tongue on her. He's half out of the car; his ass is in the air; his knees are on high school parking lot blacktop; it must look absurd. But she doesn't care. It's good. It's not exactly what she wanted but it's close.

She tilts upward to increase contact. His beard against her thighs, soft. She keeps her hand splayed against the crown of his head.

And then her phone starts buzzing in the pocket of her wadded pants. It intrudes, reminding her of her life, of the people in it, of the perils and dangers. A tiny frown creases her forehead and all at once she's sick of Ulysses being down there. She wants him on top of her again, the weight of him serving as a form of obliteration. She wants him up inside her, for real, suddenly sick of his tongue lapping at her.

"Ulysses," she says.

He looks up. "Yeah."

"Fuck me already," she says.

"Listen," he says, breathless. "I don't—I don't have a condom."

"It's OK," she says.

"I don't—"

"It's OK," she says again, firmly. She looks up through the rear windshield, out at the sky. She doesn't look at him. She's not sure she could bear to see whatever expression of concern he's wearing on his face right now. "Just—just shut up and come here."

He clambers in, lowers himself down, his jeans still tangled around his ankles. She grips his briefs by the elastic and yanks them down, just enough to let his dick out. It presses up against her.

"Now," she says.

He lifts his hips, positions himself with his hand, and then—he's there, at last. She makes a sound that is not a word.

He thrusts in her only a few times and then he blurts out, "I'm going to come."

"Do it," she says. A very distant part of her raises some objection that she can't really hear.

"Don't make me," he says. He sounds close to tears, somehow. "Don't make me."

She can feel him try to pull out. She puts her hands on his ass, clamps him to her. "Fucking *do it*," she says.

And he does. There's a moment, there, where she thinks she might come, too, riding the feedback loop of his lust. This moment rises, manifests enough to take the shape of a possibility, graspable, and then she experiences that same sensation that she felt earlier, the unsettling sensation of somcone's eye on her, from afar, and the moment slips away and is gone. A little disappointing but—oh well. Wanting a different outcome is not going to do anybody any good.

"All right," she says. "Get up."

He peels himself off her, stumbles back into the parking lot, pulls his briefs and jeans back up, looks around nervously to see if they've been caught. She doesn't wait for him to finish surveying the horizon; instead she climbs out of the car, too, dragging her pants and her panties along with her. She reaches between her legs and flicks a glob of semen, then another, down to the surface of the parking lot. She expends the effort necessary to ignore the voice of recrimination that's piping up, uninvited.

She turns her pants one way, then another, trying to get them oriented so she can step back into them. During this process her phone slithers out of her pocket, hits the blacktop. She frowns. Once she's dressed she picks up the phone, checks the screen—it's not cracked, so there's that small mercy at least. She checks the notifications, looking to see who called while she was fucking Ulysses.

It's Donald. Missed call and voice mail.

Well, shit, she thinks.

She forces herself not to show any immediate reaction, and instead she just calmly gets into the passenger seat, as Ulysses settles himself into the driver's seat. After taking a second to get collected she looks over at him, wondering why nothing seems to be happening. His keys are in the ignition but he is not reaching for them, instead he's just resting his hands on the steering wheel. She looks over at him, and finds herself startled by the look on his face. He's looking at her with something that she could only describe as gratitude. She doesn't want him looking like that. He could look satisfied. Let him gloat a bit, even, that would be fine. Totally casual? That would be OK, too. But this look? It reveals too much. Too much need in it, a thirst that the fucking didn't slake. She's embarrassed by it, embarrassed for him. Unable to meet the look, she turns away, glares back down at her phone instead.

"So, um," he says.

"So what," she says.

"Do you want to talk," he says. "About what just happened?"

"No. Just"—she waves her hand in the air—"just drive."

A beat, long enough to register hurt, then: "Fine."

They make their way out to the parkway again, wordlessly. She contemplates the phone in her lap, the voice mail on it. She visualizes some ideal version of herself acting cool, just deleting it. All she would have to do would be to make one simple set of gestures, magic in their way, and then she could finally say she'd done it: she'd finished: finished forgetting her past, finished forgetting the people in it, the people who used to matter.

But she doesn't do that. Instead she holds the phone to her ear and she listens.

20

MINTY

Maja and Pig drive north, in pursuit. It's a slow pursuit, though, taken at a pace that's practically leisurely. They don't exceed the speed limit. Maja notes this, takes it as an indicator, a good sign: a signal that Pig, at long last, has decided to trust her. Maybe it's the progress that they've made over the last few days, or maybe it's the fact that last night she finally drew a line that Pig wouldn't cross, but he seems, this morning, to have a newfound respect for her: he seems to finally believe that she can do what she says. This has calmed something in him. He still has the usual hunger in his eyes, but it's tempered with a sort of lazy satisfaction: the look of an animal that has every reason to believe that it will be fed. This look glows through the bruise which even this morning continues to spread, broadening outward from the bridge of his nose, a mask made of blood draped across his face in the night. She imagines tiny ruptures, inside his head, unhealed, continuing to bleed. She could find them if she wanted to, get her mind inside them, wear his pain as her own. If he even is feeling any pain. She assumes it's agonizing to be walking around with a smashed-up face like that, but if he's uncomfortable he gives no sign.

She still knows so little about him. Which means she's still at risk. She mustn't allow this sudden calmness to lull her into believing that she knows what's going to happen next. The future, as ever, is unwritten.

The tank of the town car is near empty. They leave the highway, find a gas station, and pull up to the pump. He counts out four wilted fives and hands them off to her, sending her into the market to prepay. She doesn't object; she needs some food anyway. All she's put in her body today was some water and a little cup of motel coffee.

She feels a closed-circuit camera record her as she approaches the register and puts twenty on pump three. *Don't worry about it*, she tells herself. *No one knows you're here.*

She wanders the aisles looking for protein. She hopes for tuna, but there's none to be found. She handles nutrition bars, bags of beef jerky, tubes of cheese in a pouch. Each elicits a sort of shudder from her as she considers the means of their production. Rapidly losing her appetite, she opts for a hard-boiled egg, packaged in a plastic case. Then, in a sudden burst of goodwill, she selects a bag of Starlight Mints for Pig.

"Thanks," he says, seemingly genuinely, as she returns to the pump and flings them across to him.

She gets back into the car, egg in hand, half-expecting Pig to head into the market himself, pick out something more substantial to eat. But he just slides into the driver's seat, pushes the key into the ignition. Before he can turn it, she speaks. She's going to learn at least this one thing before they go any further.

"OK," she says. "The candy."

He pauses. "Yeah."

"May I ask a question about the candy?"

He considers for one nearly imperceptible instant. "Sure," he says.

She considers what she truly wants to ask. "My question," she says, "is *why*. Why the candy."

The bruised tissue around Pig's eyes crinkles as he smiles, revealing his pleasure at having information that she doesn't have, that she wants. "I like sugar," he says.

"I believe you," Maja says, "but I don't think that's the whole story."

Pig raises both palms, feigning haplessness.

"No one likes sugar that much," Maja continues. "Enough to subsist *entirely* on sugar."

"That sounds," Pig says, "like you're asking *how*."

"I'm not asking how," she says. "I'm asking why."

He makes an assessing face, measuring the request. "OK," he says, finally. "I can show you something. I guess you've earned it."

He starts the car, shifts into drive, but he doesn't go back out onto the road. Instead he pulls around the back of the market, beyond the air pumps, out to behind the Dumpster, finally parking next to a long succession of milk crates, stacked into towers.

He tosses the mints back to her. "I'm gonna need a thing," he says, getting up and exiting the car. She watches in the rearview as he goes around and opens the trunk.

When he returns, taking his seat again, he has his pistol in his hand. He drops it in his lap, all the while watching her face, clearly trying to gauge the response that she's clearly not offering.

He takes the bag of candy back from her, tears it open. Fishes two mints out, pinching one in each hand.

"OK," he says. "Now check this out."

He lowers his jaw and pushes the mints into either side of his mouth, begins to chew, filling the car with the surprisingly loud sound of splintering crystals. As he grinds away, he reaches back into the bag and takes another pair of mints out, presses them back between his molars to replace the first, pulverized pair. Gnashes on them. And then another pair goes in. At this point Maja becomes curious as to how many of these things can be consumed by one person in a minute. But then two more go in—she's already begun to lose count—and her curiosity begins to crumble, revealing something like dread behind it. Horror. Because watching him continue to push them in there: it's horrifying. There's no better word. It seems inhuman, as though his face is just an automatic component in some kind of consuming machine.

You've worked with some fucked-up people, says the Archive, *but am I* wrong *to think that this guy maybe takes first prize?*

No, Maja thinks. *Not wrong.*

Little shards of candy are falling out of Pig's mouth now, bouncing down into his lap, gathering around the gun.

Pig pauses for a second, after he's chewed up what might be the seventh pair of mints. About half the bag gone. He lets out a little moan of protest, the first sign of resistance to eating that she's ever seen in him. He wipes his mouth with the back of his hand and a long string of saliva comes away from his lips.

"OK," he says, maybe not to her. He's staring down at his chest. "It's happening." He takes a deep breath, as though he's near completion of a Herculean labor.

"What's happening?" she asks.

Pig nods heavily, pushes in a final pair of mints, crunches them up. "Magic," he says, around the mouthful, his voice thick and syrupy.

"Magic?" Maja asks.

"Abracadabra," Pig says, making a flourish in the air with one hand while he grips the pistol, tightly, in the other. He musters a grin. And then he vanishes.

21

LISTENING

Ollie hears Donald's voice, for the first time in a year.

"Hey, Ollie," she can hear him say to her voice mail. "It's me, um, Donald. I know it's been a long time since we talked and I'm—I'm sorry about that. I just heard about what happened last night and I just, I don't know, I just wanted—"

He sighs.

"I just wanted to hear your voice, and to know that you were safe. I know I've been pretty shitty to you this year, and I know that I don't really deserve anything from you. But I wanted to say that I was thinking of you, and that I hope you're all right, and that if there's any way that I can help you through this you can feel free to give me a call. You know. If you wanted. That's it, I guess. Bye."

A confusion of emotions rises in her. On one level, she feels touched—it surprises her, to hear him express his regret; she'd always assumed that he was living now behind a wall of righteousness, impermeable to remorse. But on another level she feels angry—she realizes that she was waiting, as she listened to that message, for some news, any news, about Jesse, about how he was doing, any reassuring detail, anything that could maybe erase that vision of him in his room, in clown makeup. She feels enraged by the notion that Donald could break a year of silence and somehow neglect to say something as basic as *Jesse is doing well*. As she thinks over this dissatisfaction, forces it to take a shape, she admits something to herself: that what she really wanted to hear is not just *Jesse is doing well* but something more meaningful, something she could hold on to. What she really wanted to hear is *Jesse misses you*, something that would match the part in her that has been saying, this year, *I miss Jesse*. Something that would validate the voice in her that has been saying *I have to get back to raising my son*. The voice that she's been trying so hard not to hear.

"I miss Jesse," she says, out loud, into the air of the Buick.

"What?" Ulysses says.

"Nothing," Ollie says. Wait, though. Just a moment. Something falls into place within her.

"I changed my mind," she says.

"Changed your mind what?" Ulysses says.

"I don't want to go to your place," she says. "I want to go to Illuminated Farms. I want to see my kid."

Ulysses frowns. "Been a while since you've been out there, hasn't it?"

"Yeah," Ollie says. "Not since—well, you remember." He should, anyway. She'd run to him when she had nowhere else to go, showed up in his driveway holding a gym bag filled with her literal dirty laundry on the night that everything with Donald went to shit. Ulysses coming out to meet her, his arms open to hold her. She could barely see him standing there, that's how overrun she was with newly minted images of Donald's face falling from incomprehension to dead-eyed blankness to contempt. An image of him pouring too much whiskey into a heavy drinking glass and then the image of him downing it and then the image of him turning the empty glass in his hand and then the image of him throwing it through the kitchen window. It took some time to find a place inside her where she could stuff all that shit away.

That place inside her opens up now, for the first time in a long time, and she remembers what she felt, the night she confessed: not sorrow, not even remorse, really, that would only come later, once she realized the extent of the consequences. What she felt, at the moment, was embarrassment. *Surely we can handle this like grown-ups,* she remembers thinking. *It's only sex. That's all we're talking about here.*

She remembers feeling almost disassociated while watching his reaction: the very idea that her fidelity could be important enough, in its absence, to evoke sudden violence in this otherwise gentle man seemed strange to her, based on a misunderstanding so profound that it must be willful. After all, she'd told herself, each of them had fucked other people, in the years before they'd met, and this fact presented no special difficulty for either of them: If all the other guys she fucked in the past just didn't matter, then how could fucking Ulysses now destroy everything?

She tried, vainly, to explain to Donald what she meant: if you just rearranged the timeline, moved her offending actions to some faraway point, back in the past, their true significance would become clear, they would stand revealed as meaning nothing, absolutely nothing. It wasn't until later that she realized that time doesn't work that way. It's not like a pile of photographs that you can shuffle. The distance between things matters. When you're talking about time, that's, in fact, the only thing you're talking about.

"You been back there since then?" Ulysses asks.

"Nope," Ollie says.

"So I gotta ask, then," Ulysses says. "Are you really so sure Donald's going to be all that happy to see you, showing up unannounced?"

"I don't know," Ollie says. "I'm not sure it matters."

"It matters to *me*," Ulysses says.

"What?" Ollie says, baffled.

"You know," Ulysses says, "I haven't even *talked* to Donald since all that shit went down. So I'm not sure he's going to be all that thrilled to see *me*, *especially* if I'm showing up with *you*."

"I don't care about that," Ollie says.

"Of course you don't," Ulysses says. "'Cause that's your whole thing."

"What do you mean? What's my whole thing?"

"Your whole thing," Ulysses says, "is that you only give a shit about yourself."

"I want to see my kid," Ollie says.

Ulysses doesn't respond to this, he just rolls on: "You've always been like that. You make decisions and then expect everyone to fall into line around you, and you don't give a shit about how anybody's going to feel about those decisions."

"Look," she says—just saying something to say anything, so that she doesn't have to pause to consider whether there's validity in his charge—"if you feel so worried about what Donald's going to think when he sees you, go ahead and drop me off at the end of the fucking *driveway* and I'll walk the last fifty feet on my own—"

"It's not that," Ulysses says.

"Well," Ollie says, practically sputtering, "if you're so worried about whether Donald wants to see *me* I'll just—I'll just call him up, and tell him I'm coming and—" As if on cue, her phone starts to ring. She looks at the screen: it's Victor again.

Ulysses takes advantage of the gap. "That would probably be *polite*," he says, "but it's not that, either."

Ollie thumbs Victor's call away. "Well, what the fuck is it then?"

"It's *me*," Ulysses says. "It's the way that *I* feel that you don't ever think about. You know? When I heard that you were in trouble I felt *worried*. When I thought I could keep you safe I felt *proud*. When I thought you might come stay with me I felt *excited*. I felt *happy*, OK? But to you I'm just, whatever, I'm just a guy who you can fuck in a parking lot and then say, *Y'know what, sorry, take me to some other guy's place*. It's like I'm not even a person to you. It's like I'm a dick and a car. And, yeah, sure, I'm a big strong tough motherfucker and I don't look like I can be hurt real easy but I honestly don't believe that you took even five seconds to consider whether your decision might have actually, you know"—he drops his volume here—"hurt me."

"OK," Ollie says, quietly, because she has to admit that that's true.

235

They drive on for a few minutes, neither of them saying anything.

"Look," Ulysses says, his tone softer now. "After you left Donald, and you were staying with me—? That was—I know it was a tough time, but—"

"Don't," Ollie says.

"Just let me get this out," Ulysses says. He checks the rearview mirror, shifts into the passing lane to get around someone. "It was a tough time, but I helped you. I helped you get on your feet and get out of there. I got you hooked up with Jon, and with, with Angel—and you know why?"

"Because I was the best Goddamn butcher you'd ever seen?"

This manages to pull a microscopic chuckle out of him. "Well, yes," he says. "But you know why else?"

"'Cause you wanted me out of your hair?"

"*Girl*—" Ulysses says, exasperated. "That's—you have it wrong. You have it exactly, one hundred percent, back-assward wrong. Is that really what you think?"

"Probably not," Ollie says, slumping down in her seat a bit.

"I got you out of there," Ulysses says, "because you looked like you were *done*. Done with farm life. Done with trying to figure out whatever you were trying to figure out here in the Valley. Done with—being a mom."

"Of course I wasn't done with being a *mom*," Ollie says. "You're not ever done."

"Yeah, well, you looked like it," Ulysses says.

"I probably did," Ollie concedes, after a second.

"Look," Ulysses says. "What I'm trying to say here is

that the time that you were there, when I was waking up to you in my bed every morning—? I loved it. I loved every second of it. I could see it wasn't working for you and so I knew I had to let you go and that was hard as shit, but even knowing that—? Even knowing that it was *still* the happiest time in my life, and not a week goes by that I don't hope that you'll change your mind and come back up there to be with me. And so, yeah, there you have it, I guess."

He sighs. She sighs. "OK," she says, after a minute. "I get it. I do. And I'm sorry. I don't—I don't really know what's happening with my life right now. I'm caught up in something totally crazy and it's getting people killed. It still might get *me* killed."

"I hear you," Ulysses says. "And I'm sorry to be putting more on you right now—"

"No," she says. "It's OK. This is gonna sound weird, but I think it's the right time. It's like—there's nothing like being close to death to make you realize how much—just how much *shit* from your past never got dealt with. How many fucking loose ends you have. And I think whatever's going on between us qualifies. It's a thing that I've been try-ing *not* to think about, trying *not* to figure out. And I get that that's hurtful."

"OK," Ulysses says, a little cautiously.

"But, listen, Ulysses, I can promise you something. I can promise you that I *will* think about us. That I will figure out what we are doing. That we will figure it out *together*. You're right to ask me to. Help me get to my kid, and I can promise you that I'll do it."

Ulysses adjusts his grip on the steering wheel but

doesn't say a word. She doesn't know if he's thinking about it, or refusing, or agreeing, or what. She waits, but before he gives any sign of what he's thinking her phone starts to ring.

"Jesus Christ," she says, pulling it out of her pocket yet again. It's Victor, and the fact that he's called her twice in the past five minutes causes an ominous feeling to lurch up inside her: it probably means that something actually urgent is happening. "I gotta take this," she says to Ulysses's cryptically impassive face.

"Did you listen to my message?" is the first thing Victor says to her.

"Of course not," Ollie says. "What's up?"

"We have a—" He says something that gaps out as the Buick slips between a pair of rising hills.

"What?" Ollie says.

"A problem," Victor says. "We have a problem at the apartment."

"What is it?"

"It's the portal. To the Inside. I think it's coming open again."

"What? How can you tell?"

"I'm in the kitchen—? The air looks weird in here."

"Weird how?"

"I don't know," Victor says. "It defies most of the words I'd use to describe it."

"Try," Ollie says.

"If I had to try," Victor says, "I'd say the air in the kitchen is *darkling*."

Ollie shakes her head. It doesn't matter. "Victor, you know what to do. You have to banish it."

238

"I'm not sure I can do it," Victor says. "You—" He gaps out again.

"Listen, Victor, I'm losing signal," she says, loudly, hoping he can hear her. "But you can do it. You know how. We've done it twice already. You just have to do it on your own this time; I can't come help. Not right now." No response. She's not sure if they're still connected but she forges on. "Find a tool. Whatever's your best thing. Is Rufus still there? He's good at this shit; get him to help you. Just get the thing gone."

Her phone bleats; the call's been dropped. She sighs heavily.

"Everything all right?" Ulysses says.

"I do not know," she says.

"You need me to turn around?" he asks.

She considers the question for what feels like a very long time.

"No," she says, finally.

22

TRICKY

Maja blinks at Pig's seat, empty except for the half-eaten bag of mints. She waits a moment to see if he will return. The moment elongates, becomes a minute.

That's a good trick, hazards the Archive.

Quiet, Maja thinks.

She looks for Pig, widening her surveillance beyond the car, encompassing the gas station, its market. No sign of him. She goes wider, looking out over the territory they've covered today, out over the whole state. She sighs, knowing she's going to need to go wider still. She can look across the whole planet when she needs to, but it brings her back to feeling like she did when she was a kid, hiding in her closet, projecting her awareness halfway across the globe, looking for places warmed by the sun. Stretching her consciousness that way makes it feel thin, fragile, like so much flung gossamer: she didn't mind that sensation so much when she was a spacey kid but as an adult it leaves her feeling vulnerable, psychically flensed. But Pig's vanishing act has unnerved her, so she does it. She scans the world for Pig's unique prickle. Nothing. Her sense of apprehension doubles.

She reels back in, looks for signs of him in the local past, signs she knows should be there—the traces of his presence at the pumps, for instance. Even these seem to jitter in her mind, degrading as she tries to review them. It is not merely as though he is not here. It is as though he has never existed. It is as though he has gone somewhere outside of space and time entirely.

And then suddenly he's back, sitting right there, grinning at her, as though he's never left. Except, she realizes, as her attention ranges over him, it's not as though he's never left. It's as though he has just come into the world for the first time. It's as though he is brand-new. There is no history on him, not a single thing she can read.

Except—wait—there is something. If she looks deeply she can find the usual shadowed layer of fragments that she gets from him, the Cubist photographs that comprise his past. But there's something else, too. More recent information. Facts about where he went, what he did when he was there. She can feel them slipping away, though, like dreams upon waking. She concentrates, closes her eyes, even as Pig opens his mouth and begins talking to her, hoping to apprehend the important details before they can deliquesce. Hoping to turn them into things that she will be able to remember.

She gets two pieces of information.

One: the pistol in his hand has been fired. She tries to get more history from it but she fails. Wherever it's been is someplace that she can't follow.

Two: he's been near the blade. She doesn't understand how this could be possible—he doesn't know where it is, or how to get to it; that's the whole reason they've hired her—but she's sure of it, she can feel its signatures all over him, surrounding him like an ambience or a tint.

He's saying words. He's saying, "That's the thing, see. Everybody loves sugar. I'm talking the whole *world*. And it's because of energy. If sugar does *anything* it does that. It gives you cheap, fast energy. And magic—all magic *is* is just working with energy. Get enough energy and you can arrange it into patterns and then you can do stuff with it. Eat enough sugar and you can keep yourself alive—that's the easy part. You can do other stuff, too. You can punch a hole in the world."

She opens her eyes, fixes him with a glance. He stops talking. "You were with the blade," she says.

Pig breaks off, raises his eyebrows in a bland expression of interest. "What's that?" he says.

"The blade," Maja says. "You were with it. Just now. You—observed it."

"Not exactly," Pig says.

"Don't lie to me," she says. "I can't do my job if you lie to me."

"I'm not lying to you," Pig says.

"You went away and now you're back and I can feel the blade all over you. Its flavor. So how are you not lying to me?"

"I didn't say *no*," Pig says. "I said *not exactly*."

"Explain," Maja says, out of patience.

"Man," Pig says, rolling his eyes, "I liked you better before you became a person who asks so many questions." He says this, although Maja's not actually sure that he did.

"Explain," she says again.

"Fine," Pig says, shrugging. "The blade we're looking for—? It's not, it's not—how would you say it?—it's not a *stand-alone* thing. It's a *piece* of a thing."

"A piece of—?" She frowns. "A piece of what kind of thing?"

"It's a piece of a larger blade," Pig says. "It's the tip. Of a sword. That was broken." He shifts here, moving into a singsongy mode that sounds like he's reciting something, a sequence of facts that he's recited to people for a long time, or perhaps had recited to him. "Broken in 1803, by slaves, at the Battle of Vertières, in the colony of Saint-Domingue. Broken into six major pieces."

"OK," Maja says. "So the blade that I'm after—it's one of six."

"It's six of six," Pig says.

Maja blinks.

"The piece that you're after is the last one," Pig says. "We have the others."

"We," Maja says.

"The Foundation," Pig says.

"Righteous Hand," Maja confirms.

"Yeah," Pig says. "My father and me. That's why we hired you. To find the last piece. We're rebuilding the sword."

He gives off the impression of being slightly bored now, seems to be winding the conversation up. But Maja's not ready to quit just yet; she's still puzzling through what he's saying.

"OK," she says. "So the signature I'm picking up off of you right now—"

"It's the other pieces," Pig says. "The rest of the sword. I just went to the place where we keep it."

"But it's not a place," Maja says, after a moment.

Pig looks at her. "I'm not sure I follow you," he says, something faintly teasing in his tone, like he's playing dumb and wants her to know it.

"If it's a place," Maja says, "I should have been able to find you when you were there. If it had been anywhere on earth I should have been able to find you."

"I don't know if I'd say it's *on earth*, exactly," Pig says.

"Where is it?" Maja asks.

"Well," Pig says. "If it's not a *place*, is *where* really the question you want to be asking?"

"When?" Maja asks, thinking of Pig's sundered history. "*When* is it? Are you traveling to a different *time*?"

"It's not a place," Pig says. "It's not a time."

"Then what is it?"

"What," he says. "That's the question. *What* is it. It's sort of all around space and time. It's like—if you think of everything that happens in space and time as happening on a stage, everything that we know about happening as part of like, a put-on, a show—theater—then this thing, this thing that I'm talking about, is sort of like backstage, like the miles of service corridor back there, like the trapdoors and pits and shit down *under* the stage, the catwalks up *above* the stage. It's all the fucking *apparatus* that we don't normally see as we stumble around, existing blindly, groping from one minute to the next. All the fucking mechanics that keep the show running. People who do magic call it the Inside."

She nods. She feels satisfied by this explanation; it's like

snapping one more piece into a puzzle that's she's been trying to complete for years. Because she knows the space he's
describing. She's never entered it, like Pig just did, but she
knows that it's what she's accessing when she traces the histories of things, their passage. It's where all the records are
kept. It's how she can do what she does.

"You gotta watch out, of course, 'cause, you know,
there's weird shit that lives in there: like monsters? They die
good enough when you shoot 'em"—he holds up his pistol by way of illustration before shoving it down into his
waistband—"but then twice as many come back at you; it's
pretty fucked up. But that kinda works in our favor. They
seem to want to guard the space so you can exploit the shit
out of that, use 'em like a built-in security system. As long
as our prop closet, or whatever you want to call it, is surrounded by like a teeming mass of a million angry worms, I
can sleep pretty easy trusting that no one is gonna fuck with
my sword."

"The prop closet," Maja says.

"To stick with the theatrical thing," Pig says. "The met-
aphor or whatever the shit."

"I get it," Maja says.

"It's, how would you say, *apt*," Pig says. "Because the
sword is exactly like any other prop. You want to keep it out
of view until it's time."

"Time for what?" Maja says.

"Time for it to come on stage," Pig says, starting the car
again, "and do its thing."

"And what is that?" Maja asks. She has to tread cautiously here: this is the kind of question that normally she

would never put forth. Part of what clients like about her, usually, is that she doesn't ask them why they want what they want. But this case is different. The blade is powerful: she remembers the fireworks that went off in her head when she looked directly at it. And she feels the beginnings of a reservation at the idea of putting something that powerful in the hands of Pig—who, like the Archive said, might take first prize among all the fucked-up people she's ever worked with. So she asks, even though it feels to her like stepping out onto an expanse of thin ice. "What is its thing? What is it meant to do?"

Pig seems to take no offense to the question; he just answers. "It's *meant* to build an empire," Pig says. "An empire for the white race. It's meant, as my dad puts it, to be a weapon fit for the hand of a king, a king before which the inferior races of the world will bow, as they did in ages past, blah blah blah."

Maja tries to envision it: Unger as the head of an empire, Pig as his heir. Improbable: but if she's learned anything from studying the history of Europe it's that the people in power almost never match your model of what the people in power should, ideally, be like.

"Do you think it'll work?" she asks. "Do you think it will serve that purpose?"

"I don't know," Pig says, merging back into the flow of traffic on the highway. "I do think it'll fuck shit up pretty bad, and as far as I'm concerned, that makes it worth giving it at least a try. 'Cause shit right now is boring as hell."

23

GAPS

As they wind deeper into the cleft of the Valley, Ulysses proposes a plan. He agrees to take Ollie to the farm, and he proposes to drop her at the end of the driveway and he'll sit there and wait for some reasonable span of time. Just in case it doesn't go well.

"Five minutes," Ollie suggests. That'll be enough to make sure that they'll let her in. That's the thing she's been afraid of, all this time: that if she ever went back to the farm, back home, they wouldn't let her come in. She remembers the last night she was there, stumbling down the porch steps with her bags clumsily slung over her shoulders, leaving; she could hear Donald close the door behind her and in that moment she knew, or thought she knew, that he was closing it permanently. *Don't ever come back here*, he'd screamed, through the broken window. Exile, banishment: she felt these things as truths, deep in her body, indelible. It's only today that she's been able to consider the question of whether she was wrong. Just considering the question is terrifying, but she's trying it. Maybe she wasn't in exile. Maybe Donald never had the power to banish her after all, the power to cut her off from her son. Maybe she was foolish to have extended that to him. On that night, that final night, he had loomed large in her mind, taking on a terrible status, that of a god or a tyrant; but maybe he was just a guy, a guy who was angry and sad. Maybe they were just two people who needed to work their shit out. Maybe they still could. She feels like she'll know the second she knocks on the door.

"Five minutes is all I need," she says. Ulysses gives her a look.

"I'll wait an hour," he says. "In an hour you can actually know something."

It takes less time to get there than she thinks it will. In her memory the distance between the farm and the city seems vast. One hundred fifty miles! When you live in the city, and home and work and everyone you ever spend time with all fall within a circle no larger than ten miles in diameter, anything outside of that begins to seem impossibly far away, some sort of fabled distant land. But then you get in some-body's car and then it seems like you're there, right away, you're seeing the sign made out of a disused barn door, you're reading the words that you yourself helped to paint: ILLUMINATED FARMS. It seems like it took almost no time at all, to close the gap.

Ulysses kills the engine. Ollie looks at the familiar length of curving driveway, flanked by a pair of unruly sycamores.

"You're sure you want to do this?" he asks.

"Maybe *want* is the wrong word," Ollie says. "But no. Yeah. I'll be all right."

"I'll wait here," Ulysses says. "You know. In case you're not."

"I appreciate it," says Ollie. She pinches the bridge of her nose for a long time. Then she opens her eyes and gathers up her messenger bag, with Guychardson's box safe inside of it. With her free hand, she opens the door, and then steps out into the driveway and begins to walk. She doesn't look back.

The house comes into view. She can see that the windows are open. She can see the stirring of curtains, curtains that she made. She can hear the hum of a fan. And as she draws closer she repeats Ulysses's words, *You're sure you want to do this.* Not quite a question when he said them. She repeats her answer: *Maybe* want *is the wrong word.*

And as she takes a step onto the porch, she thinks: *Of course* want *is the wrong word.* This is the last place she ever wanted to return to. She's spent a year trying to forget everything about this farm and her life here. A year spent trying not to fix the past. Because it's stupid to try to do that. You can't fix the past, not unless you cheat, not unless you're willing to cut space and time and fight the faceless monsters that live back there. And she won't cheat.

So why are you even here? she asks.

Because this isn't trying to fix the past, she tells herself. *This is fixing the future.*

She stands there on the porch, where she used to sit. She remembers the things she used to do here: sorting potatoes into plastic bins, knocking dirt off turnips, holding her child on her knees.

She crosses the porch, stands in front of the door. She does not knock. She cannot bring herself to knock. She's passed through this door probably thousands of times and never once lifted her hand to knock on it.

This is my home, she tells herself.

Not anymore, it isn't, comes the reply.

Nevertheless, she lifts her hand and puts it on the handle of the door. She opens it and sticks her head in.

She tries to call out *hello* but her voice doesn't seem to want to work in here. The word comes out as a whisper. Maybe it never comes out at all.

She steps the rest of the way inside. The vision she had a few days ago led her to expect some of the mess she sees here, in the kitchen: the drift of cardboard boxes stacked against one wall. Loose bits of air packaging collecting in the corners. The counter overtaken with a spread of dirty pots and pans.

She crosses through, into the dining room. The table still has Donald's compound bow on it, now restrung. She drops her bag on the table just like she used to do, at the end of a long day, just to feel what it feels like to give in to the habitual, once again, after this long year.

It doesn't feel bad.

And then, just like he used to do, Donald walks into the room. He walks into the room and he looks at her.

And when he sees her he stops walking, and it's not like it used to be at all. It wouldn't be, it couldn't be, it can't be. Of course it can't. He appears, for a moment, to hold his breath. He blinks very rapidly.

"Holy hell," he says finally. "Are you OK?"

She thinks that maybe this is the question she would most have wanted him to ask, although she doesn't have an answer.

"I saw what happened—" he begins. "At Carnage—"

"Yeah," she says. "I got your message. And I just—I hope you don't mind that I'm here—"

"No," Donald says, taking a step closer to her. Closing the gap. "Not at all—"

"It's just—it just felt important—to see you and Jesse—"

Donald comes in to hold her.

"Is this OK?" he asks, as his arms go around her, in the old, familiar way.

"I think so," Ollie says. "I don't know," she says next, although her arms are going around him, too. "Is it OK for you?"

"I think so," Donald says, murmuring it down into her ear. "I—yes."

Looking over his shoulder, she watches as Jesse enters the room. Her son, standing there, at last. He's not wearing clown makeup, for which she experiences the briefest moment of gratitude, a moment dashed when she witnesses the expression on his face when he first sees her. It's an expression of confusion, maybe even alarm: the look of seeing your father embraced by a stranger. She will never forget seeing these emotions cross the face of her child upon her reappearance. She will remember the sight for the rest of her life.

The expression itself passes quickly, however; it's replaced by surprise, elation. "Mom—?" Jesse blurts.

She releases Donald and opens her arms, hoping that her son will come to her, nearly praying, incanting in her head a loop of *please, please, please. Let him come to me*. And he does. He slams into her with all the ferocity that his boy's body can contain, and she wraps it in her strong arms.

And Donald wraps his arms around the both of them, and just like that the circle—the circle of Ollie and Donald and Jesse, broken long ago—reforms. Maybe not forever. Maybe just for a moment, just for as long as it takes for this moment, in which they hang together, to resolve. Maybe the moment will end, and they'll rise, and they'll begin to argue, and the circle will come apart again. Ollie doesn't know. They could break apart at any time. But for right now she holds Jesse, and Donald holds them both, and all three together they wait for the future to hit.

24

HERE

Maja and Pig came off the highway a while ago, and have been driving along a two-lane road flanked by thick stands of trees, by occasional long walls made of stone. She watches out the passenger-side window and observes the topology of these stacked stones as they flicker past: the softened edges of granite taken from creeks, the harder edges of bluestone cut from the earth. She begins to derive a sense of the hundreds of quarries in this part of the state: she holds their interrelationship in her head like a map. A network of holes in her mind. A sense that, taken together, understood as one shape, they would form some single system, a set of secret passageways, interlinking at some depth to which she has not yet delved.

She recognizes this as an error, a fantasy of escape. The dream of having some place where she could deny the awareness of whatever lies ahead. Really just a wish to return to her childhood closet, the place where she used to hide. Not that hiding ever helped her, not that it ever made the future less frightening. The only thing that ever helped was just to keep looking, clear-eyed, toward whatever was yet to come.

And so she blinks the fantasy away impatiently and turns her attention away from the passenger-side window and looks instead out through the windshield, straight at where they're going. She reconcentrates on the trace of the blade, which passed up this very road, beneath the arches of these trees, through this August light, less than an hour ago. Its trail so clear.

They descend into a vale, shadows drifting across the car. Before long, a driveway comes into view, twenty yards ahead, flanked by a pair of giant sycamores. The trail of the blade emerges from a Buick, just barely visible beyond the second of the big trees, and leads up the driveway.

"Stop the car," Maja says.

Pig pulls over onto the shoulder.

"It's here," she says.

Pig kills the engine. "This is it, then," he says. "End of the road."

It never pays to be certain, Maja thinks, but she remains silent.

Pig pauses, and an unusually reflective expression troubles his face.

"Quiet around here," he says, after a minute's gone by.

"Yes," Maja says.

"That's probably good," Pig says.

"Yes," Maja says again.

"I wanna check something," he says. "Get my phone. It's in the glove box."

Maja roots around among the filthy maps and manuals

in there until she finds a clear plastic bag containing Pig's phone and its battery. She hands it over to him. He reassembles the phone, powers it on, waits a solid minute for signal. He gives a single grunt of satisfaction when he finds none and he disassembles the phone again, puts the two pieces back into the bag, and tosses it onto the dash.

"OK," he says.

He exits the car, and Maja follows him. Together they stand at the edge of a roadside thicket of trees, peering through branches and leaves, to get a view of the farmhouse that lies beyond.

"In there?" he asks.

"Yes," Maja says.

Pig spits into the dirt.

They head back to the car, around to the trunk. Pig pops it open and Maja watches as he rummages in there for a minute, until finally he gets his hands on the case containing the carbine rifle, hauls it up into his arms.

The Archive notices something. Hears something. Footsteps on road gravel.

Hey, um, it says.

Maja looks away from Pig and then she sees the man for the first time, the man who is standing there, twenty feet away from them. Startled, she jerks; in an attempt to recover she quickly pulls knowledge out of him, figures out who he is: he's the driver of the Buick, the one who brought the woman here. Stupid to have missed him before, stupid to have been too focused on the blade's path up the driveway to have bothered looking inside the car—fucking *stupid*.

"Shit," she says.

Pig looks up, alerted by the word slipping out of her unguarded mouth. He sees the man, and his face breaks into a wide, malevolent smile.

"Howdy, neighbor," he says.

The man looks from her, to Pig, to the rifle case in Pig's arms, and back to her again, his eyes narrowed with suspicion.

"You ain't my neighbor," the man says, after a beat. "So why don't you tell me if there's a thing I could *help* you two with."

Pig sighs, lowers the case down onto the roadside. "How about this," Pig says, from his crouch. "How about you help me by dying when I shoot you in your fucking face?"

He stands, draws the gun from his waistband. But Ulysses has already turned and started running up the driveway. Pig aims sloppily, as though he already knows he'll miss, and he fires. The noise cracks the air, but the shot misses by a mile. He squeezes off another shot, seemingly out of pure perversity, at Ulysses's vanishing back.

Pig scowls. "OK," he says. "I think it's time."

"Time for what?" Maja asks.

"Time," Pig says, "to switch to the big gun."

25

SAFE

The front door of the house crashes open. Ollie shrieks, but it's only Ulysses: he bursts through the kitchen and appears in the doorway. Thank God he's safe. But of course he isn't safe. None of them are safe. She heard the gunshots. She knows what they mean.

He followed us, she thinks. *I don't know how he did it but he followed us.*

Everyone is speaking at once. Donald is looking angrily at Ulysses and saying, "Jesus, *him?*" Ulysses is looking at her, bellowing, "There's a man with a gun." Jesse is looking from the face of one adult to the next and crying out, "Mom?"

Ollie, for her part, says, "We have to get out of here." She says this almost automatically, just to have some response. Just to say something. Even as she's saying it she can feel how worthless it is. Because where could they even go? She turns around and looks through the glass of the sliding door, looks across the weedy sprawl out behind the house. Yes, she can plot a path along which they could flee:

across the field, toward the safety of the woods, into the dark spaces beyond. But then what? How long before he catches up to them again? He followed her all the way out here, to the heart of the house at the farm, the safest place she can imagine, a place she'd hidden even from herself. There's nowhere else to go. She doesn't want a different direction to run in; she wants a way to make it end.

But she doesn't know how to make it end.

And that's what she's thinking when she sees him loom up in the field, the pig-headed man a demonic silhouette, ablaze in the sunset, she sees him raise a rifle and begin to take aim—

"Get down," she shouts. "Under the table." And she turns, and grabs her son's hands, and together they drop. There's a confusion then: human limbs jostle for position among the chair legs. It seems like everyone's made it beneath but before she can be sure the back door bursts. Chunks of tempered glass scribble and bounce across the tabletop, like a curtain of noise draped above their heads, drowning out their screams.

Fuck, Ollie thinks, as the rifle continues to pop. *Fuck.* She brought this here, this pig-faced thing, this unstoppable appetite, she brought it to the one place she cared about and now it's going to devour them, all of them, one at a time. Unless she does something.

She clambers out. The thing is there, at the door, kicking at the chunks of glass still standing in the frame. She lifts a chair by its leg and flings it at the thing. The thing shoulders the chair away, fumbles with slapping a new clip into the rifle. They have just a moment.

"Come on," she screams. She reaches under the table-top, gets her son's hands, yanks him out. She looks into his face as he stands, and she feels so sorry: sorry for her presence, and the disaster that it's brought upon them; sorry for her absence, a disaster of a different sort. But she's surprised to see the expression on his face. It's frightened—it's terrified—but beyond that she can see trust. After everything, he still trusts her to get them out of here alive. And she wants, very badly, to be worthy of that. It's exactly enough to keep her moving.

"Go," she says. She turns away from the thing coming through the door, puts her back between it and Jesse. She puts her hands on Jesse to help propel him. She looks at the table, sees her bag lying there among the glass, but she can't take her hands from her boy.

Ulysses is out; he's already in the kitchen, heading back the way he came in. Donald is last to emerge.

"Get my bag," Ollie screams over her shoulder, as she pushes Jesse around the corner, into the kitchen. She's not going to let this fucker get Guychardson's knife, the shard, whatever it is—she's not going to let this thing get its hands on something with that kind of power. She does not want it to have the power to rule.

"What?" she can hear Donald yell, behind her.

"My *bag*," she says, but there's no more time—she and Jesse barrel through the kitchen, through the mudroom, out onto the porch.

In the driveway there's a woman. Pale face and a ruff of dark hair. This woman stands there, empty-handed, watching Ollie. And Ollie remembers her. It's the woman she bumped into on the street, last night, outside of Carnage. But it's not just that she recognizes her from sight alone. It's more than that. It's that she recognizes the feeling of this woman *seeing* her. This woman has had her eye on Ollie for days now—watching her, perceiving her, *tracking* her—and all at once Ollie knows it. She doesn't know the exact nature of the witchery but she knows that this is the woman who made it possible for her to be found.

She releases her son and begins to advance on the woman. She's not quite sure what she'll do if she reaches her, but something. She will dig out the woman's eyes with her thumbs. Something. In response to Ollie's advance, the woman bolts, runs to the end of the driveway, beyond the woodpile, around the corner of the house. Ollie takes one step, prepared to follow, to enter pursuit, but then she catches herself, opting instead to use the moment to quickly take stock, count heads, make sure everyone's safe. To figure out a way to put some distance between themselves and the thing in the house with the gun.

Jesse's by her side. Ulysses is ahead of them, on the lawn, in a half crouch, hands on his knees. Donald is behind her; he's just exited the house. Ollie looks to see if Donald has her bag. He doesn't.

Fuck, she thinks.

However, in his hands instead is his bow.

We can work with that, Ollie thinks, after a moment. *We can end this.*

26

ESCAPES

Maja sprints around to the rear of the house, breathing hard, arms pumping. She knows the blade is still inside; she knows that once they get it all of this will be over. And so she plunges through the shattered back door, into the breached house.

Pig is there, in the ruined room, holding his rifle; he whirls to face her, the eyes of his mask like little dead circles drilled in the world.

"Where is it?" he says.

"In the bag," Maja says, pointing. And he sets the rifle down on the table, amid the broken glass and plaster, and he lifts the bag with both hands and upends it. A lacquered box falls out, and he tears the lid from it. And then he has the blade in his hand. After all this time, it's finally in his hand. He raises it before him, brandishing it, and actually seeing it, with her own eyes, up close—it's—it's the most intense thing she's ever seen. It's like a piece of a star. It carves an incandescent shape into her field of vision as he moves it.

It seems to be drawing forces of history toward it, inexorably pulling them into the room, through time. She can feel fates flowing past her—the fates of soldiers, of slaves, of nations—they flow past her and drain though the knife, filtered off to elsewhere.

Pig begins to use the blade to carve a hole in the air. When it's reached a suitable size he forces his free hand in. She watches his arm vanish, inch by inch, boiling away into nothingness. He pushes and pushes until he's in up to his shoulder and then, with a roar, he withdraws, pulling his arm back into this world, and bringing with it the rest of the sword, the base, complete except for its broken tip. He holds the base of the sword in his left hand and the missing piece, the point, in his right hand, and something happens in the room, the force of the gathered fates redoubles, the flow no longer just draining and eddying but instead beginning to twist, to seethe, to form a vortex. Her hair begins to stand on end.

The broken sword wants to be repaired. It *longs* for it as though it had a heart. The pieces pull on one another with yearning. The missing point twists free of the wooden handle that someone, long ago, set it into in order to disguise it as an ordinary kitchen knife. Pig flings the useless, disintegrating handle away and the point floats out of his hand, floats quietly upward, seeking its proper place. The point turns gently in the air, and the room, around it, seems to saw nauseatingly, teetering atop some swell of history. Excess time gushes into the room through every available opening. It's heavy, like syrup, like blood. You could drown in it if you weren't careful, Maja realizes.

She watches the point find its proper place at the top of the sword, watches an old dormant magic, the magic that forged these materials, knit the pieces back together again, into a whole, which Pig holds aloft. And then she has to close her eyes. She can't look directly at it, not anymore. Her hair begins to coil. Her nose begins to bleed. A chorus of indistinct voices churns up into her consciousness; a shearing force rips at the edges of her mind.

"We win," she can hear Pig say.

And then there's a sound, a wet impact, like a boot stomping on a rotten log, and whatever magic was accumulating in the room stutters for a moment; Maja opens her eyes, snapping back to reality.

Pig has been hit in the chest with an arrow.

She blinks, she turns. She follows the line of the arrow's path back out through the door, all the way back to a man standing outside with a bow, fifty feet away.

Pig, still holding the sword in his pose of triumph, opens his mouth as if to say something, but all that emerges is an angry hiss, the sound made visible by the droplets of blood that fleck its edges. He uses his free hand to go for the rifle, lying there on the table, but as he reaches out the arrow puts pressure on something inside him, and he groans and stiffens, unable to bend. He fishes at his waistband for his other gun, but his hand isn't quite working correctly: the pistol tumbles away before he can fully get a grip on it, and it bounces away under the table. He closes his eyes, and for just a moment he wears an expression that is utterly ordinary, that of a man thwarted by small indignities: the look of a man, weary at the end of a day spent on fools' errands, who has just witnessed the last train of the evening pulling out of the station without him.

And then he opens his eyes, and sets his face into an expression of grim determination, and he puts both hands on the hilt of the sword and lifts it, groaning, and he uses it to continue work on the hole which still hangs in the air, widening it. An escape route?

She turns, looks outside: the man out there is readying another arrow. She backs away, glass crunching underfoot, putting some distance between herself and the shattered door. Defenseless, she backs up until she bumps the table, and then she edges around it, continuing to back up, hoping to get out of the room, keeping her eye on the man with the bow.

Forget him, warns the Archive. *Where's that woman? The woman who wants to kill you?*

And Maja looks, and realizes—the woman is right behind her, having crept in through the kitchen, and before Maja can react the woman reaches up and tightens her hands around Maja's throat and begins to squeeze. With the pressure comes a jolt of information, literally being throttled into her. She learns the woman's name: Olive Krueger. *Ollie for short.*

Don't fucking touch me, Maja thinks.

Maja reaches up and grabs the woman's wrists and tries to pry herself free. But that means more contact. And Maja's not wearing her gloves. Stupid, stupid. She doesn't want to touch this woman but she needs to breathe. So she digs in. She has to.

Ollie's hands on her throat, her hands on Ollie's wrists:

they're joined at four points, a tight knot, a shape that information flows through. Maja's pulse hammers desperately at the center of it.

She starts to pick up Ollie's history. She can't help it.

Stop it, she thinks, but it doesn't stop.

She learns of Ollie's love for her son, its shape congruent with the shape of Maja's love for her brother. She learns the son's name: Jesse. Images of Jesse burst open inside her then, polluting her, filling her with noise, traces of a boy who is not hers, who was never hers, a thousand false records filed into the Archive, scattering the pieces that are Eivind.

No, Maja thinks, in the face of the confusion. *Don't you fucking take that from me. Stop.*

But it doesn't stop. Still more is forced into her as the two women struggle there in the doorway. She learns of Ollie's sadness at having lost Jesse. This sadness also finds its echo: it locates Maja's own sadness, her own loss, and begins to take it over. Feelings that are not hers flood into her, find their matches in the feelings that *are* hers, and they bind, like the molecules of a drug finding their receptors. Like spores from an invasive plant, finding niches to colonize, threatening to usurp that which properly belongs there.

Please, Maja thinks, as her vision begins to tunnel. But still it doesn't stop. She gets memories of Ollie's childhood, flashes of a city, New York City, experienced through the eyes of a child who was alone and scared. *These aren't my memories*, Maja thinks. *This isn't me. Please. Please stop.*

And then, as if her plea had been heard, Ollie releases her, drives her down to the floor with a swift hard kick to the small of her back.

What did you do to me? Maja thinks, as she pushes herself up to her knees, her hands in glass. *What the hell did you do?*

She looks up at Ollie and tries to remember that she's not looking at herself.

She presses her bloodied fingertips against her bruised throat, as though she could take the knowledge that has been thrust into her and dig it back out.

Take it back, Maja thinks. But Ollie's turned away from Maja. She's looking at Pig now. Maja follows her gaze and sees that Pig's managed to use the sword to cut a slit in the air that's the height of a door. An entryway to the Inside. If he gets in there there's no telling where he could end up.

And Ollie perhaps understands this as well, for she lunges at him, her hands extended, but she's too late: he escapes through the gate and is gone from this world.

Ollie hesitates at the edge of the rift for a moment, just for a moment, and then she follows Pig, as though she were passing through an opening in a curtain.

They're both gone. Maja is alone in the room. The portal twists in the air, a ribbon of ink. Maja stands, advances on it warily, although the closer she gets to it the more familiar it feels. If there's anything about her past that she knows for certain, anything that's been left unpolluted by the memories that Ollie just forced into her, it's this: she's been living adjacent to the Inside for a long time, learning how to ask it questions, learning how to receive the information that it has seen fit to gift her, over all these years. It feels almost like a friend to her. And right now—hurt and confused, her head stuffed with a shifting heap of mirror shards—she wants help from a friend.

She can find Ollie, in there. She knows she can. And once she finds her, she can make her take it all back. There has to be a way. She just has to cross the threshold. It's either that or stay here and get shot full of arrows.

And so she takes one step forward. She steps in.

27

INSIDE

Ollie has her eyes closed. She's doesn't know what she'll see if she opens them. She's afraid to.

But you can only be afraid for so long. This is a thing she's told herself again and again in her life. It's OK to be afraid. But at some point you have to be done with it, and it's only then that you can get to work.

She opens her eyes.

Her first thought is that she's inside the belly of a whale. She is somewhere dark and red and vast and vaulted, a space bounded by curving riblike columns that yawn upward, presumably joining somewhere far above her. Between every set of ribs is the entryway to another vault. She tilts her head and suddenly she feels like she's in a chamber in a cathedral; the space seems slightly more sane if she can understand it as a kind of impossible architecture, replicating itself uncontrollably. Except no: it's not architectural because it's so clearly animal. Except it's not animal because it's so clearly architectural. It's all of the above. It's none of the above. It seems to breathe even though it doesn't move. It seems wet even though it isn't moist. It's a building that houses a beast that's swallowed the building. It's leviathan.

It smells like sweat: her own sweat.

She keeps her eyes open. She takes a step forward, just to see if she can move in here. The galleries of infinite space around her reel vertiginously. It is as though she is trying to make her way down the corridor that opens up when two mirrors face one another. She reaches out, clutching for a support that is not there, and she can feel the gesture echoed, reflected, amplified through the spaces around her. She understands this, distantly, as a form of power, but has no clear idea on how to utilize it.

She looks down, hoping that she'll stabilize if she keeps her eyes on her feet, on the floor. Except what's beneath her isn't really a floor: it's a kind of shifting tissue, a design that seems to squirm, like an intricate carpet that, when seen out of the corner of your eye, reveals itself to be a seething field of insects. Just beneath its surface she can feel larger beings forming and reforming themselves—tendrilous things, massive starfish, faceless gnarls of unearthly tissue—she can feel them gathering beneath her feet, threatening to rise, the risk becoming greater with each additional moment of hesitation.

She lurches forward, or what feels like forward, although it somehow also produces the sensation that a reflected version of herself, a twin, is moving backward. She tries to focus on what she's after, why she came in here in the first place.

The pig-faced man, she thinks. *You have to find him. You can't let him get away with the sword.*

As she articulates this desire, the chambers around her

seem to revolve. She advances through one vast arch—feeling refracted versions of herself advancing and retreating in the spaces around her—and she finds herself in a new vault. And there's the man.

She's face-to-face with him. She thought she'd be afraid but he doesn't look fearsome anymore. He looks tired. He's holding the sword at his side in one hand; his other hand is wrapped around the shaft of the arrow embedded in his chest. He heaves every time he tries to take a breath. His shirt is dark with blood. He's not moving. He turns his head slowly from side to side, seemingly unsure of where to go next. His mask is pushed back on his forehead. Finally his small eyes fix on her, an uncomprehending rage burning in them.

"What the fuck are you doing here?" he croaks, crumbs of dried blood flaking from his lips. "You don't belong here. You're not even supposed to *be* here."

"Tough shit," she says, and she tackles him. Her body puts pressure on the arrow in his chest as he falls, and he moans. The sword falls from his hand, clatters away. She wants it, but she also wants to make sure this shitbag stays down. Straddling him, she punches him in the face once, twice, breaking open the skin across her knuckles as she strikes the teeth in his mouth. She knocks the mask from his head. With her other hand she grabs the shaft of the arrow and yanks on it, twists it, hoping it'll fuck something up inside him. He howls, and, momentarily satisfied, she leaps free, hurries over to where the sword has fallen, and she lifts it up.

She tests the sword's balance and heft in her grip. It's

lighter than she expected. It feels good. It feels natural. And more than that: she can feel that it offers her some measure of protection in this space, some degree of control.

She turns back, holds the sword out before her and watches as the man slowly clambers back to his feet, maybe readying himself for another round. *Come on*, she thinks, *come at me. I've killed pigs before.*

But he doesn't come at her. He just stands there, glaring at her, hate and confusion in his face.

Finally she can see something resolve in him, as though he has settled upon something to say, as though he has prepared some curse to direct at her, one final weapon to wield. He gets as far as opening his mouth, but at that moment the ground opens up beneath his feet. A massive worm rises, a segmented tube, thick and twisting, as wide around as a rain barrel. The man's legs disappear into the wide funnel of the worm's fang-ringed maw; he's in the beast now, all the way up to his waist, and his face, for the first time, turns to fear. He looks imploringly at her, a terrified entreaty to which she does not respond.

And then the worm contracts, just once, and Ollie's ears fill with the terrible wet splintering sound of the man's legs being chewed, pulped. And the worm expands outward again and the man drops further into its mouth. Only his shoulders, his head, and one arm remain outside.

Ollie steps closer. She looks down into the fading light of the man's eyes. Even now he seems to be attempting to muster a look of contempt. But then the worm crunches down on him with another hideous contraction and it's over; all the human expression and animal appetites in his face drain away forever, and he slides down into the throat of the thing and is gone.

She tightens her grip on the hilt of the sword, intuiting, correctly, what is going to happen next.

The worm rises up. It twists and aims its mouth at her and lunges. She sidesteps it, and she draws the sword back, and she looks at the alien meat of the worm's body as it begins to loop around for a return lunge, and she summons up all of her knowledge of butchery, she makes her assessment, she calculates, she finds the right vector, the right moment, and she strikes.

It's perfect. The cut is perfect. The sword passes perfectly through. The two halves of the worm thrash wildly for a moment, splashing her with gallons of black ichor, and then they fall, and are still.

She scrubs her eyes clear with one hand. The air around her has begun to throb, as though by wounding the worm she has wounded the space itself. Maybe she has. She can feel it beginning to gather its energies against her, as though she were an invading pathogen within the system of an enormous body. And she knows then that the sword won't protect her indefinitely. She knows she has to hurry. It's time to go.

But go where?

She looks ahead, examining the corridor that stretches off before her. There's something lying there, something she recognizes. It's a serving platter, her own serving platter, the very one that she and Victor threw into the Inside two nights ago, bearing a payload of monstrous eggs. The eggs are nowhere to be seen now, but that's definitely her platter. She stoops down, picks it up, just to confirm that it's real.

When she stands up again she can see into her kitchen. She's looking out at it from the other side of a portal, the one that Victor warned her was reopening, the one he was going to try to close on his own. It looks like he hasn't been successful. In fact she can see him, there on the far side, pacing around the room, reading some incantation out of an ancient-looking tome, casting nervous glances seemingly right at her.

"Victor," she calls out. "Hi." It doesn't seem that he can hear her. But she knows that she could take one step forward and she'd be back in the Bronx.

So—she's beginning to get it. You can use the Inside as a way to take shortcuts across space. You could go wherever you wanted. All you'd need is something that made it easy to carve your way in, and something that made it easy to carve your way back out again, somewhere else. And something that could help you to banish the holes you'd made, once you were through. Oh yeah, and ideally something that could protect you against the horrible monsters encroaching on you from every angle. And the sword in her hand does all of those things. The sword can cut through space better than anything else because it makes all of those things possible.

But it wasn't just that the sword could cut through space, she remembers. It was also that the sword could cut through time. That was what everyone kept saying. And so—you should be able to go not just *wherever* you wanted, but also *whenever*—?

She looks to her left. Another series of ribbed chambers, but as she peers into the murky reaches of this corridor she understands that she's looking back in time. That if she went down there, she would go back into the past. How far back, she doesn't know. There doesn't seem to be any end to it.

You could go back, she suddenly thinks. *You could go back and fix the mistakes you've made.* She would have wanted to do this, once. But now she's not so sure. Maybe she shouldn't grasp at the chance to undo the errors of the past. Maybe it's nobler to stay in the present, return to the shattered, broken farm, do the work of picking up the pieces, sweeping up the glass, making a future that might work.

She turns around, just to double-check that there's still a path back to the farm, that the portal the pig-faced man cut remains open. And then she jolts: for standing there behind her, just a few feet away, staring at her with a face tautened by rage, is the pale woman, the dark-haired woman. The observer, the finder. The witch.

"Fuck," Ollie blurts, and she hurriedly gets the sword up. She holds its quivering length between them. She glares down the blade at the woman.

But the woman doesn't advance upon her. Instead, her eyes flick to the mess on the floor; Ollie watches her reconstruct a narrative from the segments of the worm, the spilled pile of smashed parts that once was the pig-faced man, and the hundred little maggoty things that have risen to devour it. And then the woman looks back at Ollie—assessing for one long, searching moment—and whatever fight was in her seems to go out. The expression on her face passes from anger to resignation: *It's over.*

Kill her, Ollie thinks. *She brought all this grief to your door; as long as she walks this earth you'll never be safe.* She tightens her grip on the hilt of the sword. But she doesn't move.

277

It's the woman who moves first. She takes a few steps, moving around the edge of a wide circle, of which Ollie is the center. She is careful to stay out of range of a lunge. She seems to possess an eerie familiarity with the disorienting space; she moves through it with something like confidence even though she doesn't have the protection of the sword. She positions herself at the mouth of the corridor that leads back to the past. She peers down it, turning away from Ollie.

Don't let her get away, some cautionary part of Ollie thinks. *If you do, she'll never stop coming after you, never stop coming after you and your family. She'll never stop until she has the sword.*

But then the woman looks over her shoulder, looks Ollie in the face one final time, and Ollie knows that she's wrong. The look in the woman's expression is pleading, desperate. *I need to go back*, it seems to be saying. *Please just let me go.*

Ollie recognizes the yearning in this woman's expression. It matches something in herself. And she understands, then, that what the woman wants is different from what the man wanted: it has nothing to do with getting the sword or coming after Ollie or ruling the world or whatever. What the woman wants is to fix some mistake, to heal some long-ago wound, something small, something personal. She can read it, plain as anything, right there on the woman's face. And even though there is a part of Ollie that wants vengeance, that wants to take this sword and run the woman through, in an attempt to extract a terrible justice for the violence that this woman brought into her life, there is another part that speaks calmly, and gently, and Ollie listens to what this part is saying. It says, *You could just let her go.*

She gives one tiny nod.

And, seeing this, the woman goes. She turns away from Ollie, and takes a step forward, and then another, and then she begins to hurry, breaking into a sprint toward whatever the past holds for her. Ollie blinks once and the woman is gone.

It's time, also, for Ollie herself to go. She can feel the space gathering up for an assault on her. She has to move. She turns away from the past and looks back out at the farm, the present, the ruined dining room, right there, one step away.

To be frank, the present looks like a mess. There's broken glass all over everything, but the mess is not confined to that one room. Its boundaries extend: they reach out to encompass the entire farm, in its fallen state; they reach out to encompass the people she loves, the people who are the closest thing she has to a family: Jesse, cowering somewhere, terrorized by the day's events, damaged in who knows what fashion by her long absence, broken, a sad sick clown on the inside; Ulysses, angry at her, his accusations of her selfishness still stinging; Donald, the long year of silence between her and him, the gulf that she wants to bridge with no clear knowledge of how, all the disappointments and betrayals and miscommunications, not a single thing among all that shit that she could reliably call a foundation, a thing on which she could build. She looks away, back over her shoulder, back to her kitchen in New York, but of course the mess reaches there as well, encompassing the people who she couldn't help, Guychardson, Angel, the dead. The mess is the exact shape of her entire life. There's no escape from it.

But maybe, she thinks, maybe she doesn't need to escape from it, not any more. Maybe she's ready to face it. To work. To build a world that she can inhabit happily, a future.

She thinks the word a second time: *Future*. And, slowly, she turns, just one half step, and looks down the fourth and final corridor, the last path leading away from the crossroads where she has found herself. The path that leads into the future.

Just give me a hint, she thinks at the path. *Just a glimpse. Show me how it all turns out*. She aims the sword in its direction as though something monstrous might come charging out at her, some horrific fate given form.

But what trembles into view before her are not terrible fates. They're just images of a life, her life. She sees herself working hard in the kitchen at Carnage, using her knives to carve out cuts that the chefs will see as artful. She sees herself in the apartment with Victor, the two of them laughing together, concocting schemes. She sees herself in a car, making the drive between the city and the farm; she sees this happening many times, trying to make peace with Donald, trying to close the gap between her and her son. Eating meals together. Trying to fix the mistakes she's made, to be a better person. She sees herself held by Ulysses; she sees herself held by Donald. Beyond that, more hazily, she sees Jesse getting older; she sees his face changing from the face of a boy into that of a teenager into that of a man. Even further out she sees another child, another son, a beautiful black child, with Ulysses as the father—

And then the visions snap away, and the path is back

to showing her nothing, just room after room in endless sequence. Ollie feels a pang as they're all swept away: she wants
to know more. Are these all the same future? Or are they a
gallery of possible futures? Can she somehow realize them
all, or will she have to choose between them? She doesn't
know. But the pang passes, and what it leaves behind, like
a gift, is hope. A sense of hope. For the first time in a long
time she believes, really believes, that the future could turn
out well. All she has to do is do the work.

And then it's time. The chamber begins to quiver,
threatening to collapse in on itself, and a thousand nubs rise
from the floor; it turns from carpet into tongue. Her impression that she's in a room suddenly slides away, replaced by
the impression that she's in a mouth, and she stands there at
this junction, in this place that lives inside space and time,
and she grits her teeth and closes her eyes and readies her
body and takes a step. Stepping back outside. Committing
to the mess. Ready to begin.

28

HOMES

Maja wakes up in the bed of her childhood home. She blinks.

A map of the constellations hangs above her bed. She pinned it there when she was ten. She lies there for a minute, looking at the familiar shapes, persistent through time, exactly as she remembered them.

She is eighteen years old.

She is forty years old.

She raises her hands in front of her face, flexes her young fingers, forms them into fists.

She sits up in the bed, looks over at her small white desk, the neat pile of school books, the row of six candles she's placed at the desk's edge, arranged in order of color. Everything in its right place.

She rolls up one sleeve of her nightshirt and then the other, checking for the thin black bands of her tattoos. They're gone.

It worked, she thinks.

Relief wells up within her, so abrupt and so overwhelming that her body physically jerks. There's a layer of sadness down within her: a layer that she's operated on top of for so many years that she has forgotten that it wasn't always there. And now that strata is breaking up, coming apart, flowing up and out of her face, which is suddenly wet with tears.

What time is it? she thinks, with sudden panic. *Please don't let me be too late.* But she knows it's early. She can tell just from the position of the square of morning sunlight above her desk, surrounded by dappled bits of color thrown by the crystal pendant that hangs in her window.

She gets up. She goes out into the hall, and crosses into Eivind's room. He's in his bed, asleep.

The Archive speaks to her. It has a new voice now, garbled and damaged and partial from the day's events. But it's still there, in her head. *Hey*, it says. *I recognize that guy.*

It's good to see him, Maja thinks.

Why don't you say hi, says the Archive.

In a minute, Maja thinks. And for a minute she just looks at him. Just until she stops crying.

Then she speaks. "Eivind," she says.

He stirs.

"Eivind," she says again.

"What do you want," he says, without opening his eyes.

"Look at me," she says.

He blinks himself the rest of the way awake and lifts his head to look at her. She's never been so happy to see this dour expression.

"Are you going to the graveyard today?"

He lets his head drop back to his pillow. "I have no idea," he says.

"Are you planning to go out, though? To take photographs?"

"I just woke up," Eivind says. "I have no plan whatsoever. The future is all potential, is an unwritten page, et cetera." He churns the air with his hand.

"I need you to promise me something," Maja says. "I need you not to go to the graveyard today. I need you to promise not to go."

Eivind must hear something in her voice. The import of a forty-year-old voice coming through the mouth of an eighteen-year-old, something, for he props himself up on his elbows and looks into her face, searchingly, maybe just trying to figure out if she's putting him on.

"Promise me," Maja says.

A spooked expression jumps across his features for a second, as though he's seen something. "OK," he says. "I promise."

And she believes him. And because she believes him she can leave him there, at home, safe, while she gets on her red bicycle and rides it through the center of town and up into the hills. She remembers the way.

She rides until she reaches the ugly house with the yellow siding and the orange shutters. She leans her bike against the stone wall across the street. She sits there and looks.

Inside the house there's a boy. Once upon a time this boy killed her brother. He used an aluminum bat that is right there, leaning up against the jamb of the house's front door. Once upon a time she used this bat to split the boy's skull. Once upon a time she threw this bat into the sea, and it was never found, the end.

Only now it's not the end. It's the beginning again. And maybe she's changed the story by making Eivind stay home today. Maybe.

She moves her bike behind the wall. She crosses the street.

She goes up the garden walk and steps onto the stoop of the house. She picks up the bat, feels its weight in her hand, renews her sense of the way it amplifies the actions its bearer could take. She could just simply remove it from the equation altogether, take it down to the sea and throw it in preemptively. It would be another way to change the story. It could be enough.

It could be.

It's hard to be sure, of course. You can't be sure. Or, rather, there's only one way to be sure.

The boy is alone in the house. The door isn't locked. She didn't actively look for these facts, but the Inside offers them to her. They are relevant.

She is forty years old. She is eighteen years old. She is eighteen years old and she has been given a decision to make. And she stands there in front of the door to this house with a weapon in her hands, as she has once before, in a different future, and she waits, and knows that when it's time, she will know what to do.

About the Author

Jeremy P. Bushnell is the author of *The Weirdness* (Melville House). He teaches writing at Northeastern University in Boston, and lives in Dedham, Massachusetts.